She was close enough that his mind wandered, careless of the blades, thinking that under her tunic and vest she had breasts. Now he could see her face, the angles of it as sharp and cleanly sculpted as her sword. Yet thick lashes edged her brown eyes, disguising some of the hatred there.

"Surrender now?"

Panting, she shook her head. Yet her lips parted, tempting him to take them. She was, after all, a woman. A kiss would be mightier than a sword.

He pushed her arm down, pulled her to him and took her lips.

She yielded for a breath, no more.

But it was long enough for him to lose his thoughts, to forget she held a sword and remember only that she was a woman, smelling of heather….

In a flash she turned as stiff as a sword and leaned away— though her lips did not leave his, so he thought she only teased.

When he felt the point of a dirk at his throat he knew she did not. Had he imagined the echo of the bedchamber in her voice? No more.

Ret…
Harlequin

Introducing a powerfully dramatic,
gloriously sensual family saga from

Blythe Gifford

The Brunson Clan

The family that would kneel to *no one*

Descendants of a proud warrior Viking,
the Brunson family rules the Scottish borders.
How long can these two warrior brothers and their
sheltered sister hold out against the king?

Man on a mission, John Brunson is coming home in
RETURN OF THE BORDER WARRIOR
November 2012

Out of her depth at court, Bessie Brunson is
CAPTIVE OF THE BORDER LORD
January 2013

Black Rob Brunson seizes his enemy in
TAKEN BY THE BORDER REBEL
March 2013

Be sure not to miss any of these tales.

BLYTHE GIFFORD

RETURN of the Border WARRIOR

HARLEQUIN®

entertain, enrich, inspire™

Recycling programs
for this product may
not exist in your area.

ISBN-13: 978-0-373-29714-6

RETURN OF THE BORDER WARRIOR

**Did you know that these novels are also
available as ebooks? Visit www.Harlequin.com.**

To all those who still battle nightmares.

Thanks to Matt G and Matt G and Michael and Francisco and the rest of the gang at the Big Bowl.

And to the hillbilly poet, who really did help.

Author Note

For several years now I've written stories about characters born on the wrong side of the royal blanket. They do not have a family in the conventional sense, and for most of them at least one of their parents is unknown or shrouded in mystery.

This story, and the ones that follow, take me on a new path. After years of resisting, I have embarked on a series of connected books, centering on a family of reivers on the Scottish Borders. In few other places and times has loyalty to family been so fierce and strong. There are no bastards—royal or otherwise. Everyone knows his or her parents and siblings well.

And that, of course, is part of the problem....

Silent as moonrise, sure as the stars,
Strong as the wind that sweeps Carter's Bar.
Sure-footed and stubborn, ne'er danton nor dun'
That's what they say of the band Brunson
Descendant of a brown-eyed Viking man
Descendant of a brown-eyed Viking man.

The ballads echoed in the hills along the Borders
for so long that some confused them with the
wind's song. After a while, no one knew how long
they had been sung. No one knew the people, now
gone, who had been sung of. They knew only the
whisper of the legend, as much a part of the land
as the scent of heather in the autumn.
And just as delicate.

But once, long ago, the songs were new and the people, real.

Chapter One

The Middle March, Scottish Borders—
late summer 1528

Something was wrong. He could tell, even from this distance, though he could not explain how.

John had not set eyes on his family's brooding stone tower in ten years. Not since he'd been sent to the court of the boy king. Now that king was grown and had sent him home with a duty to perform.

One he meant to complete quickly, so he could leave this place and never return.

A shaft of sunlight cast sharp-edged shadows across the summer-green grass. His horse shifted and so did the wind, bringing with it the sharp, painful wail of keening.

That was what he had recognised. Death. Someone had died.

Who?

He gathered the reins and urged the horse ahead, thinking of the family he had left behind. Father, older brother, younger sister. His mother was dead these twelve months. They had sent him word of that, at least.

His sister was the only one he cared to see again.

No surety that they mourned a family member. Others were part of the tower's household. But he galloped across the valley as if the time of his arrival might matter.

At the gate in the barmkin wall around the tower, he was challenged, as he had expected. The man was not one he recognised.

Not one who would recognise him.

He removed his polished helmet to show friendly features, glad of cool air on his face again. 'It's John Brunson. *Sir* John now, knighted by the king.' He had waited years and miles to say so. 'Tell Geordie the Red his youngest son is home.'

Tell him I'll not be here long.

The man leaned back on his pike. 'There'll be no telling of anything to Red Geordie Brunson. He lies dead in his bed.'

And John, silent, couldn't summon up even the pretence of sorrow.

John or Sir John, there was no convincing the man to let him in. Despite the fact that people were gathering for the wake, they made him wait until they fetched his brother, Rob, to verify his identity. He could not blame them. That was the way of the Borders.

In truth, he'd found little more trust in the men surrounding the king. They were just less obvious about their suspicions.

Rob, bearded now and taller and broader than John remembered, stood on the wall walk, arms folded in doubt, letting John sweat beneath his full harness of armour. It was as much for his moods as his dark hair that they'd called him Black Rob. Now, new lines scored his brow and John wondered how many of them had deepened since he woke to find himself head man of the riding clan.

'You claim to be my brother?' Even Rob could not recognise him with a glance. John had been twelve, only half-grown when he left.

'Aye. You're looking at the son of Geordie the Red.'

'A Storwick could say the same.' His sceptical disdain was everything John had remembered. And hated. 'What brings you here?'

He did not ask what brings you *home*, as if he would not call Brunson Tower John's home, either.

But everything was different now. Instead of begging Rob's permission and asking his help, now John would tell his brother what must be. 'I'm sent of King James, fifth of that name.'

His brother snorted. 'That's no talisman of entry.'

Ruled by his advisers for the last fifteen years, the young king's name struck no terror on the Borders. But John knew the king well enough to know that it would. And soon.

'Look at my eyes and you'll know me.' Johnnie Blunkit they had called him. The only Brunson with blue eyes.

'If you're a Brunson, then what's your father's father's father's father's name?'

He searched his memory, blank, then tried to summon the ballad of the Brunsons. Only the opening lines sang in his head.

Silent as moonrise, sure as the stars,
Strong as the wind that sweeps Carter's Bar.

There was little else he remembered of his people. And less that he wanted to.

'I may not be able to name my great-great-grandfather, but I remember well enough, Black Rob, how you tried to teach me the sword. Your own blade slipped and I've still a mark on my rib to show for it.'

Some of the ladies at court had found the scar quite appealing.

Rob's frown did not ease, but he jerked his head to the guards. The gate opened, creaking.

John rode in, searching for something he might recognise. Was that the corner where he and Rob had practised with dagger and sword? This the spot where he and his sister had buried their toys? It felt no more familiar than any of the succession of castles he and the king had slept in over the years.

And no more welcoming.

A slender young woman with flowing red hair stepped into the courtyard. 'Johnnie?'

Bessie.

His sister, at least, knew him. When he'd left, she had been eight and they had been the youngest together, united against the world.

Now, she was a woman grown.

He swung off the horse and hugged her, letting her squeeze him back, holding the embrace longer than he would have because it gave him something to do. Time to think. And a moment's illusion that he still belonged here.

'Ah, Johnnie, I always told them you would come home.'

He held her away so he could see her eyes. Brown, like all the Brunsons except his, but today, red with tears.

He shook his head. 'Not for long, Bessie.' Never again. 'I'm Sir John now. I ride beside the king.'

Rob, down from the wall, clasped his arm, without warmth.

'I must talk to you,' John began. 'The king wants—'

'Whatever the king wants, I'll not hear of it now. It will wait until we've sent Red Geordie to rest with our forefolk.'

It was always thus. All work, all life would stop for the 'dead days' before burial.

Well, that might be the way of the Borders, but the king had no time to wait.

Still, John held his tongue and followed Bessie into the tower. His heavy armour clanked in protest as they climbed the stairs to the central gathering room.

'I found him in his bed,' Bessie said, as if she thought John would care, 'when he didn't come to break fast. Died in his sleep he did, with no one to receive his last words.' She whispered, as if to speak aloud would make her cry. 'Snatched away without a moment to say fare-well.' Her voice shook. 'Yet peaceful he looked, like he was still asleep.'

'No death for a fighting man,' Rob muttered behind him.

At the door to the gathering hall, Bessie paused. 'I must make his body ready.' She gave John another brief hug, then climbed the stairs to the floor beyond, where his father lay dead, hovering above him like an evil angel.

She, at least, mourned Geordie Brunson.

They entered a crowded hall, the yawning hearth half filling the outer wall. But instead of sorrowful mourn-ers, he first faced a table surrounded by half a dozen warriors.

'This is my brother, John,' Rob announced, with no acknowledgement of his knighthood and no hint that he might have come for any other reason than to mourn his father.

One by one, the men rose to greet him. Toughened by war and hard living, wearing vests of quilted wool and boots of well-worn leather, each man took his hand, took him in, and gave him trust because he was a Brunson. No other reason given and none needed.

The last one, slender shouldered, sitting with his back turned, rose last. And John saw, astonished, that he faced a woman.

Her brown eyes did not meet his with the warmth of the others.

'This is Cate,' Rob said. 'These men are hers.' He said the words as if it were no more remarkable than blooming heather.

She was tall and spare and blonde as the brown-eyed Viking who, legend said, was the father of all Brunsons. Nose sharp, chin square, cheeks hollow with more than hunger, neither face nor body showed a woman's softness.

A woman who refused to be one. How did he treat such a woman?

He thrust his hand to shake hers, as he had the others, but she did not reach out, deigning only a curt nod. He returned it, his hand dropping awkwardly to his side as he suppressed his resentment. Then he broke away from her stare, his gaze falling, without deliberate intent, to search for breasts and hips. He found only edges, no curves. No comfort for a man there.

And based on the expressions of the other men, none sought.

'Are you a Brunson, then?' he asked. She looked like some cousin, long forgotten.

She lifted her chin and gave a quick shake of her head, ruffling her cropped hair. 'I'm a Gilnock.'

The Gilnock family were distant kin, descended from the same brown-eyed, bloodthirsty Norseman as the Brunsons—and the only family on the Border more unforgiving than his own.

'But she's under our roof now,' Rob said. Under Brunson protection, as might happen when a child was orphaned.

With a quick motion, she dismissed her men and moved closer to Rob and John.

'I must speak with you, Rob,' she said. Her voice surprised John. It was lower than he expected, the words round and deep and shimmering as if she were whispering secrets in the dark. 'Your father died with his word unkept. What happens now?'

'He was not your father,' John retorted, wondering what had been promised. Yet she seemed more a Brunson than he, as if she had donned men's clothes in order to usurp his place.

'He was my headman,' she answered, looking at the new headman when she answered. 'Sworn to protect my family.'

'A Brunson gave you his word,' Rob said, anger edging his words. 'It will be kept.'

On the border, a man's word was good after death. At court, it might not be good after dinner.

'When?' she asked.

'After he's buried,' Rob answered. 'It must wait.' He looked at John, the glance a warning. 'As must other things.'

Cate caught the look and turned to John. 'You do not

come because of his death?' Her eyes, assessing him, seemed ready to judge his answer. Not for this woman the warmth he usually felt from her kind. She seemed as cold and fierce as his brother.

Rob might want him to wait for the burial, but his father was dead and the king alive. And impatient. 'I bring a summons from the king.'

'You mean from his uncles or his mother or his step-father?' Rob looked no more willing to listen than Cate Gilnock.

John understood his hesitation. James, six years younger than John, had been king since birth, but he'd been under the control of others for the sixteen years since then. 'From none of those. It's his personal rule, now. No one else's.'

They sat, silent, thinking of all this meant.

'A man with much to prove, then,' Rob said.

Did Rob speak of the king? Or himself?

Cate's lips twisted in a smirk. 'So what message is so important that your bairn king would send you here, all dressed in armour, to tell us?'

The harness and badge he'd been so proud to wear had impressed the beauties at court. 'He's your king, too.'

'Is he?' She shrugged dismissal. 'I've never met him, never sworn my allegiance. My family and my own right arm keep me safe, not your king.'

'But he will.' He fought the tug of her voice, a strange combination of scorn and seduction. 'He commands our men to join him in war against the traitor who has held him captive for the past two years.'

The 'traitor' had once been a duly appointed regent, but all things change.

Cate, not Rob, jumped in to answer. 'And the wee

king sent you to tell us, did he? You might have spared your horse. Brunson men will ride for no king of Fife. They ride to fulfil the promise of Geordie the Red and put Scarred Willie Storwick dead in the ground.'

He wondered what the man had done to earn such vengeance, but it mattered not. If that was his father's promise, it would be broken.

'The king commands you to fight his enemies, not each other. There'll be no more raiding and reiving and thieving of cattle and sheep. I come to carry out the king's will.'

And to earn his place at the king's side, but that would not sway them.

'And do you also come to stop the sun from rising of a morning?' The curve at the corner of her mouth was a poor substitute for a smile.

If a man had said it, John might have answered with a fist to his gab. 'The king wants—'

'The king doesn't rule here.' Rob's words were low and hard, his expression the one that had earned him the nickname *Black*. '*We* do.'

I do, he might have said, for his brother would be the one to say where the Brunsons would ride.

Yesterday, the decision would have been his father's.

'Surely your loyalty does not rest with the English king?'

'My family holds my loyalty,' his brother said. 'Who holds yours?'

He and his family had parted ways years before. Nothing had made that more clear than returning to them. 'We all owe loyalty to the throne. Scotland must be one country or it will be no country at all.'

'I owe nothing to your bairn king,' Cate said, heading for the door. 'Go back and tell him to leave us be.'

No one followed her.

John looked back at Rob, waiting for a decision, but his brother seemed frozen with grief. The son most like his father, Rob had been prepared all his life to lead the family, but uncertainty lay beneath the stubborn set of his jaw.

Borderers had long held themselves above the king of either country.

No, now was not the moment to force a sorrowing son to choose between his father's promise and the king's command.

But if Cate released Rob from his father's promise, then the choice would be easier. John would have to wrestle only with his brother's stubbornness instead of with a dead man's ghost. No, in order for the Brunson men to ride east to meet the king, Cate Gilnock must drop her demands and step aside.

So John would persuade her to do exactly that.

And quickly. The king was expecting John to deliver Brunson men before the first frost.

Brew was served and the sharing of stories began, stories of Geordie the Red at his best. And his worst.

Refusing to share in laughter and tears he did not feel, John left Rob and the rest in the hall and went in search of a place to stow his gear and his armour.

Avoiding the floor where his father's body lay, he made his way to the open sleeping room on the upper level. He had travelled alone, without even a squire, for speed and secrecy, so he wrestled his armour off by himself.

He would certainly not beg his brother for help.

Instead, he pondered the problem of Cate Gilnock.

For the few days of the wake and burial, he would leave Rob to mourn and turn his charm on the woman. By the time his father was in the ground, he'd have her ready to release Rob from whatever promise she'd been given.

She looked and sounded like no woman he had ever met, yet underneath, he had no doubt that she was the same as all the rest. With the right handling, she'd be persuaded to peace.

Reason would be useless, of course. Near as useless as, he feared, it would be against his brother. But there were other ways.

His family might confound him, but women did not. He knew how to flatter and cajole them, how to overcome their feigned resistance, and how to coax a smile or a kiss. He and the king had shared their fill of women and John had even taught the younger man a thing or two, though in truth, the king needed little teaching in this realm.

He headed down the stairs to find her, a smile returning to his face. No doubt Cate Gilnock had never been wooed by a man before, acting as she did. All she needed was a honeyed word and a winning smile and she'd soon be releasing Rob from the daft-headed promise his father had made.

And Brunson men would be riding to join their king.

Cate forced herself to walk down the tower's steps when she left him, though everything in her screamed to run. She only ran *towards* things now, never away.

Fear only encouraged them.

But this one, with his smooth tongue and his knightly armour, this one scared her as none had in years. Not because she thought he would hurt her body. She'd let no man do that ever again.

And if one did, she would not let herself feel it.

No, it was because of the judgement she saw in his eyes, criticising the rough armour she had forged around her life, carefully as bits of iron hidden between the quilted layers of her jack-of-plaites vest.

If he knew the truth, it would be worse.

She escaped to the stables, where her sleuth dog had been banished until the burial. Usually, Belde was ever at her side, holding her fear at bay, but a dog in the house with the dead could be killed if he got too close to the body.

She would let herself be killed first.

Tail wagging, Belde sniffed her from the toes up, his usual greeting. It took longer this time, because he caught an unfamiliar scent.

'That's a new Brunson you smell,' she muttered, scratching behind his ears. A Brunson who threatened the fragile barrier that protected her. 'Bite him when you see him.'

Intent to understand the new scent, the dog didn't lift his head. She wrapped her arms around his neck and buried her face against his reddish fur. There would be no tears, but this creature would be the only one allowed to see her sorrow.

The men accepted her silently. Braw Cate, they called her, and if she was not exactly a comrade in arms, none of them saw her as a woman. That part of her had died and she would let no one resurrect it.

Especially a blue-eyed Brunson.

She lifted her head and settled a firm expression on her face.

Sorrow would be left on the dog's coat.

* * *

John found her in the soft, grey light of the afternoon doing something he'd never seen a woman do: waving a sword at her fading shadow in a corner of the courtyard.

He watched her from the doorway, more baffled than ever. She was slim and strong. Bone and sinew bent to her will. This was not, he could tell, the first time she had lifted a blade, but the sword, more than half her height, was one a man needed two hands to wield.

What kind of woman tried the same?

Quietly, he unsheathed his dagger and crept around the edge of the yard. It was no match for her sword, but confronted with a weapon in a man's hand, she'd no doubt gasp and blush and step aside.

She heard him before he got within a sword's length and whirled to meet him. He lifted his weapon and crossed it with hers.

'Surrender?' he said with a smile.

Instead, she knocked his dagger aside. 'Never.'

Then, lips set, eyes narrowed, she pointed the sword at his chest, as if to make a touch.

Or something even more deadly.

He tightened his grip on the dagger and took a step back, wishing he still wore his armour. On his guard, he countered her, exhilaration warring with annoyance as they circled each other. He had learned to fight in this very yard, learned because it was a matter of life and death, but his style had been polished beside the king, who had picked up an adult sword at thirteen.

Partnering with King James, guided by the same master, he had developed swift elegance that allowed his opponent to increase his skills without either fighter being hurt.

Even disadvantaged by his weapon, he should be able to toy with this woman until she lowered her blade.

Yet she knew none of those rules. She swung her sword with the bluntness of a warrior astride a hobbler pony, fending off an enemy brandishing a pike. Her sword's thrust carried urgency, even passion, that somehow stirred his blood.

Even his loins.

He jumped just in time to escape a touch. Now was not the time for distractions. He had expected a playful joust. Instead, he faced a warrior.

He swung high, but she held up her sword, turned sideways, to block his stroke. A clever move, but lifting the two-handed sword had strained her strength and when she lowered it, her arms shook.

Seizing on her weakness, he attacked and they crossed blades again. Prepared now, he leveraged his strength against her sword. Though she kept her grip, he pushed the blade away, coming close enough to feel her chest rise and fall, nearly touching his.

Close enough that his mind wandered, careless of the blades, thinking that under her tunic and vest, she had breasts. Now he could see her face, the angles of it, sharp and cleanly sculpted as her sword. Yet thick lashes edged her brown eyes, disguising some of the hatred there.

'Surrender now?'

Panting, she shook her head. Yet her lips parted, tempting him to take them. She was, after all, a woman. A kiss would be mightier than a sword.

He pushed her sword arm down, pulled her to him and took her lips.

She yielded for a breath, no more.

But it was long enough for him to lose his thoughts,

to forget she held a sword and remember only that she was a woman, breasts soft against his chest, smelling of heather…

In a flash, she turned stiff as a sword and leaned away, though her lips did not leave his, so he thought she only teased.

When he felt the point of a dirk at his throat, he knew she did not.

'Let me go,' she said, her lips still close enough that they moved over his, 'or you'll be bleeding and I'll leave you to it, I swear.'

He eased his arms from her back and she pushed him away, wiped her mouth and spat into the dirt.

He touched the scratch she'd left on his neck, grateful she had not drawn blood.

Her eyes, which he had thought to turn soft with pleasure, narrowed, hard with fury.

'It's a Brunson you're facing,' he said, trying a smile. 'Not a Storwick.'

She raised both sword and dirk, the larger wobbling in her grip. 'It's a man I'm facing who thinks what I want is of no consequence if it interferes with his privileges and pleasures.'

Had he imagined the echo of the bedchamber in her voice? No more.

He raised his eyebrows, opened his arms and made a slight bow. 'A thousand pardons.' Words as insincere as the feelings behind them.

She frowned. 'You are a stranger here, so you know no better. And because you are a Brunson, I'll let you keep your head, but I'll warn you just once. You will not do that again. Ever.'

She lowered her sword, slowly.

You are a stranger. She was the Brunson, besting

him with a sword, displacing him at the family table. His temper rose. 'And what if I do?'

The blade rose, this time, not pointed at his throat, but between his legs. 'If you do, you won't have to worry about bedding a woman ever again.'

He swallowed, gingerly, his body on fire. Only because she had challenged him. Nothing more. No man could desire such a woman.

'Then have no worries on that score, Catie Gilnock,' he said, flush with anger. 'When next I bed a woman, it most certainly will not be you.'

Cate watched him go, struggling to keep her sword upright. Only when he was safely inside the tower did she lower her blade and raise her fingers to her lips.

He had dared to kiss her. And for just a moment, she had felt what other women must.

What she had thought never to feel.

After the raid, after her father died, after…the rest, she had been mercifully numb. Months were a blur. Some days, the only sensation she felt was Belde's nose, nudging aside tears she didn't remember shedding.

Then the numbness faded, and the fear came.

Bit by bit, day by day, she fought it. Piece by piece, she built a wall to hold it back.

Now, no one questioned why she was not like other women. But Johnnie Brunson did. His careless smile was a cruel reminder of doubts she had smothered and regrets she had suppressed. When he looked at her, they haunted her anew. Who she had been. Who she could never be. All the things she wanted to forget, the questions she did not want to ask, wanted no one to ask.

The questions she would never answer.

She carried her sword back to the armoury and polished the blade, reluctant to rejoin the wake and see him again.

Surely she would not have to fight Johnnie Brunson for long. He'd soon learn that no outlander could dictate to a Borderer who or how he could fight. This land, these people, were beyond the whims of a king.

But fight she would, and keep fighting until Scarred Willie Storwick lay cold beneath the ground. Not, as most thought, because of what he had done to her father.

Because of what he had done to her.

Chapter Two

John watched Cate return to the hall and join her men near the hearth without so much as a glance his way.

The wake was in full swing and John was surrounded by strangers. Rob had gone upstairs to sit with the body, which was never allowed to be left alone before burial. Soon enough, John would have to face his father's corpse, knowing the sightless eyes would never see the king's badge of thistle that John had so proudly pinned to his chest.

It seemed to impress no one here on the Borders. Not even the Gilnock wench.

In truth, he had not planned to kiss her, but when she refused to surrender, when her eyes clashed with his as strongly as her blade, he found himself…roused. Even then, he had expected little more than the taste of cold steel. But her lips, thin and sharp as her tongue, warmed, drew him in…

And then rejected him.

She might not have meant it as a challenge, but that was his body's translation.

Women did not refuse Johnnie Brunson.

He watched her, surrounded by her men, wondering

what kind of a woman she was. Flaxen hair framed a face hard, sharp and spare as the rest of her. At least, that's what he had thought until he was close enough to feel her breasts against his chest and see the sweep of her thick lashes.

He forced his thoughts away from rumpled sheets and throaty laughs. She did not seem to offer stories of her own, but she laughed at the others and encouraged them to tell their own tales.

In that, at least, she seemed a woman. She was likely as changeable as any he had known. All he must do was figure out how to change her.

Beside John at the table, the men who had ridden with Red Geordie were swapping stories of Storwick cattle stolen and recovered and stolen again and making promises of the cattle they would steal in Geordie's memory.

John did not waste breath to argue. Black Rob would decide when, where and if they raided again, but John must not force that choice too soon.

When next John turned to look for Cate, she had gone.

'Would you sit a watch with him?' His sister's voice, soft, came over his shoulder.

He turned to see her, and Rob, faces scored with grief, behind him.

'It should be kin beside him,' Rob began, as if John were kin no more.

'Rob, please.' Bessie's voice was weak and weary.

He met his brother's eyes, clashing as they had, even as boys. 'I am as much his son as you are,' he said. At least, that was what he had told himself whenever he had doubts. 'I will take my turn.'

He rose. No other choice. He must face his farewell.

Alone, he climbed the stairs and paused at the open door to the room where his father lay. The candle that would burn throughout the night flickered on the chest by the hearth.

And at the foot of the bed, Cate Gilnock sat, head bowed, as if *she* were kin with the right to sit with him.

Anger pushed him into the room to claim his place. His brother, his sister, even the men who rode beside Geordie the Red were closer to him than John was. That, he had accepted.

But not this woman, this interloper.

'I sit with him alone,' he said, voice cold.

She jumped up and reached for her dagger, stopping only when she recognised him. 'If you cannot respect his word, you should not sit with him at all.'

Her words twisted inside him, sharp as a blade. 'Alone,' he said, not trusting himself to say more.

Wordless, she lowered her blade and stepped outside.

His father lay in the curtained bed where he had died, arms at his side, wrapped in white linen. John could hardly imagine his gentle, doe-eyed sister having prepared the body for burial, but here he lay, even in death, his face as fierce as in John's memories.

He took a step forwards. He should pay his respects. He should pray for his father's soul as Cate no doubt had done. Or perhaps he should be fearful that the man's spirit, vengeful, might still haunt the room. He should feel…something.

Instead, he felt as if he stood in an empty room.

Hard to even picture this body as his father, straight, strong and spare of speech with no time for his youngest boy except brief minutes to drill him in the wielding of the staff and sword. He had not been the son favoured with the old man's care and training. John had been the one pushed from the nest and sent to the king, his loss mourned no more than that of a cow or a sheep.

And in ten years, never a word sent except notice of his mother's death, as if John had ceased to exist once he had left Brunson land.

Well, he was back and his father, in truth, was dead as he had been to John for the last ten years.

Taking a step closer to the bed, he was swept with a wave of grief that weakened his knees. Staggering, he gripped the corner post of the bed to stay upright. He thought Rob was the one who needed to grieve, Rob the one who needed time to adjust to his father's loss before he shouldered the demands of the head of the family.

Now, John faced the truth. *He* was the one for whom it was too soon. Too soon to accept that his father was gone. Too soon to release the glimmer of hope he'd felt as he rode across the hills, proudly wearing his armour. Hope that he might make peace with the man at last.

Too late for that now.

Peace, if peace were possible, would have to be made with his brother.

The air stirred behind him. The room was empty no more.

'When did you last see him?' Cate's voice.

He did not turn, but spoke the memory. 'I was twelve. He sent me to Edinburgh, with just enough men to assure I'd arrive safely. We rode as far as the burn, crossed the water, I turned back to wave...'

But his father had already left the parapet and, in that moment, left his life.

John shook his head, stood straight and turned his back on the body in the bed. There would be no reconciliation now. 'I last saw him ten years ago.'

Shadows and candlelight softened her face, until he believed, for a moment, that she understood.

Or did he see only pity for a man who did not belong to his family?

He bristled against it. *She* was the one who did not belong beside the deathbed. 'Why are you praying over my father as if he were kin? Where is your own?'

'Dead as yours.' Whispered, words more vulnerable than any she had yet spoken. 'At the hand of Scarred Willie Storwick.'

Now. Only now did he understand. 'So you picked up his sword and his men and vowed vengeance.'

She didn't bother to nod, and when her eyes met his, the woman's softness was gone and he faced the warrior again. 'And your king will have no men of ours until I've had it.'

Her words, a vow, chilled him, but hot anger rose to wipe out the feeling. This stubborn woman was his enemy, as much or more so than the Storwicks across the border. 'The king will have his men, or you'll wish he had.'

She sniffed. 'I'm not afraid of your king.'

'I was not speaking of the king.'

Her eyes widened and he regretted his threat, but her obstinacy had swamped all his plans of persuasive charm.

He leaned closer, this time resisting her lips. 'But the king, too, knows something of revenge. That's why he's going to destroy the man who's held him captive these last few years.'

'If he's a man who knows revenge, he will know why I need mine.'

'He won't. Not if it stands in his way.'

He wanted to best her now, as he'd been unable to

do in the yard. 'So if you're of the Brunsons, you'll do as we do. The king will have his men. I am here to make sure of it.'

'Johnnie!' Bessie stood at the door, the faintest hint of judgement in her voice.

How long had she stood there, silent as a wraith, watching?

And what had she seen?

She did not wait for him to ask. 'You've travelled long today. Get your rest. I'll sit with him.'

He walked out, silent, without a backward glance at the bed.

Or at Cate Gilnock.

'Did you see to the dog?' Bessie moved so silently, it always surprised Cate when she spoke.

'I tied him,' Cate answered, returning to sit on her stool. 'With the horses.'

'I'm sorry you must be separated.'

Silent with surprise, Cate blinked. She thought she had fooled them all, that they judged Belde only a dog, valuable for tracking and nothing more.

Bessie pulled a stool beside Cate's and sat, then let her head fall into her hands with sorrow, or fatigue.

Cate reached out to touch her shoulder, uncertain how to help. 'Let me get you something.'

Bessie shook her head without opening her eyes. 'They'll be here, coming and going all night.' Her voice soft, still. Then, she sat up, straightened her shoulders and met Cate's eyes, coming to herself in a way so similar to her brother's that Cate blinked. 'I'll sleep later.'

Bessie was the woman every man expected: chaste, quiet, placid and peaceful. One who looked out on the world with an open gaze, as if she knew and was perfectly content with her lot in life.

And though the two women had shared a room and a bed for near two years, Cate still knew no more of her than that.

'Your brother is not like the others.' He threatened the defences that had served her so well.

Bessie nodded, not asking which brother Cate meant. 'We were close when he was a boy.'

Cate could see that they would be, both lean with rust-coloured hair, unlike Black Rob, who favoured his mother's people.

Then, Bessie smiled, sadness banished. 'We called him Johnnie Blunkit.'

'Blunkit? Why?' She could not imagine this angry man dragging a blanket behind him.

'Because of his eyes.'

'Ah.' Blunkit fabric was a soft blue-grey, remarkably similar to the colour of John Brunson's eyes. 'He must have hated that.'

'Later, aye—' Bessie nodded '—he did.'

Cate shook her head, trying to picture this strong knight as a youth. 'I don't remember him.'

'You must have seen him when he was younger.'

'When?' She would have been no more than ten when he went to court, Bessie even younger.

'A wedding, a year, maybe, before he left. I cannot remember whose, but the tower was full. Everyone had come to celebrate.'

Cate tried to summon the event and had a dim memory of two lads in the courtyard, crossing swords. The taller—it must have been Rob—had the advantage, but John gave no quarter, fighting harder when he accused his brother of holding back.

'So long ago.' She was no longer the giggling girl of nine who knew nothing of the world's horrors and still thought to be a bride one day. 'I had forgotten.'

'He was not like the others.' Bessie nodded towards the bed where her father lay. 'Even then.'

Cate shook her head. Perhaps Bessie no longer knew her brother. 'He's like enough.'

He was a man. One whose first thought had been to kiss her.

When John returned to the hall, the fire had burned low and the raucous conversations had quieted. Some men dozed.

He accepted a mug and took a wedge of cheese, the first food he'd had all day. So simple, the things that kept a body bound to the earth.

Rob sat alone on the stone window seat. He did not move or speak when John joined him.

He wasn't sure what drew him back to his silent brother, but he had faced the truth: his father was truly gone. The triumphant return he'd hoped for lay shattered at his feet. There would be no reconciliation.

It was the king's favour he must seek now, not that of a family who had never granted it and never would.

His father, Cate, his brother. Each had judged him and found him wanting. The king would not—not when John brought three hundred Brunson men to fight at his side.

Cate walked into the hall and another man rose to take her place in the dead man's room. This stubborn woman, determined to oppose the king's will, was haunting him more than the things that should have been: his father, the king, his mission.

She was nothing like the women he had known at

court, any of whom seemed ready to flip their skirts for a chance to bed a king's man. Even those women already wed.

'She's a skittish one, isn't she?' he said to Rob, nodding towards the other side of the hall where she stood with one of her men.

'Cate?' Rob shrugged. 'Maybe.'

John took a sip, waiting.

His brother said nothing more.

He gritted his teeth. Silence was not the way at court. There was always chatter, even if the words were meaningless.

Even if they were false.

He forced another question. 'Why is that, do you suppose?'

Another shrug. 'Not for me to say.'

'Not for you to say or not for me to know?' Was Rob hiding something? With as few words as the man used, it was hard to tell.

Then, Rob turned his head to look at John with that familiar expression that needed no words to say *Little Johnnie Blunkit*. 'She lost her father to the Storwicks. Do you expect her to be dancing?'

'No,' he said, refusing to yield, 'but I don't expect her to dress like a man and wield a sword, either.'

Rob shrugged and made no answer, but his face spoke his grief. He had just lost a father. He was not dancing. And if John forced him too soon, he'd not be sending men to the king, either.

'She has no mother?' John said, cracking the silence.

'Dead. Years before her father.'

'Brothers? Sisters?'

Rob shook his head.

She had no family, so she stole his. Well, she could have them.

'When did it happen?' His brother delighted in making him beg for each scrap. 'Her father's death?'

'Two years ago.'

Longer than he had thought. Long enough that she should no longer be in grief's grip. 'How?'

Rob sighed, finally accepting John would ask until he was answered. 'She said little. It was about this time of year. They were still in the hills with the cattle when Scarred Willie came. Killed everyone but Cate. Took the cattle.'

Killed everyone. It was not the way of the Borders, such killing. But the woman's life had been spared, as was right.

'Could you not chase him down?'

'We didn't find out till weeks after.'

'Why not?'

'She buried them, her father and the others, before she came down from the high land.'

John studied her again, the woman who could barely keep a blade upright. How had she summoned the strength of body and heart for that? 'And then?'

'We tried,' Rob growled, as if John accused him of shirking his duty, 'but the Storwicks denied his guilt and the English Warden wouldn't hand him over for trial.'

The Borders had their own laws, enforced jointly, on occasion, by royally appointed Wardens on both sides of the border.

'And even if he had,' Rob continued, 'it would have been his word against hers.'

'So Father promised her the justice the Wardens

wouldn't.' Suddenly, he saw hope, something that might persuade Rob, persuade all of them, to the king's side.

'The king has appointed a new Scottish Warden.' John leaned forwards. 'I carry the papers with me. This one will insist Storwick is brought to justice.'

Rob snorted. 'One Warden's no different from the next. Scots or English.'

'This one is.' John's statement was more emphatic than his certainty. He knew little of the man. 'You must give him time to prove it.'

'*I* must?' Rob near shouted. 'You left us and now you come back and tell me what *I* must do?'

'I didn't leave. Father sent me.' He lowered his voice, hoping Rob would follow.

He did not. 'Well, I didn't see you running home when you turned one and twenty.'

'And I saw no invitation.'

'You don't need an invitation to come home, Johnnie.' All the arrogance of a big brother was in his voice.

'For no better a welcome than I've had, I do.' Out of the corner of his eye, he could see that conversation in the hall had stopped.

'Well, what have you done since you arrived but yammered about what the Brunsons must do because your precious king says so? You might at least have given your father the grace of his burial.'

His plan to make Rob's decision easy had already gone well awry. 'We've little time. The king needs our men in East Lothian by mid-October.'

Realisation reflected in Rob's eyes. He rose. 'Well, Johnnie, *my* father is more important than *your* king. He, and you, can wait for my decision until we've laid Geordie the Red in the ground.'

Rob turned his back and walked out of the hall.

And when John looked up, everyone was watching, silent.

Including Cate Gilnock.

Chapter Three

It was no day for a funeral, John thought, as they gathered outside the tower's walls the next morning. The sun looked downright cheerful to see the man put in the ground.

To Bessie fell the role of leading the procession to the burial ground, as her mother would have had she been alive. Awed, John watched his sister calmly assume yet another duty. When last he had seen her, she'd been a lass of eight. Now, she seemed a woman who had already seen, and accepted, all the sorrow life could offer.

His brother stepped up to the coffin, first man to be ready to heft it to his shoulder. John moved to take his place on the other side.

'I've five other men already,' Rob said.

'None of whom is his son,' John said, warning them back with a glance. Estranged as he might be from his father, from the family, this was his role, his right.

His duty.

The others stepped away, not waiting for Black Rob's permission. In this, John had the right.

He took his place and at Rob's nod, they lifted the coffin to their shoulders.

Bessie led them from the tower, singing of sorrow in a song that needed no words. Cate fell in behind her, ready to lend an arm if she faltered. Next to his sister, Cate, with her cropped hair, loose pants and knee boots, seemed as young as a lad.

The burden rested heavy on his shoulder as the men found their common step. Arms raised, he steadied it with both hands, feeling as if his father's weight held him fast to the earth. But he would not be the first to cry off. And in the mile between the tower and the burial ground, they only paused once to let the coffin down.

The Brunson burial ground perched on the leeward side of a hill beside an empty church. The grave had been prepared beside his mother's. All there was to do now was to take the body from the coffin and lower it into the ground with ropes.

Not for them the priest and the prayers, the laying on of hands, the final rites that might have eased his father's passage. A few years ago, the Archbishop of Glasgow had banned the riding clans from the church and cursed them to eternal damnation with a vengeance that would have made a reiving man proud.

The priest had left.

The Brunsons remained.

So at the end, his father was laid to rest with only his family and the land he belonged to. Perhaps, he thought, as they consigned his father to the earth, this was more fitting.

John looked out across the valley his father had loved. Grey clouds had gathered atop the hills, shielding the sun, and he felt a stir of unwelcome emotion. This earth, this clay, had made him, too.

Yet now, he was a stranger to it. His brother and the others who rode it daily could find their way on a moonless night. To him, it was like a woman he had not yet bedded. The soft hills, the surface he could see, beckoned, but he did not know what parts of her body would respond to his touch. Hadn't found the hidden places.

He found himself watching Cate, wondering what hid beneath her disguise. She embodied every dilemma he faced: a family who had disowned him, a land that kept its secrets, a way of life at odds with everything he wanted.

And yet, something about her tugged at him, tempting him to peel back her layers, to discover her secrets. And something about her made him mourn what he had lost.

The ancestral melody began. Bessie and Rob joined voices to sing the ballad of the Brunsons. The song that had come down from ancestors no longer remembered, except through song.

This is the story, long been told
Of the brown-eyed Viking, man of old
Left on the field by the rest of his clan
Abandoned for dead was the first Brunson man
Abandoned for dead was the first Brunson man.
Left for dead and found alive
A brown-eyed Viking from the sea
He lived to found a dynasty.

There were verses unnumbered, names and stories of the Brunsons since the first, and when the last had been sung, Rob stepped forwards to sing alone.

I sing today of Geordie the Red;
A Border rider born and bred
A man more faithful never found

*Loyal to death and then beyond
Loyal to death and then beyond.*

The last notes faded. The song had been sung. His father laid to rest and his legacy created. Loyalty. But did Rob sing of loyalty to king or to kin?

Or was he still struggling to choose?

They walked back to the tower even more slowly than they had left. Ahead of him, Rob and Bessie leaned towards each other, shoulder to shoulder, eyes on the life ahead of them.

A life in which he had no place.

Cate, to his right, was dry eyed, but none wearing the Brunson brown and blue had more vengeance in their gaze than she. More vengeance, he thought, than sorrow.

No, Rob would not, *could* not yield, he feared, as long as Cate held him to his father's word. She was the key.

Well, women were changeable. The king's own mother had sided with the English, the French and the Scots in turn, changing sides as easily as she changed husbands. This Cate would be no more steadfast if he gave her the right persuasion.

He just had to figure out what persuasion that was.

Last night, the hall had been full of talk, laughter and tears. Today, the guests were gone and only Rob's and Cate's men remained. And the silence of sorrow.

John escaped the tower, even the courtyard, unable to feign regret he did not feel. Outside, in fresh air, he would be able to think clearly on the challenge of Cate Gilnock.

He did not need her acceptance. He did not need,

or want, to touch the woman. He simply needed her to release vengeance he still did not fully understand. He feared, however, that peeling away her layers could be even harder than peeling off her clothes.

Beyond the tower walls, the Galloway ponies dotted the field, left to feed themselves until the coldest weather came.

Let them find their own forage, his father would say. *Makes them strong.*

He paused to pat one of the bays on his broad, sturdy chest and the pony let him, nosing for a treat. John held up empty hands. 'Not today, boy. Next time.'

In apology, he swept his hand down the reddish hair of the beast's back, feeling warmth beneath his palm. When they were boys, Rob used to challenge him to mount a pony bareback and race around the tower. John won often enough that Rob dropped his dare. He beat his brother because he was more flexible, able to communicate with the horse, rather than forcing the creature to his will.

He grinned. He could probably do it still.

Seized with the memory, he murmured a word or two and stepped away to allow a running start. The pony waited patiently as John approached, jumped, then pushed himself up and swung his leg over to settle astride.

Well trained, the pony lifted his head and waited his command. No saddle held John on. No reins helped him guide. And no armour separated him from the feel of his mount's muscles, flexing beneath him.

He guided with his legs and, by shifting his weight, headed out to where the Liddel Water skipped down the valley. He was surprised to discover that, once mounted, he remembered paths his head had long forgotten.

Following the stream, he saw Cate in the distance, wading across in water that reached near to her waist. She carried a wad of cloth and kept glancing downstream, as if looking for someone.

Instead of calling out, he stopped the pony in a thicket of trees where they could not be seen, curious.

She dropped the cloth on the other side of the stream, then waded back across. Man she might try to be, but now he knew the truth. Now, he could appreciate the shades of ash and flax mixed in hair that did not reach shoulders too slender to be mistaken for a man's. And as she climbed out of the stream, wet cloth clung below her waist, drawing his gaze to the place her legs met and putting him in mind of what might happen if she spread them for him. Strange that a place normally hidden behind a skirt should be so tempting when clothed in breeches.

Pausing, shoulders hunched, she looked from tower to valley to hillside, as if wary of danger. Storwicks could be around any bend, true, but it was early in the season and still daylight. An attack was unlikely.

His pony, trained to be silent and invisible, did not draw her eye. Then she turned her back on him and ran downstream to disappear around a bend and into the trees.

Baffled, he urged the horse ahead, slowly, uncertain whether to follow. What was she doing with—?

Before he could finish the thought, a sleuth dog in leather harness burst through the bushes, pulling Cate behind.

The beast weighed more than she, if John were any judge. Nose to the ground, the dog dragged her with him as he followed the trail she had laid, turning abruptly to cross the water where she had, and pouncing on the bundle of cloth with his tail wagging when he reached the opposite bank.

Well trained, he thought.

'Good, Belde,' she said, pulling a treat from her pocket for him to gobble. 'Good dog.'

And then she petted him with more affection than she'd shown to any two-legged creature.

As they crossed the stream again, he dismounted and walked closer. But before he reached her, she heard his step over the rushing water, whirled and drew her dirk.

Not drawn for him, he realised. She was a woman wary of any sound. He held up his hands, palms toward her, a gesture of peace. 'No enemy. Only me.'

She did not lower the blade. The softness she'd shown the hound did not extend to him. They reached the bank and the dog bounded over to him, then put his nose to John's waist and started sniffing him up and down.

John pushed him away to no avail. 'What's he doing?'

'Getting to know you.'

He took a step towards her and the dog, between them, started to growl, the hair on his neck standing straight.

'What do you want?' she asked. After four trips through the water, she was soaked. Only the quilted jack-of-plaites vest disguised her sex.

He raised his eyes, fighting irritation. 'Not a kiss. I promise.' He had told her flatly he would not bed her. Could she tell her body was not listening? 'Call off your dog and put down your dirk.'

She sheathed the blade and her eyes flickered to the pony, standing patiently behind him. 'You're riding Norse. He's a fast one.'

Her tone gentled, as when she had spoken to the dog.

'Do you work with the ponies, then?'

'Aye.' She walked over to the pony and stroked his neck. Her dog followed and sat squarely between Cate and John.

Physical persuasion was futile, but the four-legged creatures seemed to be the chink in her armour. 'You're good with the animals.'

She threw him a look of disgust. 'I've found them to be kinder than people.'

An odd statement. 'I never thought animals had any feelings at all.'

'At least they don't kill their own.'

He did not remind her that she was the one ready to kill Willie Storwick. 'What possible quarrel might one sheep have against another?' He laced the question with a smile, bending towards her.

The dog rose, growling.

'Sit, Belde,' she said, grabbing his harness.

The dog looked at her, wagged his tail and sat.

John eyed him warily. Drooping ears and a wrinkled face gave the dog a lazy look, but he acted as if he would kill, if she asked.

'He's very protective of you,' John said.

'To the death,' she answered, meeting John's eyes. The gentleness she showed to the animals did not extend to him.

He raised his brows. 'A sleuth dog usually has an English hand on the leash.' And behind him, a pack of riders tracking the reivers across rock and water.

'Not this one.' Cate wasted no more words than his brother.

'How did you get him?'

Something softened around her eyes, as if she was thinking of a smile. 'Da stole him.'

John nodded. It was the only honourable way for a reiver to get anything.

Her memory, apparently, was a good one. 'He had been tracking Da, but he slipped his leash and lost his tracker. When he found Da, he was so pleased he just sat there wagging his tale while Da rubbed his head.'

She had kind feelings for the beast, that was certain. 'He does not wag his tail for me.'

'He does not know whether I am safe with you.'

I do not know whether I am safe with you, she might have said.

'You must tell him…' He met her eyes. If he could get the dog to like him, maybe the woman's trust would follow. 'Tell him that you are.'

She swallowed, then looked down at the dog. Her breath came faster, but she did not speak.

'How would you do that?' He kept his voice soft, not wanting to force her. 'How would you tell him?'

She did not look up. 'I would tell him you are a…' She glanced up, studying John, as if uncertain he deserved the label. 'That you are a "friend".'

Looking into the mirror of her eyes, he suddenly wanted to be worthy of the name. 'I am.'

Though her eyes reserved judgement, she turned back to the dog. 'Friend,' she said firmly, then spoke over her shoulder. 'Reach out to him.'

He held out his hand and Belde sniffed it.

'Friend,' she said, as the dog licked his fingers. 'John.' Then she smiled. 'He should not growl at you again.'

John hoped the same would be true of Cate. 'How long have you been working with him?'

'Three years.'

Only the dog brought softness to her eyes, so he

would talk of the dog. 'Was he with you the night your father was killed?'

The joy that had touched her face shattered.

Fool. Speak of something else. 'The ponies? How long have you worked with them?' Would she deign to answer?

She shook off the sorrow. 'Longer. I had no brothers, so my father depended on me. And once he was gone…' The darkness returned, and with it, all her barriers. Then she faced him again, head high. 'We've the finest horseflesh on the Borders. Sturdy and tireless. They've been known to ride sixty miles without a stop.'

Long enough to leave Scotland after sunset, foray deep inside England and return home before the sun rose. In fact, without such mounts, there would be no reiving.

Yet in her talk of the ponies, he had heard a flash of pride. Better that than fear or anger. 'You do a fine job, I'm sure.'

Instead of the smile he had wanted, she turned back to the pony, blinking against tears.

'There now.' He walked up behind her, put his hands on her shoulders and forced her to turn. 'No need to cry at a compliment.'

Belde stood to all fours, growling.

'Quiet, beast,' he said. 'Friend.'

He wrapped both arms around her in a hug, thinking she would smile as most women did when cajoled.

Instead, she brought her knee up, squarely between his legs.

Hard.

He dropped his hold and doubled over, biting back a curse.

Teeth bared, the dog barked. Cate groped for his fur

coat, without looking where her hand fell. Instead of his pain, he saw hers. There were no tears, but horror had replaced sadness and he wasn't sure whether she saw him at all.

'Cate!' He tried to stand, barely able to hear himself over the dog's baying. 'What is it?' She looked as if she were staring at spirits.

Cate knelt beside the barking beast and clasped her arms tightly around his neck. Then, as if her prayers for deliverance had been answered, her face relaxed, her eyes met his, and he saw Cate again.

She lost her parents to the Storwicks. Do you expect her to be dancing?

But that had been two years ago and death was no stranger to these hills. Her fear was beyond that.

She rose, her hand never leaving the dog's fur, and gathered his leash. 'I must go.'

And she turned her back, clearly intending for him not to follow.

But, with a slight limp in deference to the ache between his legs, he did.

His brother might disdain him. This woman might detest him. But he was not a man to be feared by women, even by one who clearly had much to fear. He grabbed her arm. 'Stop.'

She did, but pulled her arm away so he was no longer touching her. The dog growled again, but she stilled him. 'I told you—'

'Listen to me,' he began. 'You may not like me. You may not want to lose Brunson men to the king's business. And I understand you want no kisses, but I am a Brunson and you're under my family's protection, so you needn't pull a dirk every time I am close.'

'It's *you* who must listen,' she answered. 'I warned you and you act as if you are a man without ears.'

'I heard what you said.' Lucky, he thought, that she had used her knee and not the dagger she'd threatened him with last time. 'And it was a kiss you warned me against, not a simple touch.'

'Then let me make it clear enough that even you can understand my meaning. No man touches me. Ever.'

He remembered again that first day, when she refused his hand. Strange even then, he had thought. And now he had seen the fear behind it. 'I am not a man who hurts women. Ever.'

She stilled then, accepting his gaze with those deep-brown eyes, come from some common ancestor. A sigh escaped. 'I know,' she said finally, a whisper.

The whisper reminded him of the kiss, now so fully forbidden. He swayed towards her, then stopped himself before the dog could take a chunk from his leg.

'Go then,' he retorted, wincing and wanting to clutch himself again. He'd have to walk the pony back from here.

She did, but he called out before she was beyond earshot, 'And don't let that beast growl at me again.'

She looked over her shoulder with that barely-a-smile crooked corner of her mouth that made him think she might be laughing at him.

He might not be a man to be feared, but some man was. He wondered who. And why.

Chapter Four

Cate had a long, hard fight with herself as she ran away from him, back to the tower.

She had not allowed a man so close since...

Since *then*.

Though the Brunsons were family, they did not treat her as her father had, hugging her goodnight or ruffling her hair in play. Red Geordie was sparing with a hug, even for his own children.

That suited her. Here, she was protected, but no one tried to come too close.

Except this man, who knew no better than to put comforting arms around her shoulders.

She had stiffened at his touch, braced against the fear that would come and steal her mind, afraid she might spear him with her dirk before she could stop herself.

It did come, the fear, her old enemy, then left near as quickly as it came. And if she wounded his manhood and his pride, at least she didn't leave him bloody.

Because his embrace had not felt like an attack, or even the prelude to a kiss. Instead, held against his chest, she had felt warm and comforted.

Safe.

When had she last felt that way?

Braw Cate, they called her. Cate the Bold. They thought her brave and bold and unafraid because she dressed in breeches and waved a blade.

She was not fearless. She was terrified.

Only with sword and dagger in hand did she dare to face those fears. Only when breeches disguised her womanhood could she rise from bed to face the world. Only with Belde within reach of her hand could she survive the most ordinary day. Going beyond the tower walls, as she must to train him, took every bit of her strength. And when she did, she always kept a clear view and an eye open for the enemy.

Now, this man had touched her and, for a few minutes, she had not felt fear.

And that frightened her more than anything else.

Inside the tower, with Belde at her side, she entered the hall, empty of mourners now. Black Rob sat alone, shrouded by mourning, looking every bit of his name.

Her heart ached for him. For all of them. She had lost a father, too.

She did not often speak idly with Rob. It was not their way. Words were worth no more than air. Necessary for breath, a menace in excess.

But today, she wanted words that might help her understand this tall, lean, blue-eyed stranger who bore the Brunson name. He barely seemed their kin, though he and Bessie shared a certain slant of the eye, an arch of the brow that spoke of pride. And action.

Bessie had told her of the boy, but it was the man she sought to understand, the man who was getting too close, not only to her body.

She hovered beside the table, waiting for Rob to look up.

When he saw Belde, he smiled, the first one she'd seen from him all day. 'So you've let the beast inside again, eh?'

She nodded and sat across the table. The dog lay down beside her, close to the hearth, as if glad to be back.

She let the silence lay a while. Rob waited for her to speak.

'So,' she began finally. 'John comes home.'

Not a question. That would be too difficult. Too personal. It would indicate she cared.

The smile disappeared. 'Aye.'

Belde stretched out, his yawn a squeak in the silence.

She tried again. 'He's been gone a while.'

'Long enough to change.'

She looked up and his eyes met hers as if he knew why she asked. 'Change?'

'He's no Brunson now.'

She might have agreed an hour ago. Certainly, his tongue had little Brunson in it and his ideas did not belong to the Borders. But he was as stubborn as the rest of his kin, that she was sure. 'Maybe not, but he shares your blood. Nothing replaces that.'

Ever.

She was here, safe, only because Red Geordie had taken her in. It was their code. It was how they lived. For family. For loyalty. For kin. To be cast away from the family was to be a broken man, wandering alone like the outlaws who prowled the no man's valley of the Debatable Land.

Even Johnnie did not deserve that fate.

Rob's shrug said the same. 'Maybe, but he won't be here long.'

'Because you want him to leave?'

'Because he doesn't belong.'

She sighed. Johnnie had said as much. Her sense of safety was an illusion. He'd return to court, where he belonged, beside that king he spoke of and surrounded by the kind of ladies who would people such a place.

And she'd still be here. Alone.

Barely able to walk, John watched Cate and her dog disappear through the gate. After he'd recovered, he limped back to the tower, leaving the pony to graze near the west gate. He wondered whether her dagger might have inflicted less damage than her knee.

Understanding women had never been so difficult before. Living beside the king, he had never had to spare an extra thought for them. Women were fickle, accommodating creatures, ever ready to please you, in bed or out.

At least, the women at court were.

His sister was not like that, of course. And his mother had not been, either. Perhaps Border women were as different as their men. He'd ask Bessie about this Gilnock woman. Subtly, of course. He would not want her to feel forced to choose between her brothers.

He found Bessie in the courtyard's kitchen hall, kneading a ball of light brown dough with calm, rhythmic strokes and blinking against tears.

Heedless of her sticky hands, he gave her the hug Cate had refused and she rested her forehead on his shoulder. 'Are you all right, Bessie?'

She shook her head, not lifting it. 'I knew we would lose him one day. Every time he went on a raid I prepared, but not…not for this.'

Some men prayed to die peacefully in their sleep. Brunsons were not among them.

He patted her back, not knowing what else to do or say, until she raised her head and forced a smile. Then he let her go and she straightened her shoulders, turned back to her breadmaking and pummelled the helpless dough into submission.

He wandered the kitchen, for there was nary a stool to sit on, wondering how to broach the subject of Cate. Finally, inspecting a large hanging carcass of beef as if to give it his approval, he glanced over at her, as if the thought had just occurred to him. 'That's a great beast she has, that Cate.'

'She's always with him. Close as some are to their kin.'

Closer than others. 'So she lost her family, then.'

'Aye.' She did not look up from shaping a loaf.

'Was she so...' What word would capture it? 'Bloodthirsty?' Aye, there was the word, though it did not match the woman with fear in her eyes. 'Even before?'

Before what? Her father's death or something else?

Bessie was slow to answer. 'Have you ever known a Borderer who was not?' she said finally.

No. He had not.

Then why had he thought he could turn her from her own vengeance to young James's? Now that he was here, he remembered what his years with the king had erased.

An eye for an eye.

It was the only Bible verse his father ever knew.

'He always hoped you would come home, you know.' She said it as if she had followed his thoughts.

He shook his head, fighting the longing her words

evoked. Only Bessie would think so. A woman could weave entire cloth out of words a man never spoke.

It was too late for peace with his father. And now, Rob was head of the family, as he had been destined since birth. There was no place for John here, being beholden to his brother while they both tried to wrest a living from the same, stingy earth.

Maybe that was why his father had sent him away.

'You and Rob are not comfortable, are you?'

He started, wondering for a moment whether she really were fey. Quiet, watchful, she had always had a way of reading people, of knowing the things that went unsaid, especially the ones you wanted to hide.

But then, Rob hadn't bothered to hide his disdain.

'We're different, Rob and I.'

'He's alone now, Johnnie.'

The thought surprised him. He had assumed his brother knew his place and embraced it. Yet his father and Rob had been the pair, even when Rob was growing. His father had spent hours with his first born, teaching him to ride, to fight, to follow the trails when the moon was dark. Showing him the best places to hide the cattle. Telling him how to deal with a head-strong follower. Neither spoke much. A nod. A shrug. A grunt. These communicated as much as words for a talking man.

A good thing, since both of them had rust in their throats.

And in a battle, he had no doubt, they would have fought with one mind, finishing each other's thrusts without needing to confer.

And now, Rob sat alone.

Well, that hadn't sent him to Johnnie's side, but it explained why he seemed frozen between John and Cate's tug of war.

A sudden vision stunned him. 'Does Rob plan to marry?'

A sigh. 'Marry who?'

'Cate Gilnock.' Did every conversation lead to her? He paced abruptly, bumped his head against a hanging pot, then swatted it in irritation. That would explain Rob's loyalty to her, even beyond that of kin. 'They seem well matched.'

A slight smile touched Bessie's lips, as if she were enjoying a joke he did not understand. 'Too well. There's no spark there, not the one that a man and woman feel.'

He ignored his relief. Then another thought nagged. 'Is there someone for you?' His little sister, grown now. Past time for her to find a husband. 'Is that how you know about men and women?'

She finished shaping another loaf and lined it up beside the first. 'I know,' she said, stopping to face him, 'because there *is* no one for me.'

He tried to remember the men who shook his hand yesterday. Fingerless Joe, Odd Jack, the rest. No, none of them would be good enough for her.

He faced Bessie's future for the first time. What would happen to her? As her older brother, he had protected a shy, delicate, pliable sister. That was not the woman who faced him now. This woman had strength any man would be lucky to have beside him. Strength he had never seen in the women inside Stirling's walls.

Strength like Cate Gilnock's.

Unwelcome thought. 'You could come back to court with me.'

'Could I now?' She put her hands on her hips and

then presented her plain wool skirt as if to curtsy. 'And wouldn't I look so lovely meeting the king?'

'We could find you something…else.' What did he know of women's clothes? How to take them off.

She dropped her skirts and returned to her bread. 'You've a good heart, Johnnie Brunson. Don't ever think you don't.'

No. She was right. Court would welcome her no more than his family had welcomed him. The women in Stirling, perfumed and curled and expecting to be waited upon, would barely nod to her. Even the wench carrying the king's bastard would mock Bessie Brunson, he feared.

'And so does your brother,' she said, bringing the talk back to a subject he'd hoped to avoid. 'If you would give him a chance to show it.'

'More than he's given me.' There seemed no truce between what he wanted and what Rob did.

But he had to find one—a truce with Cate and then with Rob—or he might never see Stirling again.

'Why don't you stay with us?' she said, turning to face him. 'Come home, Johnnie.'

'My place is with the king.' This was not his life. Hadn't been for years.

'He wants you to stay, you know.'

He searched her eyes, then shook his head. Only a sister's foolish hopes. 'No, he doesn't.'

He started pacing, ducking the pots this time. He had not come home. And he had not come to the kitchen to talk to Bessie about Black Rob Brunson.

'Cate says she wants to avenge her father. Is that all?'

'Storwicks are no friends of ours,' she said, sounding like the Borderer she was.

'I mean to Cate. Is there something more?'

Bessie didn't look up from the dough. 'Why do you ask?'

Because of the fear she carries with her. Fear she seemed to be able to hide from the rest of them. Was it his to reveal? 'Her eyes are...haunted.'

'I thought you said she was bloodthirsty.'

'Aye. That, as well.' A contradiction. 'That's why I wonder—'

'Don't be asking me these questions,' she said, and he saw a reflection of his mother's expressions in her raised eyebrows. 'Cate's the one you must be asking.'

He sighed. He'd rather confront his surly brother than brave Cate's knee again.

As he climbed the tower stairs, he heard raised voices in the hall.

'Now! A raid in his honour. He would want it.' One of the men. He could not tell which.

John hurried his steps. So soon, they returned to reiving. He heard a murmur, his brother's steady voice, though he could not make out the words. Would Rob say yes or no?

'There's enough of us,' someone else said. 'We could go.'

'The moon's half-full.' He could hear Rob clearly now. 'The night still short.'

'And our horses swift.' Cate's voice. 'We could get to their tower and back before the dawn. And if Scarred Willie is there—'

As John reached the top of the stairs and entered the hall, he saw Rob surrounded. His brother's face of strength had few differences from his face of grief, but John could see them. If Rob carried his grief into battle, the enemy would have an advantage.

'Red Geordie is barely in the ground,' John called out. 'Can you not give him a moment's peace?'

Rob, Cate and half a dozen of his men turned to look at him. Even the dog tilted his head, quizzically.

Cate scowled. 'It was not peace your father wanted.'

Rob's face of strength returned. John waited for a scathing rebuke, for he was arguing for the very respect for the dead he'd ignored yesterday, when Rob wanted the same.

'Johnnie's right. Return to your homes.' He looked at John with an expression that might have been warning or thanks. 'The time for riding will come soon enough.'

Cate's look said she blamed John, but the men had cattle still in the hills and homes to return to. One by one, they took leave, giving a hand to both brothers, the grip of John's hand less hearty this time.

Cate's men, seeing her look, did not shake at all.

No matter. Rob had resisted a call for revenge. Perhaps he was ready to listen to reason instead of vengeance.

'I would speak to you, Rob,' he said, when only the three of them remained.

Rob nodded towards the table, and Cate started to follow him.

'Alone,' John said.

She looked to Rob. He nodded, a signal for her to leave them.

She glared at John before she did. The woman who had trembled in his arms less than an hour ago had disappeared. Only the defiant warrioress remained.

He searched her narrowed eyes, wondering which Cate was the real one.

She leaned closer. 'Are you walking straight again,

Johnnie Blunkit?' Her growled whisper was soft, meant only to reach his ears.

Angry heat rushed to his cheeks as she passed him on her way to the stairs.

Johnnie Blunkit. The blue-eyed baby.

Words he had tried to forget ever since he'd left home. Not ones he wanted to remember as he faced his brother.

Although there were only three years between them, Rob, older, had been the favoured one. Tall, strong, taciturn, with their mother's dark, straight hair and the Brunson brown eyes, he had wielded weapons, but never words.

Words had been left to blue-eyed Johnnie, the gowk in the Brunson nest.

So John learned to talk. Even as a bairn, he told stories and jokes and did tricks to make them laugh. It was the only way he knew to gain their approval.

And sometimes, when Black Rob wielded his sword, or his fists, too quickly, clever John was the one who made peace.

So they sent him away, a gift to amuse young King Jamie. That's when he knew: all his clever words and funny tricks would never earn his father's approval. And when he arrived, he discovered a six-year-old king who needed a big brother of his own.

He also found that while a glib tongue might get you out of trouble, it could also get you in—trouble you needed a strong sword to escape. So gradually, he became as his brother's equal with a blade.

At least, that's what he told himself as he joined Rob at the table, though to confront his brother with words was little easier than to face his sword. An untrained fighter, clumsy with a blade, could do untold, unintentional damage.

So could a man ignorant of words.

John settled himself across the table. Rob met his eyes, silent, waiting for him to speak.

Perhaps a different argument would sway him. Perhaps he could remove Rob's dilemma and make the king his only choice. Maybe his brother would be relieved. Even grateful.

'Have you thought, Rob, about what happens after you hunt down Willie Storwick?' This was not swapping stolen cattle. Everyone on the Borders did that. Killing like that would continue for generations, kept alive in song. Borderers had a name for it. Blood feud.

'Scarred Willie should have thought of that before he killed Zander Gilnock.'

'Of course, Cate could change her mind.' He leaned back, folding his arms, and shrugged. 'Women often do. Then you'd be free to send men to the king instead.'

'So *that's* your plan.'

Never try to fool a brother. 'What do you mean?'

'You think to seduce her into helping you.'

He battled the vision of Cate, naked beneath him. 'A woman like that? No.' Though he had, once, foolishly, thought exactly that. 'But women are changeable.'

At least, the ones he knew had been.

'Cate?' Rob near laughed. 'You know nothing of her if you think that.'

'I know something of women.'

Rob leaned forwards. 'Do you now? Well, you know nothing of the Borders.'

Cate and this country, both unexpected mysteries. But it was no mystery what he must do here. 'I know enough to do as the king commands.'

Rob studied him, confusion on his brow. 'The king must have made some pretty promises to turn you into his lackey.'

The king had made no promises, but he had hinted at a wealthy bride and a position in the royal household. Cupbearer or Pursemaster, perhaps. 'There's no dishonour in serving the sovereign.'

'Well, I hope you enjoy whatever bauble he gives you,' Rob scoffed. 'Your king offers us nothing we cannot get ourselves.'

'Food in your belly, wool on your back, a stout wall and roof? Aye, all you can grab for yourself. But not the time to enjoy them. Only the king's peace can give you that.'

Rob blinked and something shifted behind his eyes, as if he glimpsed a different life. John held his breath. Did his brother finally understand?

Then, Rob cast his eyes to the floor above, where, until yesterday, his father had slept in his own bed. 'Only God can give you that, Johnnie.' He shook his head. 'Only God.'

'And God sends us the king to do his bidding on earth.' He leaned forwards to grip his brother's forearm. 'Help him, Robbie. Help him.'

But the Rob he recognised faced him again. 'I'll leave the helping of the bairn king to you, Johnnie. Just don't think that wearing his wisp of a badge will let you lord it over the rest of us.'

John winced. 'I've never thought that.'

Rob smiled. 'Have you not?'

John sat back, suddenly wondering. Why else had he returned?

He had ridden home wearing the king's badge, carrying the king's word, expecting finally to garner his father's respect. Or at least his attention.

Instead, he was Johnnie Blunkit again. Or worse. An outlander, no more part of the family than a Storwick.

But John had *seen* that outland, seen a life beyond these hills. 'I know what the king plans. Scotland will face England as an equal.'

'You think he'll defy his Uncle Henry? *He's* the one who's been stirring the families across the border.'

It was true. The king's uncle, the English King Henry, eighth by that name, was using the reiving families of England to keep the Scots occupied. 'Because he has no respect for us.'

'No. Because he *does* respect us. He respects our swords.' Rob leaned forwards. 'And I mean to be sure we *keep* that respect.'

John gripped his fists in frustration. 'It's been two years since Gilnock's death. Why is it so important to avenge him now?'

'Because now, I'm the head man.'

Pride, stubbornness—everything he knew of his brother was in those words.

He felt his voice rise, ready to shout. 'I need to know why.'

Rob gave a snort. 'If you'd not abandoned your family these last ten years, you would know.'

'If my family had not abandoned me, I would care,' he snapped.

Rob blinked.

John pressed on. 'Two years and Father didn't hunt the man down. Didn't you ever wonder at the reason? Didn't you ever think he was trying to avoid a blood feud?'

'And you think to force us to ride where the king

bids us instead? The last time we did that, ten thousand Scotsmen lay dead on Flodden Field, along with the foolish king himself. That's a mistake we won't be making again.' Rob pressed his palms flat on the table and rose, done with listening. 'Your king can wait for Brunson men. We ride after Willie Storwick within a fortnight.'

He cursed himself for a fool. Instead of easing Rob's decision, he'd forced it. 'And join the king after?' If they found the man quickly, they could still meet the king in East Lothian by early October, though John would have to soothe his sovereign's temper when he discovered they'd taken vengeance against an English Storwick.

'I've not decided.' Rob's lips curved, less in a smile than in a sneer.

Not a defeat, then. Rob had not said no.

'Ride with us, Johnnie. That is, if you're not a fazart.'

Fazart. The worst kind of coward.

John stood now, shaking his head. It wasn't death that he feared. 'I will not join you in vengeance. Not when I promised the king I would stop it.'

Rob, who rarely smiled, did. 'Ah, and promises must be kept, eh?'

A rueful smile touched John's lips and, for a moment, they shared it. 'Perhaps I've a drop of Brunson blood after all.'

'What happens,' Rob said, finally, 'if you can't keep it, your promise to the king?'

He had not faced that unpleasant prospect before. 'If I'm a careful and lucky man, I'll never lay eyes on King James again.'

'And if you're not?'

John liked the king and the king liked him, but he did not fool himself. Friendship and sentiment did not rule a king, not even this one. He'd cut down any enemies who stood in his way.

And any friends, as well.

'If not, my happy life could be a short one.' That was the fact of it. Now Rob knew.

John wondered whether he'd care.

His brother crossed his arms and shook his head. 'Then I can only wish you luck, Johnnie. And that you enjoy it while you can.'

Chapter Five

The nightmare visited her again, carried on the scent of heather.

Cate sat up, struggling against him, feeling the scream rattle in her throat, ready to escape. Just in time, she opened her eyes to find Belde nuzzling her side, as if he had tried to wake her.

Next to her, Bessie slept like one dead. Cate released a sigh, grateful, and slipped out of bed. She would not be able to close her eyes again this night.

She wrapped herself in a length of plaide and crept quietly down the stairs. Belde trailed her. Even in the dark, with most abed, there were few places to be alone. Someone would be awake on the tower's parapet. Another guard would walk the wall. The hall would be full of snoring men. But she had prowled the tower at night often enough to find a perch at the curve of the stairs where there was a hole in the wall for a lookout. There, she could sit, watching the hills, to be sure no one was coming.

As she approached it, she heard steps coming towards her. She had not brought a candle, needing no light to find her way, but this was not a footfall she recognised.

She gripped the dirk that was ever by her side, comforted by Belde, who was right behind her, but did not growl. Was it someone the dog knew? She slowed her steps.

Stopped.

He did the same.

She took a step.

So did he.

Her heart beat fast and the blood in her ears almost drowned the sound. Was someone beyond the curve of the stair? Ready to take her again?

No. She would not let that happen. She would run him through first.

She held out the dirk and rushed down the stairs, blade poised to hit a man in the belly.

But just before she reached him, a hand grasped her wrist, tight as a manacle, and jerked her arm up, pulling her closer. 'What the hell are you doing, Cate?'

Her body still carried the dream's fear. It took two breaths, three, before she recognised John Brunson. And then, pressed against him, his lips close to her cheek, she felt something she had never thought to feel for a man.

Desire.

The dog pushed himself between them, sniffing John in greeting. 'Traitor,' she muttered.

John let her go quickly, and she pulled away, back against the wall, still clinging to her dirk.

Holding his hands up and well away, he spoke. 'I didn't know it was you, I swear. I only touched you to save my skin. Don't run me through.'

Shocked and disorientated, she stood shaking, slow

to recognise his light, coaxing tone. Her fingers tightened about the hilt of the blade.

He leaned forwards. 'Are you all right?'

Surprised he had dropped anger so quickly, she jerked her head, not sure whether she signalled *no* or *yes*.

'Did you hear something? An intruder?' His hand hovered over his own dagger now.

'No, no.' She found her hand on his arm, trying to quiet him before the whole tower waked. 'You just startled me.'

'Then why were you prowling the stairs?'

She exhaled her pent-up breath. 'I had a bad dream and could not close my eyes again.'

The sound of his breathing next to hers in the dark was oddly intimate. In this bend of the stairs, they were hidden from view and for the first time since she woke, she breathed easily. An unfamiliar feeling. One she barely recognised.

'And you,' she asked. 'Did dreams rouse you?'

Even in the dark, she sensed he shook his head. 'Worries, not dreams.'

The moon Rob had warned of cast faint light in through the opening in the wall. She sat, taking her favourite perch. Belde moved to the step above her and settled, warm and familiar at her back. John sat two steps below, not asking permission. His position, so close and in the dark, seemed more intimate than a touch.

She struggled for distance. 'We'll send no men to the king. At least, not until we kill Scarred Willie.'

'And when you kill him, the Storwicks will kill a Brunson and we'll strike back and it will go on until after all of us have been gone for as long as that Viking on Hogback Hill. Is that what you want?'

She shifted on the hard step and glanced away from him. She spouted fine words about family, but she had thought of Willie's death only in terms of what it meant to *her*.

At her silence, he pushed again. 'Will his death be enough?'

She faced his eyes again. 'Yes.' It must be. It must be enough to make her into a different person. She must probe this man now, not let him ask more of her. 'And you. How can you choose king over kin?'

She listened to the silence, sensing his struggle.

'The king chose me,' he answered, finally, 'when kin did not.'

Harsh words. But so, too, were the ones his brother had hurled. 'And if we do not bow to your king's command? What then?'

'I cannot return to court.'

She shrugged. If he did not go back to the king, he would stay on the Borders, where he belonged. It did not seem such a hardship.

'Is it a place so much better than here?' She knew this valley and its hills. The rest—Stirling, Edinburgh, Linlithgow—were as foreign as London.

He was silent for a long time. 'For me it is. There, I've a place. Or will.'

'And for that, you would betray your family?'

'Betray!' The harsh word sounded like a shout, echoing off the stone wall. 'Haven't the Brunsons broken every law, betrayed every agreement of God and men?'

'What would you have us do? Let them take our sheep, our cattle, our…' She could not say it. 'Take our very lives without lifting a hand?'

'I would have respect for the king and his rule.'

'The king has not punished Willie Storwick.' The king's law had not saved her. Only the strong arm of her family could do that.

'Is this the way you want to live?' he asked. She couldn't see his expression clearly, but she sensed the earnest question in his tone. 'Ever in fear?'

She opened her mouth, but no words came. How had he seen her so clearly? No one else had. War or peace, the fear never left. If she were walking the very halls of the palace, surrounded by the king's soldiers, the fear would walk beside her, grabbing her each time an unfamiliar man came into view.

'Whether I want it or not,' she said, 'I think that fear is our lot.'

Yet for these few moments beside him in the dark, she had not been afraid.

It seemed impossible that she could respond to a man again. She had thought those feelings lost for ever in that dark and ugly hour two years ago. And now, this man had come in and she felt—alive.

She rose. 'I'm going back to bed.' Where she would lie with her eyes wide open until the dawn.

'Have your dreams faded?'

'Enough.' But she did not say yes, for the truth was those dreams would never fade. They had stalked her for two years and would stalk her until the day she died.

Or the day that Willie Storwick did.

John watched her disappear up the stairs, the echo of her question still ringing in his head.

And if we do not bow to your king's command? What then?

Her question. Rob's. Forcing him to confront the fact that he might fail.

How arrogant he had been to think he could sway her, simply because she was a woman. It was not only the men of the Border he did not understand. Cate had seemed curious as she listened to him, but without a thought that she might be wrong. Stubborn as any man. And despite her dark sorrow, she was more a part of his family than he had ever been.

What would it be like to have a strong family and a faithful woman beside him? The husky, tempting timbre of her voice echoed in his head, coaxing him to visions of a bed he would never share.

At court, he'd had no shortage of bed partners, but he'd learned they sought him out thinking their next bed might be the king's. If a few months with Johnnie did not lead her to the royal favour, a woman would drift off to the next man.

And he to the next woman.

Is that place so much better than here?

The valley of his boyhood spread out before him, lapped by the dark hills edged by moonlight. She had been roused by dreams, he by worries.

Worries. A pale word for his thoughts. In the place that should be home, he was an exile facing a brother who would not bend and a woman who would not yield.

In a few weeks, the king would expect him to deliver a band of Brunson fighting men. Instead, it looked as if those men would be riding the hills, chasing Willie Storwick.

In a few weeks, it would be prime riding season. Cattle and sheep would return from the hills to huddle near the tower. The bogs would dry, the ground harden.

Then, with the moon to guide them, the riders could criss-cross the hills as if they were flat as a chapel floor.

Men as skilled as his father did not even need the moon.

His father had known this vast emptiness well. His ponies knew every trail, every burn and rivulet. Where the trees used to be and where the stumps were now. Where the sinkholes were dangerous and where the heather grew. His father, his brother, they could ride blindfolded through these hills, trusting their memories and their ponies to guide them out of the valley and home again.

Even he had recognised the rise and fall of the earth under his pony's hooves today. A harsh land, but theirs.

Not the king's. *Theirs.*

He should not be thinking Cate's thoughts. Yet tonight, something called to him, like a voice on the wind… *Silent as moonrise, sure as the stars…* It was as if during all his time away, the land had waited for him like a faithful lover, now ready and eager to seduce him all over again.

Standing, he braced against temptation. The land wanted him no more than Cate Gilnock. He had not come home. He had come to carry out the king's command.

He turned from the window, heedless of the dark. As a boy, when everything became too much, he had taken off to the hills, to the only place where he had felt as if he, too, were descended from the Viking. And he'd gladly accepted his father's heavy hand in exchange for those precious hours of escape.

Perhaps on the bay pony he could find the way there again.

Chapter Six

'What do you mean, Johnnie's gone?' Cate asked.

Cheerful sun flooded the courtyard, belying the ominous words. Bessie picked up a damp shirt and draped it over a rope to dry. A furrow between her brows marred her normally calm forehead. 'No one's seen him since yesterday.'

What if something had happened to him? The thought bothered Cate more than she expected. 'I did.'

'When?'

She looked away. 'I'm not sure. Late. I couldn't sleep. We…passed on the stairs.'

Where had he gone after they talked?

After he left her without a touch.

'That's half a day ago.'

Cate shrugged, not wanting to care. But it did not take half a day for a life to change. It did not take half an hour. 'Why tell me? Ask Black Rob to find him.'

'Rob's in the hills, helping bring the cattle down. And, despite being prickly as a thistle, you're a sensible person. More so than either of my stubborn brothers at the moment.'

Cate blinked. Bessie said little, but saw much. Had she seen Cate's own troubles?

'But finally,' Bessie concluded, 'because you're the one with the sleuth hound.'

Cate rubbed the dog's head without thinking. Yes, she'd trained Belde to track swiftly and silently. When the time came, Scarred Willie would not escape. But her fingers shook as she scratched behind his ears. If she went too far, alone, something could happen...

Might have already happened to John.

No, she would not be afraid. Belde would be with her.

'Bring me something John has worn,' she said before she could change her mind.

'Here.' Bessie dug into a basket of clothes near the washing kettle and pulled out a linen sark. 'I was going to wash it for him.'

Cate took it, hoping his scent had not been muddied when it was mixed with the other clothes. Yet once in her hand, knowing it had touched his skin, she wanted to hold it close, to pray that he was safe.

'You'll take one of your men with you,' Bessie said.

She shook her head, resisting the temptation. 'He'll be embarrassed enough that two women were so worried about him. He'll be furious if I bring a brace of men. If I find him quickly, no one else will be the wiser. Including Rob.'

John would hate that. She wondered how she knew.

'I don't like you going alone. You'll be careful?' Bessie said.

Cate raised her head and donned her fearless look. 'If I don't find him quickly, I'll come back for help.'

Her fingers shook, clumsy, as she saddled the pony and put Belde into his tracking harness. Knowing what was to come, the dog jumped with excitement. Finally

ready, she knelt beside him and held the shirt to his
nose, glad she had named John a friend last night. Belde
might pick up his scent more easily.

'Fetch! John!'

Belde tugged at the leash, ready and eager. Cate
mounted her pony, shaking. The dog would run aside,
silently, as she had trained him.

So the prey would not hear them come.

Daft as he had been to ride into the dark alone, John
and Norse had found the circle of ancient, carved stones
on Hogback Hill. No one knew where they came from.
Or how long they had been there. Some said they were
tombstones of the ancestors. Some said the place was
haunted by primeval spirits.

That was certainly the story they spread on the English side of the border. It was enough to frighten most
away from this spot.

And enough to give him pause every time he stepped
into the circle.

It was a circle no longer. Over centuries, most of the
stones had disappeared. But the ones he remembered
still waited for him. Broad at the base, smoothed to a
peak, they were just tall enough for him to rest against
while he looked over the valley.

Many a day he'd sat here, looked to the east, and
wondered what lay beyond their valley. Now, he knew.

John took his favourite seat, hoping to summon the
feeling of peace he remembered. He liked to imagine
the stones had been put there by the First Brunson.
Liked to imagine talking to the man as if he were the
father John's was not.

And during those imaginary conversations, John felt
as if he, too, were a Brunson—something he did not

feel today. He had ridden off without a word to anyone, sure no one would notice, or care if they did.

He sat in the midst of the Viking stones, watching for first light to glimmer over the hills, and pondered his fate. The future that had seemed so certain when he rode into the valley had dissolved. What was he to do now?

And as his eyelids grew heavy, the only answer he heard was a woman's husky voice, whispering secrets in the dark.

Cate had trained Belde, yes, but he had not tracked before, at least, not when it mattered. Yet with only a whiff of John's scent, he took off as if the trail were a bright red ribbon, near tugging Cate's arm out of her shoulder in the process.

'Slow!' she called.

But he was doing what she had asked, what he was bred to do, and he didn't pause, pulling her, and the pony, straight north into the hills. Blessedly, in the opposite direction from the border. She pictured John a thousand ways. Lost. Fallen. Hurt. Dead.

Then she recognised where Belde was leading her. Straight to Hogback Hill. Where she had lost her father. And everything else.

Good land for grazing, yes, but full of dangers, even before that night.

Watch for the ravine. You might fall. Don't go near the stones. There be spirits.

Yet she could not stop now because Belde was taking her straight to the stones carved with strange symbols.

She did not want to see this place again. She saw it often enough in dreams, but there was no turning back and as she came closer, a figure with a drawn sword rose from behind one of the stones.

She gasped and tried to pull the horse back, but it was too late. Belde tore the leash from her hand and loped ahead, jumping with happiness to have found his man and sniffing John head to toe in greeting.

Relief left her limp and she did not examine it closely. It could have been relief that the man with the sword was not an enemy. Or it could have been joy that John was safe.

'Good dog,' she said, sliding off the pony.

John pushed the dog aside, playfully, trying to sheathe his sword, and then looked at Cate. 'What are you doing here?'

His smile was for the dog. His tone of irritation was for her. Well, she could match it. She had barely inhaled the whole way here, battling fears he knew nothing of because she had been worried that something had happened to him. Yet here he stood, alive and well, with all his parts in working order. 'You disappeared. Your sister was worried. What are you doing here?'

'I used to come here, when I was a boy.'

Safely outside the circle, she still shivered. 'Why?'

'To think.'

She looked around the stones and back to him. 'All day?'

He looked away, a tinge of embarrassment colouring his cheekbones. 'I came last night after we talked. And then I fell asleep.'

Anger surged at his carelessness. She had subjected herself to this horrible hill again because he had napped?

'Be grateful I didn't bring my men to find you dozing.' She reached for the dog's harness and pulled him safely beyond the stone. 'Enough, Belde.'

'Well, you've found me. Now turn around and go back home.'

She shook her head. 'Bessie will have both our heads if I come without you.'

He shook his head and sighed. 'A woman as stubborn as the rest of us.'

Cate had to smile. Those who didn't know Bessie mistook quiet calm for meekness. 'Next time, tell her where you are going.'

She hung back, still outside the circle, wondering that he treated the ancient stones as if they were ordinary rocks.

'Come,' he said. 'Sit.' He held out his hand.

She looked at the stones, not moving.

There be spirits there.

Yet it was full day, and the only spirits here, it seemed, were the ones that haunted her. 'Is it safe?'

He grinned. 'No safer place on the border.'

She put her hand in his, still reluctant to step across the imaginary line. 'My father said the spirits of the old ones haunt this place. He told me never to come here.'

John barely moved, afraid to remind her she had given him her hand.

That her cold fingers still rested comfortably on his.

'So did mine,' he said with another smile, hoping to distract her. 'But most of my father's warnings turned out to be false.'

'I cannot say the same,' she said, her fingers trembling.

But she stepped across the imaginary line and settled beside him, looking around, cautiously.

'You look like him,' he said.

She looked back at him. 'Who?'

'The first of our family. The brown-eyed Viking and his kin.'

'There was only one. He had no kin.'

A lucky man.

John searched his memory. He had heard the story many times before he went to court and not once since. 'So what *is* the story?'

'It is all in the song. Do you not know it?'

The wonder in her voice was condemnation. 'It's been years. Tell me again.'

'The First Brunson came with his fellows, across the North Sea to the Northern Isles, down through the High Lands, and all the way to the West Sea.' It was a tale she knew well, but no boredom touched her telling.

He did not interrupt.

'But as they reached the sea, the Others fought back.' She gazed westwards, quiet for a moment, as if she could see the story. 'And they pushed the First Brunson and his fellows into this valley and backed them against this hill.' In her low, deep voice, the story sounded real. 'And killed them.'

The words chilled him, like a cloud across the sun. 'All of them?'

'There are stories that one escaped. Maybe two. But the first Brunson was stripped of his horse and his sword and left for dead.'

The words came back to him now.

Left on the field by the rest of his clan.
Abandoned for dead was the first Brunson man.

* * *

A man as lost, forsaken and homeless as Johnnie Blunkit.

All his life, *he* had been the one who seemed to share nothing of this ancestor, not even his eyes. Even when he made himself at home among their graves, he doubted he belonged there. But to hear that the First Brunson had been abandoned by his tribe, well, that he understood.

'He survived,' she finished, 'and made his home here. Brunsons have held it ever since.' She looked at him. 'And always will.'

Sitting beside this woman, he looked out over the valley with a rush of unfamiliar feeling. Of belonging. Of permanence. Of home.

Home was not a tower. It was the grey-blue hills that held him, the green-gold earth that beckoned him. Home was a life with a woman who would bear his children, children who would ride the land after he was gone.

He fought the yearning. He had been long enough at court to know that land was given and taken like a golden coin, used as reward, withheld as punishment.

Women were much the same. A momentary pleasure or a political alliance, but never something that would last.

Yet this woman beside him gazed out on the land as if she were as unmovable as the hills. For all her fears and faults, he could not see her allowing herself to be given, or taken, for anyone's purposes but her own.

She was looking south across the hills they must ride to reach the Storwicks. 'From here, you could see anyone who might come.'

Suddenly, he saw it all. They must have ridden up

unseen, pouncing on her and her father asleep in their hut. And she lived in fear they would come again.

Were her sword and her clothes no more than armour to give her courage?

Beside him, she whispered, barely loud enough for him to hear. 'I have not been on this hill since…'

He heard the next words as if she had spoken them. *Since that night.*

Yet she had come here to find him. And come alone.

He finished her sentence. 'Since Willie Storwick.'

At the name, her air of dreamy calm disappeared behind tight lips and narrowed eyes. 'Aye. Not since then.'

There was something more in her expression, something that made him wonder whether…

He stifled the thought. He did not want to understand her fears. Instead of looking out over the valley, thinking of her in ways he had thought of no other woman, he should be thinking of how to persuade Rob to send men east to the king.

He calculated the weeks quickly. Perhaps there was a way to satisfy Cate *and* the king. A way that would not require Brunson men to scour the hills for weeks searching for a fugitive.

'What if I could ensure Storwick was punished quickly?' He turned to her, resisting the urge to take her hand again.

For a long moment, she stared as if he had not spoken. 'How?'

'He would be tried by the Wardens of the March.'

Her sigh overflowed with disgust. 'Do you not think we tried?'

Rob had told him as much. 'But the king has named Thomas Carwell the new Scottish Warden.' John had the papers with him, and an assignment to deliver them.

'And the law says the English must hand over a criminal for trial within fifteen days of the warden's request. He'll be tried and convicted within a month.'

Time enough for the men to reach the king. Barely.

She shook her head. 'Then what? They would only set a ransom and let him free. I don't want blood money,' she said, through clenched teeth. 'I want him dead.'

That, and something more, unspoken. Some instinct told him now was not the time to ask her what. 'I will make sure that is the sentence.'

'How can you do that?'

'I will explain it to Carwell.' The king could not object to proper punishment for murder. 'Make him understand the sentence must be death.'

She raised her brows, not convinced. 'And if it isn't? What then?'

'If you convince my brother to bring it to the wardens and they do not give you justice, then I will ride to find Scarred Willie myself.' Possible, but unlikely he would have to carry through. Either way, perhaps then this woman could put down her sword and get on with her life.

For a long moment, she studied him, silently. Instead of the *yes* he listened for, he heard only the wind.

'Why,' she asked, finally, her expression sceptical, 'would you do that?'

He sighed, forced to make his bargain plain. 'So that you'll help me persuade Rob to send our men to the king.'

Bald words. And not the whole truth, but he did not want to admit the rest.

Something like disappointment drifted across her eyes. 'You give me your word you'll see him dead first?'

He thought it through one more time. If all went as planned, the Brunson band would have a week to reach Tantallon Castle, where the king waited. Not much time, but enough. 'Aye.'

'And what's your word worth?'

Her doubt punched his gut. 'Must I swear? Then I swear.'

'By what? By what do you swear?'

She had not asked this the last time he made a promise. Did she know he never expected to ride after Willie Storwick? 'By Christ's blood, if you like.'

She shook her head. 'The church has barred all reivers and cursed us to hell. Swear by something else. Swear by what means the most to you.'

He looked around. Felt the wind. Saw the hills. And realised he sat in the truest place he knew. He reached out to touch the stone, hard and real, rough and sure beneath his palm. 'I swear by these stones.'

He let himself fall into her eyes then. They were doubtful, whether of him or of herself he could not tell.

He leaned forwards, wanting to take her lips, and she seemed to bend towards him as well. He raised a hand to touch her cheek as her hand reached for his, as if some power of the place pushed them together.

Her fingers, light on his cheek, drew him closer. His lips hovered a breath away from hers. He dared to brush her cheek. Another inch and he would taste her lips...

Stiff fingers touched his mouth and blocked his way.

He opened his eyes to see hers, huge and dark. She leaned away, back straight, shoulders square. All Cate again.

And he searched her eyes, fearing he had pushed her to refuse.

Her breath rose and fell as they sat, silent. And as

the moaning wind threaded its way around the stones, he heard the whisper of a song.

Finally, she nodded. 'I agree.'

Chapter Seven

John made sure they went to Rob together, immediately, before Cate could change her mind.

They found him in the master's room, staring at the bed as if unable to accept that it was now his by right. The interruption seemed a relief.

'We must talk,' John said.

Rob crossed his arms. 'I'm listening.'

'There's a new Warden of the Scottish March, or there will be, as soon as I carry the king's orders to Carwell Castle. Cate has agreed to let Willie Storwick be brought to justice under the Border Laws instead of sending Brunson men to find him.'

'Oh, she has, has she?' Doubt permeated Rob's words and he looked to Cate for confirmation.

John held his breath.

'Aye,' she said.

He looked at Rob, as if there had been no doubt of her answer. 'The English Warden is required to bring him to Truce Day for trial.'

Rob shook his head. 'Truce Day is a waste of horse feed.'

It was the same tone of voice Rob had used when

they were boys, the same patronising look that said: *You'll learn when you're older, Johnnie.*

He'd managed to forget that look during his time away. Those around the king might not love him, but they did not underestimate him.

He strangled his anger. 'Not this time. I'll deliver the message to the warden along with the king's documents. Justice will be done.'

Rob studied them both silently.

'Well,' he said finally, 'you sound as stubborn as a Brunson, that's the right of it.'

John smiled before he could stop himself.

His smile faded at Rob's next words. 'But you might as well hunt the gowk.'

Rob had sent him on more than one futile 'gowk hunt' when they were boys.

'He has promised,' Cate said, 'that if Willie Storwick isn't hanged for murder, John himself will hunt him down.'

Rob raised his brows. 'So you'll ride with us after all, will you?'

Cate turned to John. 'He has sworn it.'

Surprise transformed Rob's face. 'Another promise to keep, Johnnie?'

'Aye.' The weight of the words sunk in. He had sworn to take on someone else's cause, one that might collide with his own. Every promise a new stone, piled on an ever-growing wall. 'But I'll need yours, too. After the trial, you must send our men to the king.'

Silent, Rob studied him. 'Are you certain that is what you want?'

'Yes.' How could it be otherwise?

'Then I promise,' he said finally. Words strong as a handshake.

John nodded, feeling for a moment the strength of Rob's pledge. Could a brother's promise truly serve as a shield against the world's uncertainty?

Rob's next words seemed to answer *no*. 'But don't come crying to me when laws and wardens and kings fail you.'

Cate slipped her hand into his. Surprised, he turned to see her looking up at him. 'Family won't. Family won't ever fail you.'

He shook his head. He could only hope this time would be different.

It was too easy, she thought the next day, as she saw to her horse and prepared her sword. Too easy to imagine burying her face in his shoulder, letting him put his arms around her.

Too easy to let him help her bear her burdens. Piece by piece he had made promises to her. One by one he was acting on them until she had even begun to believe the promises might come true.

She must not surrender to those imaginings. When the black fear came again, she must subdue it alone. That was the way it must be.

If she let him touch her, if she let herself surrender as a woman did to a man, fear would no longer live in her dreams. It would be resurrected to live in her world. Whether she willed or no, her body would resist. Her fear was rooted so deeply that she would never be able to let a man take her again.

No matter who he was.

The others did not know that, but they knew enough to leave her alone. Knew she wanted to be alone.

But Johnnie Brunson looked at her with fresh eyes. She had lived the last two years seeing her past, at least the part they knew, reflected in the eyes of every man and woman who faced her. They brought it with them and heaped it on her with every glance.

Is she all right? We must be patient. We must make allowance.

The words were never spoken, but no one, except perhaps Bessie, was willing to come closer than arm's length. They gave her the space, the time, the seclusion she demanded.

They left her alone.

But Johnnie had not witnessed that time and what came after. He had not seen her grief, her numbness. He had not watched her float through the days like a wraith.

No, he only saw what she wanted him to see. Braw Cate. Cate the brave. Cate, who feared no man. This was the Cate he knew, not the ghostly, grieving girl. And certainly not the hopeful young girl who had once played hide-and-seek at a wedding and dreamed of a marriage of her own.

It was easier, somehow, to face eyes that saw only what she had become. To see her only as she wanted to be seen. She must be sure that was all he ever saw of her.

John was ready to mount Norse the next day when she appeared, mounted on her own pony, with the dog at her side.

He blinked, surprised. 'You're not coming.'

'You're not going without me.'

Did no one control this woman? 'Yes, I am.' He mounted and started for the gate, where two armed men waited to guide him to Carwell's castle. He had learned, in the last week, not to ride this land alone. 'Goodbye.'

'Those are Gilnock men ready to guide you,' she called out. 'If I do not go, neither do they.'

He sighed. He knew only that the castle he sought was west, near the sea and Rob could not, or would not, spare any of his men from guarding the tower.

He paused, turning in his saddle. Exasperation grabbed him by the throat. 'Why must you come?' *Don't you trust me?* But he did not ask that, perhaps because he did not want to know.

A bitter look settled over her face. 'It's my vengeance you're demanding. This new warden will hear from my own lips how serious I am.'

He swept her with his eyes as she sat astride her pony. 'How seriously do you think he will take a woman dressed as a lad?'

An angry flush touched her cheeks. 'As seriously as you tell him to.'

*I've not been so far from the tower…*she had said. Yet they'd be riding much, much farther than Hogback Hill.

How brave was this Cate?

How strong was he?

'We'll be gone two nights,' he said, watching for a hint of hesitation in her eyes. 'Maybe three.'

Three nights of sleeping beside her. He had thought to escape with this trip, not take temptation with him.

Her lips wobbled and she swallowed. Then her jaw settled into an immovable line. 'So then, we shall.'

Brave enough.

He sighed, wrestling his annoyance. He did not want her with them. Did not want her to interfere with his conversations with Carwell.

Or with his sleep.

He sighed. 'Come, then, if you must.'

Her smile almost made his concession worthwhile. She fell in behind him, Belde loping at the pony's feet.

'We're tracking no one on this trip,' he called, over his shoulder. 'The dog stays here.'

She opened her mouth to protest, but he shook his head. Perhaps leaving the beast behind would be enough to make her stay home as well. 'Don't waste breath and time. That's the way of it. Make up your mind.'

She paled. Panic touched her gaze, but she nodded, finally. He sighed and gave her a few moments to turn the beast over to Bessie's care before she joined them at the gate.

'Now keep up,' he said, as they rode out. 'And keep quiet.'

To John's surprise, she managed to do both through all of a long day. They swung northwards, climbing into the desolate waste of Tarras Moss. The ponies plodded carefully to avoid the worst of the bogs, and John was grateful that the other men and the beasts knew the way across the desolate, windswept land. But inhospitable as it was, it kept them beyond the edge of the Debatable Land.

No reason to search for trouble.

Trouble, he thought, watching Cate ride ahead of him, was already firmly attached.

Low grey clouds hung in the sky, reaching towards the hills like an old man's beard. Now and then, the air would grow thick with fog as wet as rain.

As they climbed, forest gave way to scrub that clawed at the ponies' legs, but they stopped for nothing. Food was an oat cake, eaten with one hand while the other held the reins. But unlike proper reiving men, they rode all day and left the night for sleeping.

They were on the far side of the range by the time of gloaming, and bedded down by a stream after the sun set. Summer was turning to its golden end, but they lit no fire. The two Gilnock men who rode with them bedded down out of earshot, but John set his blanket within arm's length of hers.

She frowned. 'You need not be so close.'

'And if I need to protect you in the middle of the night, would you have me be out of reach?'

He hated the fear that touched her face.

'Another arm's length will be close enough.'

He sighed. Sleeping beside her would be more difficult than his conversation with Carwell. 'We should be there by tomorrow night,' he said, as he settled his pallet a little farther away. At least there, she would bed down with the women, well away from him. Not that it would keep her away from his thoughts.

He turned his back on her and closed his eyes. A futile gesture.

'The Carwells can mount more men than any family west of the River Esk,' she said finally, breaking the dark silence.

He kept his eyes shut and his back to her. 'Can they now?'

'Almost as many as we can.'

The thought gave him pause. The Brunsons had been known to put near three thousand in the saddle when threatened. The king wouldn't be seeing near that number. 'We're not here on a raid. We're here to bring the king's proclamation that makes Thomas Carwell the Warden of the March.'

'That means less in Liddesdale than it does at Stirling,' she said. 'And little or nothing to me.'

He turned over and sat up. 'His father was warden before him. He knows what must be done.' The king's hated guardian had snatched the father's post away, along with its power and purse, when he took control of the young king. It was one of the first things King James set to rights. 'When Carwell mounts men, it will be in support of the king.'

A mistake to look down at her as she lay ready for sleep. It put him in mind of things he must not think.

'Why didn't he make *you* the warden?'

'Because I didn't want it.' Did not want to be trapped here in this land he had left behind long ago.

But the truth was that the king had never asked him to take the post. And for the first time, he wondered why.

'It would have done your family good,' she said. 'Would have made us the most powerful family in the March.'

'Go to sleep,' he said, lying down again.

But as he lay there, searching for stars behind the clouds, an unpleasant truth crept over him. He had cared for the king like a brother, protecting, teaching, treating the boy's welfare as his own. Creating a family to replace the one that had left him behind.

The king had not done the same.

When John had left the court, the king was meeting with the bishops and Lords of Council. He didn't need a big brother any more.

So he had sent John back to this lawless, empty land, expecting complete loyalty, never showing the same. And the allegiance John had shown until now would be forgotten if Brunson men did not ride to join the king before the frost.

John must have drifted into sleep, but when he heard a whimper next to him, he woke immediately, ready to ask her what was wrong.

Cate's eyes were still closed.

I had a bad dream, she had told him. Apparently, it was not the first.

Asleep, she tossed from one side to the other, muttering words he could not hear. Then, she swung her arms, wildly, hitting him in the arm, then nearly missing his eye.

'Cate! Wake up!'

She sat bolt upright, still fighting frantically, breathing hard. He tried to soothe her without a touch, murmuring words of comfort in her ear, close enough to catch the scent of her, close enough to remember how she tasted…

He had promised not to touch her, but, realising she was still gripped by her dream, he grabbed her wrists to keep her from hitting him or herself again.

'No!' Anguish touched her voice. In the dark, away from her haven, she must take him for an attacker. 'No!'

In a moment, her men towered over her, swords drawn, ready to use them against him.

'She still sleeps,' he said, letting go of her arms. 'Cate! It's John. You're safe.'

At the words, she collapsed, fighting to breathe, gulping air in a sound close to a sob. Then, she went stiff and still. 'What did I say?'

What was she afraid she would say? 'Nothing. Your men are here. And so am I.'

She looked up at her men, immediately sitting straight. Immediately Braw Cate. 'You may go. It was just…a dream.'

She waved them away and he nodded in agreement. They went back to their posts.

The new day was threatening. To the east, a pale light showed through a tear in the grey clouds.

Cate reached out, patting the earth, searching. 'Where is Belde?'

'We left him behind. Do you remember?' He regretted that now. Seeing her reach for the beast was like seeing her reach for courage.

Her only answer was a sigh. She stood then, and took a few steps away, as if knowing he had been too close.

'Another bad dream?' he asked, rising to follow her.

'A dream,' she whispered, turning away from him. 'Yes.'

'I'm sorry.'

'You cannot stop my dreams.'

'Not just for that. I touched you, but only so you would not hurt yourself.' He smiled in the direction of her back. 'Or me.'

A shrug. A mumble. He could not be sure what he heard. 'What's wrong, Cate?'

'Nothing.' She raised her head. The armour that made her Cate shielded her again. 'Nothing is wrong. We're riding on a fool's journey to put my fate in the hands of a man neither of us knows. What could be wrong with that?'

'You insisted on coming. Next time, stay at home.' He wanted to grab her arm. He wanted to whirl her around and take her in his arms and kiss her and stroke her hair and tell her—

She turned and took a step towards him, as if she had heard his thoughts and shared them. But instead of soft lips, he faced hard words. 'Next time? So you have no faith in him, either.'

'Yes, I do.' He had no other choice. 'Now lie down and go back to sleep.' He moved his pallet closer. 'I'll be right beside you.'

He lay down and deliberately turned on his side, back to her, listening for her to lie down again.

Instead, he heard only stillness. Finally, he sat up.

She was still standing, wide awake, arms crossed, looking up into the hills as if watching for a band of Storwicks to sweep down on them.

'Your men are near,' he said, 'if anyone comes.'

'It was like this,' she whispered, as if to herself. 'The night they came. Damp and clouded, the smell of heather strong enough to choke you.' She shivered. 'I hate that smell.'

The thought shook him as he realised he had been savouring that smell, hungry for the scent of home.

And that he had associated it with her.

She shuddered, looking suddenly small and frail.

Over and over the same bad dream. Was it of her father's death? Or something else? Something, for a woman, worse? Red anger boiled at the thought.

'What happened that night, Cate?'

Immediately, she armoured her eyes. 'Willie Storwick and his men attacked us and killed my father and his men.'

Yet the fear she carried, the fear she tried so desperately to hide, was personal, almost as if... 'Is that all?'

'Isn't that enough?'

'It isn't enough for you to be so afraid.'

She froze then, as if he had called her a coward. 'That is all,' she said, not looking at him. 'And that is enough. I was only frightened in the dream and I only dreamed because I was outside and smelled the heather.'

Braw Cate, the Cate she showed the world, was fearless. And who was he to know or judge how frightened she should be at the memory of a sudden raid and her father's murder? Perhaps that was, indeed, enough.

'Nothing will happen to you,' he said finally.

She turned, her smile sad. 'Do you promise?'

Promises, promises. One atop the next. 'I want to,' he said, surprised that it was true.

'But you are too honest a man for that.'

'I've promised not to touch you. I've sworn to bring Scarred Willie to the warden's justice. I've promised to pursue him myself if he does not bring it about. Those are things I can promise because they are things I can do.'

She picked up the thread. 'But you can't promise that nothing bad will ever happen to me because the world is wide, life is long, and God as capricious as the west wind.'

She knelt beside him then, and put a hand on his shoulder. Startled, he felt the heat of it through the wool of his shirt.

'Make me no more promises, Johnnie Brunson,' she said, squeezing his shoulder. 'For my heart will break when they do.'

He reached to cover her hand with his, stopping just in time. So easy to break a promise. So hard to keep one.

Her smile told him she was not surprised. Told him she had no faith he'd keep any of them.

He drew his hand away. 'Come. Sleep another hour. I'll stay awake and watch for Storwicks.'

She lay down again and, at last, he heard the even breath of sleep. And as he sat, awake, watching the sun rise behind Tarras Moss, he made another promise.

That he would do all in his power to protect her.

Chapter Eight

Thomas Carwell, John was pleased to see, let them enter on the name of the king.

But then, three men and a woman posed no threat to Carwell Castle, even from the inside. Surrounded by a moat, guarded by a looming gatehouse as large as the Brunson tower, it was grander than any he had seen except the king's.

The day's ride had been long, but the land was flat and the trip easier than the day before. Carwell had greeted them hospitably and, as soon as they had been given rooms for the night, John insisted on a private meeting.

'I don't trust him,' Cate whispered as they followed one of Carwell's men through the darkening halls.

'You don't even know him,' John answered, though he could not say he knew the man, either. Their paths had crossed at court, but only briefly.

Carwell was a little older than Rob, but he had the smoothness of one who had spent time at court. Reason enough for Cate to doubt him.

But as they entered his solar, the man's narrowed eyes had the guarded look of suspicion. Carwell took

John's offered hand and they shook, clasping each other's arms.

He wondered whether the man meant it.

'You say the king sent you,' he began after offering them ale. 'To do what?'

Wary, then. As he should be. 'He's thrown off his guardian. It's his personal rule now.'

The man nodded. 'We heard.'

John struggled not to look surprised. Carwell, it seemed, still had connections at court who kept him informed.

'And he wants peace in the Borders.'

King's man or no, Carwell's lips twitched. 'Does he now? And when does he plan to stretch out his hand from on high and make this happen?'

'Now. And he's expecting your help.'

'And what does he expect me to do that I could not do last week or last month or last year?'

'He's expecting you to enforce the laws.' John handed him the king's proclamation. 'He's named you Warden of the March.'

Carwell took it, eyes wide for a moment, but an unreadable expression quickly replaced the surprise. He unrolled the gilded signet letter until the king's black seal dangled free at the bottom. A folded parchment fell on to the table. Breaking the seal, Carwell leaned close to his candle to read.

Somewhere beyond the window, in the dark, waves broke on the shore, as tireless as the wind sweeping across the hills.

Finally, Carwell leaned away from the candle. Shadows disguised any emotion in his eyes.

'What was the other message?' John asked. The king had told him of nothing but the appointment.

Carwell waved his hand. 'Personal congratulations.' He sighed. 'Would that my father had lived to see the wardenship rightfully returned to our family.'

'A Carwell may have been warden in the past,' Cate said, as if she, too, wore the king's badge, 'but what is returned must also be earned.'

This was why she had come, John thought. He would let her have her say.

Carwell raised his brows and looked at her. 'You're to tell me how I must earn it?'

A sceptical tone, John noted, but not a disdainful one.

Cate was quick to answer. 'You must hang Scarred Willie Storwick.'

'Must I now?' he answered. He did not smile when he said it. 'The man has enemies from here to Jedburgh. What is your complaint?'

John felt her tense beside him. For a moment, he was not sure she would be able to speak.

'Murder,' she said finally. 'He murdered my father.'

So they told him of the raid, the escape and of the previous warden's refusal to act. And when they had finished, the new Warden of the March nodded. 'I'll send word to the English Warden tomorrow. Storwick will appear at the next Truce Day to answer for his crimes.'

Cate relaxed into a smile, the first he'd seen since they left home.

'It must be soon,' John said. 'No more than a fortnight.'

Carwell crossed his arms. 'I see that the two of you will be doing the warden's job without any help from me.'

Johnnie smiled to soften his tone. 'It must be settled before we send Brunson men to join the king.'

Because I promised Cate. That, he would not share.

'He asks for mine as well,' Carwell said, nodding towards the king's letter. 'They'll escort you home, then ride on to meet the king.'

'Without you?' Even a warden would be expected to answer the king's summons.

He waved the 'personal' note. 'The king asks that I deal with some administrative matters here.'

Yes, Carwell, too, was a king's man, but as he and Cate left the chamber, John wondered whether their interests truly converged.

Home again, after Belde sniffed both of them to discover where they had been and with whom, John and Cate gathered in the hall to give Rob and Bessie their report.

'So it is settled,' John said. 'Storwick will be punished.'

And John's promise kept. He looked to Cate for confirmation.

She shrugged. 'He'll be summoned. He must still appear.'

John swallowed. That, he could not promise.

Rob's scowl reflected Cate's doubt, but his tone was surprisingly jovial. 'So we have a fortnight until Truce Day.'

'Aye. He and the English Warden will agree on the date and then the families will be notified.'

'Then we'll ride the day after tomorrow.'

An unpleasant prickle touched the back of John's neck. 'Ride where?'

'On a little jaunt over the mountains,' he said with a smile.

If this was what it took to make Black Rob smile,

John would prefer that he sulk. 'You said you would wait for the warden to act.'

'I said I would let him punish Scarred Willie,' he answered. 'Our little foray has nothing to do with him, although it might involve some Storwick cattle.' Rob's smile dissolved into a grim, determined set of his lips. 'Yes, in just a few days, the moon will be new, the sky fair and the wind at our backs on the trip home.'

Peace on the Borders, he had told Carwell. Now the Brunsons the first to break it. 'You say you must steal or starve, but there's no shortage in the larder today.' John looked at Bessie. 'Is there?'

She sighed. 'Winter is long,' she said finally. 'If there's no shortage today, there will be tomorrow.'

John slammed his fist against his palm in frustration. A man with much to prove. That was Rob, now, eager to mount his first raid. The one that would mark his assumption of the title head man.

'Join us, Johnnie,' Rob said, his voice suddenly alive and urgent. 'Ride with us.'

And his first thought was *yes*.

Join us, Johnnie. Sweet words he had waited too many years to hear. Was Bessie right? Did Rob want him to stay?

They all watched him, silent, waiting.

He shook his head. The king wanted more than men. He wanted allegiance to the crown, not to family feuds. 'I'll be no party to it. It's Scarred Willie I promised to punish. Not his family's cows.'

'What hurts the Storwicks hurts Willie,' Rob answered.

What hurts the Brunsons hurts you, he might have said.

But he was not a Brunson. Not in the way Rob meant.

Cate, who had been silent, rose. 'I must see to my pony before we ride. His leg was scratched as we came across the hill.'

'You're not going,' John said, as if he had the right, angry that she would put herself in the path of fear and danger again.

'Yes, I am,' she said. 'And you're not the one to say me nay.'

Had she learned nothing from the trip she had just made? 'You want revenge against anyone named Storwick, don't you? Whether it gets you closer to Scarred Willie or not.'

She turned away, not answering. As if she did not expect that he would keep his word and had taken vengeance back upon herself.

'She can ride if she wants,' Rob said. 'The decision is hers.'

But you haven't seen her, he wanted to shout. *You don't know how frightened she will be. She won't let you know.*

But *he* knew.

'If you won't come with us, Johnnie, can I trust you to keep the tower safe?'

He didn't look at his brother. It was not the tower he wanted to keep safe. It was Cate. 'If she goes, so will I.'

Wordless silence as Rob, Bessie and Cate all looked at him. He tried to read Cate's eyes. Confusion creased her brow.

Was she glad of him? Or did she care at all?

'And anger your wee king?' Cate said finally.

'When Rob first rode, he was younger than the king is now, so I'll hear no more about his age.' Yet Johnnie had never ridden. Not to this day. It was one more way in which he was no Brunson.

Perhaps it was time. Perhaps if he understood it, it would be easier to stop. 'I will go with you to steal a few cattle,' he said with grim determination, 'and to keep you from doing worse.'

To keep worse from happening to Cate.

Rob nodded slowly. 'Welcome, then, Johnnie, but there's a lesson you may learn when you ride with us. On a raid, you don't always have a choice.'

John followed Cate out of the hall and down the stairs, intending to talk to her, to change her mind, but she stayed ahead of him until they reached the courtyard.

He resisted the urge to grab her shoulder. Instead, he lengthened his strides until he walked beside her. 'I'm going with them. Now you don't have to.'

She did not stop walking and he kept pace as she strode through the gate and beyond the wall. 'My vengeance doesn't belong to you.'

'It does now.'

She shook her head, doubtful.

'I gave you my word that Scarred Willie would be brought to justice. I won't let you kill him first.'

She smothered a smile.

'And neither,' he continued, 'will I let him kill you.'

Her smile disappeared. The set of her lips was grim. 'If that's why you are coming, you can stay at home.'

It was. No need to say it. But something else niggled at him. A tremble of her chin. Eyes too defiant. Something that said—

'You've never ridden a raid before.'

She reached down to stroke the dog, a sure sign she was nervous. 'Neither have you.'

'You still don't trust me, do you?' Even she gave him

none of the credence she would give another Brunson. 'You don't think I will keep my word. You think you must do it yourself.'

She stopped walking, then, and turned to face him. They had reached the grove near the stream, the same place where he had watched her train the dog. The burbling water sounded deceptively peaceful.

'I think you are trying to help me. And I thank you for that.' Her voice did not overflow with gratitude. 'But whether Willie Storwick lives or dies, you'll be leaving the Borders and I'll be living here—' she flung her arm towards the hills '—and Storwicks will be living on the other side of those fells, for the rest of my life. So his fate means nothing to you. It means everything to me.'

Her fair hair, whipped by the wind, tangled behind her and her brown eyes had become dark holes in her face. He still did not know what to make of this woman and her mix of courage and fear. But watching her bludgeon her terror into submission made him long to prevent her from ever feeling it again.

'You're brave.' He gentled his voice, wishing he could put his arms around her. 'To ride with them.' Then he smiled, hoping to coax one from her in return.

'I do no more than any Border man would do,' she scoffed, as if blades and blood were nothing. 'It takes no special courage. Nothing to sing about.'

'What is courage, then, if not to face your enemy?' He wondered whether she would answer, whether she would give him a glimpse behind her shield.

'To lie down in darkness and face your dreams. And then to rise in light and face your day.'

Her words hit him like a punch. Aye, that was the kind of courage she needed to live when even sleep did not bring rest.

'What dreams, Cate? What dreams do you face?'

She was silent for a moment, eyes dark. But when the dog nuzzled her hand, she raised her eyes to John's and shook her head. 'Is that what the king's men do?' she mocked him, clearly, to save herself. 'Speak of their dreams?'

He had dreamed of her, he realised, but he would not speak of that. 'No. Life with the king takes courage of a different kind.'

He thought she would mock him again. Instead, her eyes touched him softly. 'Tell me.'

He had told none of them. Indeed, he had barely admitted it to himself, but she seemed to draw his words, like the vent drew the smoke from a brazier.

'The king has grown up surrounded by—nay, more than surrounded, he's been at the mercy of men who kept him alive for their own good purposes.' He had become king when still a babe, and a young king is a fragile creature. 'Even his mother changed her allegiance faster than she changed her husbands. Scots, English, French—he knew not from one day to the next where her loyalty would lie. It has made him strong, but not trustful.'

And had made John the same. Life had shown him no reason to trust family. Or women.

'Does he trust you?'

'If he hadn't, he wouldn't have sent me.' Yet with those words, he recognised why the king had sent him. It was a test, a larger one than he had realised at the time.

One that would prove where his loyalties lay.

Cate's gaze was steady, but he felt the confusion in his own. There had been no questions in his mind when he left the king. No doubts about what he must do.

Now, things were not so clear. Loyalties were tangled. That never happened to the others. Family was all. No one here ever, ever doubted that.

No one but Johnnie Brunson.

But stubborn, steadfast Cate was making him question himself, something no woman had ever done. And now, grudgingly, she had even thanked him. Something, he was sure, she had never done for another man.

But she still doubted him. Well, maybe she had good reason. Maybe she, too, was testing him, demanding no less proof than did the king.

'I gave you my word, Cate. Do you trust me to keep it?' He held his breath, awaiting her answer.

Her smile surprised him. 'Not enough to let you ride alone, Johnnie Brunson.'

Folding his arms, he matched it. 'Then we'll both be mounted, because I'll not let you ride without me.'

'You're pigheaded, Johnnie Brunson.'

'No more than you, Cate Gilnock.'

And they smiled, and shook their heads at their shared stubbornness.

That night, Cate woke with a dream more frightening than all the others.

She dreamed of joining with John Brunson. And of being unafraid.

She lay awake, staring at the ceiling, listening to Bessie's gentle breathing beside her, trying to understand. In her dream, there had been a moment of peace, a soft kiss, and then, *more.*

She had wanted more.

Nay, no dream then. Just a premonition of what would happen if she gave in to him. For in the dream, his hands were on her breasts, on her skin, stroking, comforting, exciting until she felt swept away, as if some wild spirit moved through her—

And that was when she woke. Heart pounding, afraid again.

She lay on her back, staring at the ceiling, forcing her breath to slow.

She must marry some day, she supposed, though she had put it far from her mind. As long as the tower was without a mistress, she could live here, helping Bessie with the running of it and Rob with the ponies. As long as she could train dogs and raise ponies she would have food and shelter. A life.

One that seemed worth little.

For months after the attack, she had numbed herself, feeling nothing. Food had no taste, sun, moon, music no sweetness. Her clothes hung loose and she moved in a world coloured only in grey.

She wasn't sure how long she lived that way, but one day, she heard a bird. Felt the wind. Rediscovered delight in small things she could hug to herself. A dog's tongue, grateful, on her hand. A sunrise after a night free of dreams or raids. A fire's warmth in December. These were the things she clung to, the smallest daily touchstones, asking, wanting, expecting nothing more.

Until now.

She had had few reminders of tender feelings between man and maid. Her father had been widowed early, so she had not seen kisses stolen nor heard bodies joining in the room next to hers. She could pretend they did not exist. Pretend she would never have to face them again as long as she stayed alert with her body stiff and her sword at hand.

John's arrival had changed all that.

He was a man used to easy kisses and willing women. One who had not been taught that she was not to be touched. And his very appearance roused a desire more dangerous than the body's. A desire for a life with a man. To work beside him in trust and sleep beside him in love and carry his children in her womb. Things she had forbidden herself to imagine, let alone to want.

She wanted to resent him for that, but the dream told her the truth. Promises made. Promises kept. And now she dreamt of things that could not be. Dreamt of being a woman who could love a man.

She must suppress those dreams. Master them as she had mastered her life for the past two years. For even after Willie Storwick was dead, she feared she would never be a woman who could press her body, nor even her lips, against a man's and feel joy.

And that meant there was no point in pining after a man like Johnnie Brunson who could charm a woman just by breathing. He would expect a wife eager to be charmed. One who would melt into his arms and welcome his kiss.

And she was Braw Cate—now and ever more. Not a woman who needed, or wanted, a man.

His promise to her was really, always, a promise to the king. That's where his allegiance lay. Soon, John Brunson would be back at court and married to some woman with courtly graces, leaving Cate alone with yearning and regrets as difficult to heal as those she had already suffered.

No, she must not yield. And she must make sure John Brunson got no closer. The day would come when

he would be gone and she'd be alone with her nightmares again.

Don't you trust me? Aye, there was the problem. She
was starting to do exactly that.

Chapter Nine

John mounted with the rest, in the hour before sunset.

It was a small group tonight, so they could move quickly. Come before they were seen. Go before they were heard. Only five men and Rob, John and Cate.

In the dimming light, breasts beneath her quilted jack-of-plaites vest, hair disguised by her steel helmet, she looked no more a woman than the rest.

Except to him.

The borrowed helmet on his head shifted and she reached over to straighten it.

Not a touch, he reminded himself, but he smiled. 'My thanks.'

His eyes met hers and her lips parted. Then she looked away, as if even her fingers on steel were too great a risk.

He wanted to grab her hand. To kiss her fingers. To tell her he would keep her safe. To beg her to stay home—

'Stay in the middle.' Rob's voice, speaking at his side.

She gathered her reins, motioned Belde to her side and nodded as her horse started for the gate, following the others.

'Both of you,' Rob said in a voice John could not misunderstand.

'You needn't worry about me,' John said. 'I was trained by the king's own sword master.'

'You stay close and do what I tell you,' Rob said in a voice meant for John alone. 'I don't want you straggling behind.'

'I'm not Johnnie Blunkit any more,' he growled.

'That may be, Johnnie boy, but you've never ridden a raid.'

He resented the reminder. He'd been too young to ride before he left. Or so his father said. Rob had ridden by the same age. 'Maybe not, but I'll have no trouble with it.'

'Do as you please, then, if you know so much, but if you get yourself killed, don't blame it on me.'

Rob rode to the front of the group, but beneath his angry words, echoed something beyond annoyance. Concern.

John pulled his pony beside Cate's. It was for her that he rode tonight and he meant to stay close.

'We're only there to lift a few cattle,' Rob said, addressing all of them. 'Just a little reminder and a warning. Nothing more.' He looked at Cate. 'And no one else.' Finally, he raised his voice, a battle cry. 'Silent as moonrise!'

'Sure as the stars!' his men responded.

'I ride for no cattle,' Cate muttered, so low that only John could hear.

'And you'll not ride for him,' John said. 'Not tonight.'

'But they must know where he is.'

'I promised and so did you, Cate. You gave me your word you would let me bring him to justice.'

A pout mixed with her frown as she flashed him

a frustrated glance. She trusted family, yes, but this woman was not accustomed to depending on anyone but herself. Nothing he had done so far had done much to change that.

As they rode across the valley and into the hills, John felt awkward as his brother had predicted. His own horse had been judged untrained and his armour too heavy. So he rode Norse, still an unfamiliar mount, and wore only the chest piece of his armour. The saddle's back rose high against his, a blanket rolled behind him. He carried his own short sword and dagger, but in his right hand, he carried a lance, longer than he was tall, forcing him to ride one-handed.

But for all the strange trappings, he rode lighter and more freely than when he was suffocated by his armour and, as they climbed into the hills, the pony steady and sure beneath him, something stirred within. Not quite a memory, but a hunger for the feel of hooves on the ground beneath him, sure and swift, as if he were remembering something that had been with him since his first breath.

He settled in, trusting the bay, as they rode through the dark. The miles were not long, but they were hard ones. A friendly visitor would have ridden by the water, in the valleys, to come up to the castle. Instead, they took to the hills, circling around so they would not be seen. From here, he looked down, catching a glimpse of a little village and the glow of hearth fires.

They were not raiding a village tonight.

He kept as close to Cate as her dog, but she kept her eyes straight ahead, never looking at him.

The others might want cattle. Cate wanted revenge. And he meant to keep her from it.

There was no road, but the ponies did not need one.

They were in the treeless part of the land now, dipping in and out of the folds of the hills so that if someone caught a glimpse of riders, by the time he blinked and looked again, they would be gone.

And then they came over the rise to see a small hut and the last of the Storwick cattle still left in the high country.

Scarred Willie was not a keeper of cows. There was no reason he would be near the beasts in the middle of the night.

John kept his eye on Cate anyway.

As they paused and looked down, Cate gripped the pony's reins so tightly that he shifted, trying to sense her command.

She loosened her fists and kept her eyes straight ahead, as she had done throughout the ride after that one quick glance at John. She could not look around for every threat. Looking would only feed the fear. Surrounded by men, with Belde at her pony's side, she tried not to think about where she was going.

And even though it was impossible, she thought she smelled heather. Choking her. Reminding her.

You're brave, John had said. But she was not. When Scarred Willie was dead—only then would the fear ebb and the nightmares cease.

Yet when Rob gave the nod and the rest rode down the rise towards the cattle, her fear returned in a wave. This time, not just for herself.

This time, she feared for *him*.

Rob motioned them into action with only a dip of his head and a flick of his hand. John stayed on the ridge beside Cate, relieved she did not follow. The other men swooped down, surrounded the cattle, herded them back up the hill and slipped away before a single Storwick could protest.

But as the rest disappeared, Cate lingered on the ridge. A single man rushed out of the hut, too late to save his herd. Beside him, John sensed her taking a breath, tightening her thighs on the pony, gathering the reins...

'Come.' Rob, beside them. 'Now.'

He could not. He must move or Cate would ride down and confront the man alone. 'Keep her here.'

John galloped to the hut before the man could mount and pointed the lance at his chest. 'Scarred Willie. Where is he?'

The man laughed, a sound of panic. 'I know not. He goes where he likes.'

John was aware, dimly, that Cate had ridden up behind him. 'What does he say?' she asked, breathless.

He heard the creak of saddle and boot, the growl of a dog. Was the woman dismounting?

'Stay back,' he said, glancing over his shoulder.

A glance away was enough.

The man pulled his dagger and swung. The blade hit John's left arm, unprotected by armour, and drew blood. But the man did not stay to fight. He started to run.

Towards Cate.

John swung the horse around. In the dark, it was hard to see what was happening, but he thought he heard Belde jump.

No time to dismount. No time to reach for sword and dagger. Instead, he thrust his lance at the man.

No thought. No hesitation. Just as quickly as that and suddenly, John was looking down at a dying man with the steel tip of his staff holding him to earth.

'Are you all right?'

'He cut Belde.' Her voice shook.

John started to dismount, then swayed, dizzy, nearly falling. He must be losing blood.

Rob appeared, crackling with anger. 'Come. Now.'

Cate was not ready. 'But Belde—'

'Must run with us.'

She mounted, slowly, and Belde struggled to his feet. Then they rode back over the ridge, leaving a dead man behind, along with some of John's arrogance.

You may learn, Johnnie, that on a raid, you don't always have a choice.

Contrary to plan, the ride home took longer than the ride out. Rob sent the others ahead with the cattle to hide in the gullies of Tarras Moss. That way, if the Storwicks followed the trail of blood, only Rob, Cate and John would be in danger.

Instead of keeping to the hills, they followed the easier route along the river, but neither John nor the dog could move fast. As the sky lightened, they stopped to look to the wounds of dog and man.

John kept an eye on Cate, tending to the dog, while Rob looked at his injury. Rob washed it roughly and without tenderness, tying a cloth around John's forearm to stop the bleeding.

'You'll mend,' he said, jerking the knot a little too tightly.

John winced and looked down at his arm, then up at his brother. 'Rob, I'm sorry.'

A shrug. It meant forgiveness. 'I'm riding back a ways to see if they follow us.' He looked over at Cate, then back at John. 'Go.'

John took the few steps to where she sat, the huge

beast sprawled across her lap, cradled like a baby, his shoulder roughly covered by a cloth. The dog nuzzled against her with a soft whimper of pain, a sound John had never heard from him before.

'How is he?'

She looked up, anguish in her eyes. 'How are you?'

'Rob says I'll mend.'

'So will he.' She petted Belde and slipped away from him. 'The cut was not deep. Now let me see yours.'

She turned to John, fussing over the bandage Rob had tied. Her fingers, gentle on his bared forearm, were welcome after his brother's rough treatment.

Touch. She was touching him.

She was alive and safe and touching him.

He covered her hand with his and she stilled, but did not protest. All the emotions he had stifled throughout the night flooded over him. That he could have lost her. So easily.

He raised her fingers to his lips, kissed them.

She rewarded him with a squeeze of his hand and raised her eyes to his. 'You saved my life.' Her words came slowly. She was not accustomed to giving thanks.

'It's why I came.' He put on a smile to make light of the admission.

Relieved, she answered it. 'You must stop getting yourself injured, Johnnie Brunson,' she said, taking her hand back, but without drawing her dagger or threatening him.

He reached for her hand again, pulling it back, pulling her closer. Then he tilted her head up to look into her eyes and stroked the fair hair away from her temples, her brow, and trailed his fingers down her cheek and to her neck with a touch softer than he knew he possessed.

She trembled in response and her fingers crept up

his arms, carefully avoiding his wound, but then holding on tight. Her eyes clung to his as though he were a rope keeping her from falling into darkness. They did not reflect passion. Nor did she look at him with the sultry eyes of a woman swooning and ready to spread her legs for him.

No. Instead, her eyes clung to his as though he were the last thing she might feel on earth, the last thing holding her to life.

'May I kiss you?' He had never asked a woman for permission once she had acquiesced to his embrace, but everything about this woman was different.

She did not speak or nod. She simply closed and opened her eyes.

He leaned closer. This would not be a kiss of possession. He would not ask her to surrender. His lips simply met hers, inviting her to join him.

At first, she did not respond. Then, she tried, as if her lips were still learning.

As if she had never kissed before.

The thought startled him and he broke the kiss. 'Have you never been kissed, then?' Absurd question, yet, yet…

'Not when I wanted it.'

A thousand questions, blurred by his desire. He pushed them aside. 'Do you want this?'

Silence. He could barely stop himself from saying please.

'Aye,' she said finally, then closed her eyes and leaned towards him again, lips parted.

I am not afraid. He will let me go if I ask.

Cate nearly moved her lips to say the words, words like those she muttered to herself every day. But this time, she teetered on the brink of being swept away, as if she stood on the edge of a cliff, with the wind behind her and nothing to hold on to, nothing to keep her from falling.

If she jumped, what would happen? If she lost herself, could she ever find her way back? Could she really be an ordinary woman, able to love a man?

This man?

For a moment, the answer was *yes*.

Yes to lips warm and tender on hers. *Yes* to arms firm yet gentle around her. *Yes* to kisses trailing down her throat, and hands grazing her breasts and to a world that held only his body and hers, stealing her breath, stealing her mind...

Stealing her control.

And it seemed that, even if he never touched her again, somehow, if she let him any closer, he would know everything.

And that frightened her more than ever.

Now his arms were too tight, his kisses too rough, her breath too short, and then—

No.

She pulled away, pushed him back, and he released her, more easily than she had expected.

They breathed in tandem, only their foreheads touching, which seemed for a moment more intimate than the kiss.

She braced, expecting him to protest. To grab her, to force her back into his arms.

Instead, his breath moved in and out, mirroring hers as if they were trading secrets, trading souls.

She did not risk taking his eyes, but watched his hands, unmoving in his lap. And faced that something in *her* had changed.

So close to losing him, the caring she'd ignored would not be stopped. For all these months, she had lived *for* one thing, revenge, and *against* another, succumbing to a man, ever again.

But with John, she had started to wonder. His touch was gentle, his kiss tender. When she touched his arm, she had wanted more, wanted him as a woman might want a man.

And then, dark fear rushed through her again and she knew that even the tenderest lover would never be gentle enough.

Perhaps her feelings for him were gratitude. Camaraderie. Even friendship. But they could not be the feelings of a woman who could truly love a man.

And he must never know why.

Was it lust or his wound that made him dizzy? When his lips met hers, he lost himself, felt his body reaching out to hers, felt her start to melt.

Then she'd pushed him away.

And they sat together, exchanging silent breaths, each of them on the edge of something.

A final breath and then Cate rose and walked back to where Belde still lay.

No, not walked, stomped. As if she could crush John beneath her feet. Her body was stiff as if she had never yielded in his arms. As if she never had a place to rest.

As if he were as much of an enemy as Scarred Willie.

Or she as changeable as any other woman.

Yet when they breathed together, he had felt something else. Hope? Yearning? Something soft as a whiff of heather shielded by her jack-of-plaites vest so that swords and spears and pain could never reach her.

Was it only her body she was trying to protect? Or was it her heart?

The question stunned him. A kiss, yes, but he should not be thinking of hearts and tomorrows. This woman was not one to be trifled with unless he was serious about building a tomorrow.

And he would not be here tomorrow or the thousand tomorrows that a wife would demand. No, his promise not to touch her protected him as well as her. The kiss had been a thoughtless risk. It would not happen again.

'Quick.' Rob's voice broke his thoughts. 'I saw no one behind us, but the sun is near up.'

They mounted and crossed the burn, reaching home to find that the men with the cattle had them safely hidden in the hills. He let Bessie coo over his wounds, then collapsed into bed.

He woke the next morning, uncertain of the man who had slept in his skin.

He had ridden a raid. He had killed a man. He had kissed Cate.

And he wasn't sure which of those was most disturbing.

Chapter Ten

John still wrestled with his thoughts the next morning. The king would not be happy to discover John had killed a man on a reiving raid, but a phalanx of Brunson men fighting at his side should blunt his anger. At least, John hoped so.

He paused as he passed the door of the head man's room. His brother's now, his father's no more. Yet though John had seen the man dead and buried, he hesitated, wondering if his ghost haunted the walls.

Rob saw him at the door. 'I told you to stay back,' he said, not bothering to ask for an explanation. 'You nearly got yourself killed. And her when she followed you.'

Followed him? No, that was not the way of it. 'She was ready to ride in alone.' He would make no apologies for saving Cate.

Rob frowned. 'Did she say so?'

John shook his head. She did not have to speak. He had felt her gather the reins and lean forwards on the pony. 'I could tell.'

'Why? What for?'

'Looking for him!' He lost his patience now. 'While

you're willing to risk life and limb for a few cattle, she's intent on only one thing—Willie Storwick. That's the only reason she came with us. And she shouldn't have come at all.'

'You tell her that.'

They shared a look of mutual exasperation, shook their heads at the same instant, at the same angle.

John laughed. 'You're the head man. You tell her. I can't change her.' Kisses aside, she was more steadfast in her purpose than any woman he had ever known. 'No more than I can change...'

...the wind.

And he heard, in his own words, what she had said to him that first day. Borderers held themselves above the king of either country. Family came first, the king a distant second, if he came at all. John had not believed it then. Did not want to believe it now.

Yet he had ridden beside them and killed a man as dead as any Brunson could. 'I'll not ride again,' he said.

'You can't change us, either, Johnnie,' Rob said, as if speaking his thoughts. 'Be glad I'll be giving you the men and stop trying.'

Giving *you* the men, not the king. Giving them because he was family.

'The king wants more than men,' he answered. 'He needs allegiance from all of Scotland, including the Borders.'

'You won't succeed, Johnnie.' For a moment, he thought he heard a touch of regret in Rob's voice.

And now, at least, he knew why. Because to succeed would mean changing an entire way of life.

It had seemed so easy before he left Edinburgh. Easy as delivering a message commanding them to make the king's fight their own. Failure had not crossed his mind.

Now, like Rob, it looked him square in the face.

'So what will you tell wee Jamie then?' his brother asked.

'Nothing. If I don't succeed, I'll not go back at all.' Not if he wanted to keep his head free of a noose. But he must say it with a smile, as if he spoke words instead of a death sentence. 'So then I guess you'll be forced to take in another wayward Brunson.'

Rob shook his head. 'No, I won't, Johnnie lad. If you can't live by this family's code, you're no longer a Brunson. I won't have you here.'

John turned his back and walked down the stairs. There was the truth of it. *You're no longer a Brunson.* Words his father might have said. Words that summed up what he had always felt.

And family had failed him once again.

Still, he shrugged and told himself it was no hardship. He wanted to stay no more than Rob wanted to keep him.

And outside, the whine of the wind mocked him.

'Come here,' Cate called out to him from the hall. 'I've something for you.'

She had a well-worn jack-of-plaites vest in her hand and a determined set to her lips.

'Turn around and stand still,' she said. 'I must measure you.'

'For what?'

'A proper vest.'

He bit back a smile. 'My harness is better protection than that bit of fabric and bone.'

'Your armour is too heavy for the pony and it clangs like a bell announcing our coming. If you're to ride with us, I won't have you wounded again. Slows us down.'

'I'm not going to ride again.' He did not try to soften the bitter tone. 'And neither are you.'

'You'll be riding to Truce Day soon enough. The last time we rode, you had to kill a man.' *For me*, yet she didn't say that. 'You've made me a promise, Johnnie Brunson, and I intend for you to stay alive long enough to keep it. Now I've not time to make a new vest, but I think I can recut this one.' She held it out. 'Put it on.'

He humoured her, amused, until he felt the weight of it on his shoulders, coating his chest and back. It looked deceptively like a simple quilted vest, buttoned to the neck, snug, perhaps, in winter, but no match for a sword or a dirk. Only after he had it on did he realise she was right. It left his arms free, and protected his back, his belly, and his heart, yet he could move more easily than in the unforgiving armour.

She pulled and tucked the vest around him, not meeting his eyes. No smile graced lips that stayed safely distant from his, yet she was so close, he could feel her breath on his neck as she inspected the fit of the vest at his back.

She sighed. 'I'll need to add a strip here,' she said, raising his arm, 'and on the other side.' She stepped back. 'You can take it off now.'

He did, handing it to her, relieved to have it off his body, wishing he could strip off the last few days as easily. He was no Border man. To dress as one made him as false as Cate garbed in breeches.

Yet now, Cate paused, clearing her throat as if to speak, but not raising her eyes from the vest draped over her arm. 'I should have thanked you,' she said finally. 'You saved my life.'

'It was why I came.' He could say little more.

She nodded, not raising her eyes.

Who was this shy woman before him? By the river, she had touched him. She had kissed him. Was it in gratitude because he saved her life? Or just the excitement of the raid, making her blood run hot?

It must have been no more than that, and though she had thanked and not chastised him, she deserved his apology. He had asked if he could kiss her and she had said yes. But he had promised. He should have been strong enough to keep it.

'And I must say to you that I am sorry that I…' Was he sorry he kissed her? No. He tried again. 'I gave you my word not to touch you. And I broke it. I'm sorry for that.'

Her cheeks turned pink. A blush. Something he could not reconcile with Braw Cate.

'The fault was not yours,' she said. 'I should never have…' She looked away and let the sentence drift, unfinished.

'It was not so bad as you had feared.' Of that he was certain. For those few heartbeats, she had been totally his.

Cate shook her head slowly and raised her eyes to his. 'I didn't expect…' She looked at him, then, as if inspecting the vest again, trying to make the pieces fit. 'You are not a man like the others.'

The words were a slap, a cut, a blow to the gut. Even Rob did not doubt his manhood. 'What do you mean?' He kept his voice low and his words even.

'Just that! Most men would roar and stomp and boast of their bravery. Or they would be sullen and silent. You talk. You smile. And you just stand there and calmly ask, "What do you mean?"'

'Is that what you think a man is? Someone who growls and stalks and kills like a wild beast?'

Yet he had done just that. He had killed a man without any thought except to protect this woman. And whether he had given her his word or not, he was imagining her in his arms again.

'A man,' she said, 'is someone who will avenge his family unto death.'

Aye. Now she was trying to cloak him with that duty as well as with the vest. But he had taken it on himself, given his word to this revenge of hers, even as he struggled to understand what lay behind her hate. 'Is that all you live for, then? To see your father's killer dead?'

Something strange drifted across her face. He blinked and it disappeared, but for a moment, it almost looked as she might cry like any ordinary woman. 'If I don't avenge him, who will?'

He felt a twinge of guilt on behalf of his father. If Red Geordie had avenged her, it wouldn't have been left to his sons to do.

'And what will come after that? You've built your life around punishing one man. What happens when he's gone?'

Blank puzzlement wobbled on her face, as if she had never considered the question. 'I don't know,' she said finally.

Without thinking, he snatched her fingers. Her hands had wielded a sword, bandaged his arm and measured a vest, but cradled in his, they felt small and delicate. 'You should marry,' he said, wondering what would happen to her once the purpose of her life had been fulfilled. He had a feeling it would not make her as happy as she thought. 'You should find someone to care for you and protect you.'

Someone other than Johnnie Brunson.

The thought kindled his anger. At least, anger was

what he called it. Anger because she had put herself in harm's way. Anger because he had been forced to kill a man because of her stubbornness.

'Ah,' she said with a lift at the corner of her mouth. 'Now you sound like other men.'

But she did not pull her hands away.

Instead, her eyes met his and he could see her consider the idea. Then he lost the logic of his argument. The small, cold hands in his put him in mind of warming them. Of warming her, with his lips. In his bed.

She must have seen desire darken his eyes. She pulled back and busied her fingers plucking at threads on the vest. 'There will be no marriage for me.'

'Why?'

'Because I do not want it.' She sounded as if she were trying to convince herself as well as him.

'Why? Because of what happened?'

'What do you know of what happened?' Her gaze was as sharp as her words.

'I know that women have lost fathers before and they did not lift swords and shun men.' *Had* there been something more? Something worse? He had asked her. She had denied it, but—

'And men have been fostered away from home before without abandoning their families.'

He flinched. The woman could fight with words as well as a sword. 'And does Rob know? Will he be willing to feed and shelter you for the rest of your life?' He rued the cruel question the moment he asked.

She raised her head, proud. 'I earn the food I eat.'

Her lifted chin, the shield around her heart—he saw, suddenly, that all of life was a battle for her. And that wounded him more than her words.

'Oh, Cate, life doesn't always have to be so hard.' He spoke to himself, as well as to her.

'You said the king would not take you back if you did not do his bidding. Life at court sounds no more forgiving than that on the Borders.'

'It isn't. But two people can make moments that are.' The best liaisons had playful moments as well as passionate ones. And he remembered, long ago, private laughter behind the door of the master's chamber and shared smiles across the table. 'They can laugh and sing and be happy together, even when life is harsh.'

She studied the warrior's vest on her arm, as if she might find an answer there. Then, she raised her eyes to his. 'If that is true, then I wish such a life for you some day.'

'But I want *you* to be happy, too.'

Her jaw sagged in speechless surprise. Hunger filled her eyes.

'Has no one ever wanted that for you before?' he asked.

She shook her head.

He sighed. Rob and Bessie supplied food and shelter. But happiness? They might not even hope that for themselves.

'Let me show you. There are ways for men and women to be happy.' The words galloped out before he knew whether he sought Cate's happiness or his own.

'Like our moment by the stream?'

He nodded and he held his breath, hoping.

'So it is in a woman's body you think to look for happiness?' Disappointment tinged her words.

'No! I mean...' What did he mean? He had found happy hours of mindless escape in the arms of too many women. 'You are different from other women.'

She shook her head. 'And you, Johnnie Brunson, alas, are the same as other men after all.'

And she turned away before he could admit, even to himself, that Cate's body was not the only thing of hers that he wanted.

In the hall, she pulled the table closer to the window and spread out two strips of fabric, cutting each to the size she had measured with her fingers. Then she picked up a chip of steel from a broken sword and stitched fabric around it, until it was hidden and padded between two pieces of wool.

Carefully, stitch by stitch, piece by piece, she hid the tiny bits of armour between padded cloth. One at a time. Little leftovers. A chip of bone. A scrap of broken armour. Nothing pretty. Nothing whole. Just bits and pieces, carried home, buried and hidden as an animal would collect what he needed to survive.

That was how she had survived. Building her armour piece by piece, day by day, word by word. Hiding the fear.

There are ways for men and women to be happy.

Was that still true for her? Was it still possible for her to be like other women?

What will you do when he is dead?

When he was dead, everything would be different. But when she tried to picture how, she could imagine no life other than the one she lived. Could not picture joy at joining.

Desire had flared when she kissed John, something she thought never to feel again. What if she could feel that without fear? Perhaps she ought to start finding out now.

She pushed the thought away, but it kept creeping

back as her fingers moved, silently selecting and stitching each piece into his vest.

She had trained the others, trained them so well that none dared approach her. But though John *said* she was not like other women, he still imagined her as a woman who could be touched and kissed…

And more.

She said he was like other men, but that was not true. She wasn't sure, exactly, who this man was, stubborn as a Brunson born, but gentle with her. Gentle but with insistent eyes and tender hands and compelling lips.

And when he had kissed her by the stream, for just a moment, before the fear returned, there had been only John and Cate and joy. Was life truly like that for other women?

If she let herself… If she let *him* kiss her again, she might discover whether she had healed at all. Or whether she could.

And if not, she could be Braw Cate still, for no matter what she discovered, he would be gone back to the court and its women, not here to remind her of her failure or press his success.

The realisation was not as reassuring as she had hoped.

Cate found him on the parapet that night, taking the first watch. Behind the fog, the moon was creeping back to its light, but the night was cool and damp, as if winter were testing its time.

She hugged her plaide tighter. 'A good night for the seat,' she said.

He rose from the watchman's seat, tucked against the chimney so his back was warmed, and smiled. 'Stirling Castle boasts no such luxury.'

Lantern light flickered over his smile. In a life in which smiles had been scarce, it was part of him she cherished most.

'Does your arm heal?'

He waved it, as if to brush off the question. 'It will.'

She looked out over the parapet, not knowing what to say next. Fog hugged the hills, hiding anyone who dared ride that night. But it also seemed a shield, hiding them.

There are ways to be happy. Could she learn them?

'You apologised today,' she began. 'For…' How hard it was, to speak of it when he was close, warm, solid beside her. 'For kissing me.'

'Yes.' The word was wary, as if he expected her to demand further penance.

She lifted her head, trying to see his eyes in the dark. 'You gave me your word and I release you from it.'

'You mean I may touch you?'

'Yes.' She held out her hand.

He hesitated, but then enfolded it in his. 'Like this.'

She nodded. 'And you may…kiss me.' She tried to force her coiled muscles to relax, in case he chose to kiss her immediately.

He nodded, slowly, but didn't move. 'I see. And what has changed since this morning that I might touch you and keep my manhood intact?'

Either he was laughing at her or he was suspicious. Well, she had given him reason for both. But she squeezed the hand that held hers, warm. 'You said men and women could be happy.'

'Aye, yes, hinny,' he said, in a voice as warm as his hand. 'The loving moments a man and woman spend in bed can make the rest of life worthwhile.'

It was a foreign language, the very idea. 'I do not

want that.' *Not yet*, her mind yelled back. 'But another kiss, yes, perhaps.'

'And you'd like it now?'

He *was* laughing at her. Yet he made no move, waiting for permission.

She hesitated. Was she ready? What if…?

No. No more hesitation. 'Yes. Now.'

He put an arm around her waist, gently, and stroked the hair away from her forehead with his fingertips. 'These things must not be rushed.'

His touch was light, a whisper, as if he knew not to grab and thrust. His very slowness allowed her feelings to stir to life.

He did not take her lips, but pressed his to her forehead, down her temple, nibbling around her ear, slow, soft, yet relentless. Inside something shifted, like ice breaking on the river, exposing the running stream, still flowing beneath it.

Somehow, his hands moved, too, up and down her back, stroking her sleeves, warming her skin until it tingled.

Her lips parted, expecting to meet his, but he worked his way around her face, her cheek, down her throat and she shivered. Then he came up the other side until she was impatient, reaching for his cheek to force his lips to hers.

But he escaped her touch and bypassed her lips again, ending on her forehead where he began. Then he let her go.

Immediately, she missed him.

His smile wobbled. 'We had best begin slowly.'

'But…' She was eager now. His forbearance was her frustration. He had taken her mouth before, touched her.

She had already done more, already wanted more. 'I wanted a kiss. Like the one you gave me before.'

'You did not want it…before.'

Yes, she had pulled away from him at the stream, but not until she'd glimpsed that happiness he had promised. She wanted it again.

'I won't resist. Not this time.' She clenched her fists. No matter what.

'Put your hands behind your back,' he said.

She did, slowly, immediately feeling vulnerable, then saw him do the same.

'Now I'll kiss you.' He leaned towards her, taking her lips without taking her in his arms. So all she would have to do was lean back if she wanted to escape.

She did not want to escape.

His mouth caressed hers, soft, warm, and then he tasted her with his tongue and she felt that touch in parts of her body far distant from her lips. His mouth did not move from hers and she wanted to be closer, wanted the strength of those arms so cruelly denied her. Wanted the rest of his body pressing against hers.

She unclasped her hands and threaded them under his, around his waist, pulling him to her, expecting his arms to follow. They did not. But both of them breathed harder, his tongue explored her as she wanted his hands to do—

Then he broke her hold and stood straight. 'We'll continue…another time.' His words were breathless.

She clenched her fist and raised it, not to fight him off. To pummel his arm in frustration.

She dropped her hand and looked up, absorbing his face. The lopsided smile, the eyes, grey-blue like a stone, but softer.

Had they seen directly into her? Yet no judgement

touched his gaze. He stroked her hair again with the same tenderness as when he started. His kiss had been fervent, not brutal. And it had been pleasant. More than pleasant. So wonderful that she forgot…

Somehow, he had known how to make her forget. And when to stop so that she would not remember.

She cleared her throat. 'I can see how that might make a body…happy. Thank you.'

And she couldn't even tell him all the reasons.

Chapter Eleven

Cate had no nightmares that night. And her first thought on waking was how bright the late-September sun shone.

'That's a pretty tune you're humming,' Bessie said as she rose and pulled on an extra petycote.

'Was I?' She had not thought of humming at all. Was this what Johnnie had done for her?

She reached for her comb and pulled it through her hair. It had grown two inches below her ears now, long enough that she should cut it again, but she looked at Bessie's thick, red locks, tumbling halfway down her back, and paused.

'Bessie, do you think I'm pretty?'

Bessie smoothed down her skirts with a great sigh. 'It's not me you should be asking.'

Cate turned away, feeling her face flush, and put down the comb. It did not matter how she looked, if she did not want to be noticed. 'It was a foolish question.'

'He looks at you as if you are.'

He. So even Bessie could follow thoughts Cate could not recognise as her own.

For two years, she had been sure that she would never be a woman again.

Now Johnnie had given her hope.

She did not know how to add this small spark of happiness to the mix of fear and anger that fuelled her. It perched uneasily in her breast, as out of place as the sun at midnight. It burned not like the hot, destructive rage that had driven her, but more like the warm glow of a fire on a cold winter's night, offering sanctuary from the harshness of life.

Offering the happiness Johnnie spoke of.

For those few moments in his arms, there had been nothing but her and him and the kiss. Pain, vengeance, all the things that had filled her very body for two years were pushed aside. Past pain, future worry, all gone.

But for how long?

Yes, he had shown her a small piece of pleasure, like a sunny day or a good stew. But the sun would set. A sated stomach would be hungry again.

Pleasure did not last.

She had learned that when she had used those brief moments to pull herself out of despair. They didn't last, but they served as rungs on the ladder that helped her escape the pit. Could this do the same?

She followed Bessie downstairs, trying to put him out of her mind. But she had promised him the vest, so she bent over the garment that would protect his back, shelter his shoulders and shield his heart.

With Belde at her feet, she worked in the hall, where the sole fire burned, as the household came and went throughout the day. She knew without looking when he entered the hall. She glanced over, trying not to turn her head, not wanting him to know she watched him, but he caught her eye and she turned away, embarrassed to be caught staring at him.

Her fear of him had ebbed in one way, yet today, she feared something new.

Johnnie Brunson was a man who knew too much about women. For the last two years, she had held her armour strong against the rest of the world. He was chipping away at it, piece by piece, making her want, even making her believe she might find happiness with a man.

With him.

And now, instead of being brave, she was glancing at him beneath her lashes, hoping to see some yearning in his eyes, acting as if she were an ordinary woman who might some day enjoy the ordinary happiness Johnnie spoke of so temptingly.

Scolding herself, she turned her back on him and looked down at the vest. *His* vest. *His* fault to remind her of what she could never have and would never be. She had been content before he came, with one purpose in life and that was revenge.

Now he had upset it all.

She had wondered whether she might ever enjoy a kiss again. Now she knew. She could, when he did not hold her in his arms.

It seemed her body would resist men for ever, even if her mind, even if her heart, did not.

Nothing was going to change that. Not even Johnnie Brunson.

John watched Cate for days, trying to understand this strange, maddening woman. The first time they had met, she had threatened him, swearing no man would ever touch her. And from everything he could tell, no man did. She had the temperament of a warrior and the habits of a nun.

But gradually, they had made a truce. She had shared none of her secrets, but he had come to care for her. To wish for her happiness.

And now, she had come to him, asking for a little of that pleasure he had promised. Asking him for something she'd taken from no other man.

For something that made him feel as if he belonged.

A frightening thought. There was nothing for him here. Nothing but to serve the king and leave.

But his duty had faded for the moment. All he could think of was Cate.

Why should a simple kiss affect him so? He'd kissed women aplenty. It was, as he told her, pleasant. A moment of happiness.

Why did it feel like more with her?

Because there was still something, some missing piece he did not understand. Something that lay behind her devotion to family and her quest for revenge. Something that meant he could not hold her too close or too tight.

But he had promised not to touch her and he had kept his word, for the most part, until she came to him. Until she asked him to. But now that she had, he wanted to kiss her again.

Wanted more than that.

And now, she sat, day after day, remaking a vest for him that he did not want and did not need. Working for hours as if she cared for his safety, but barely glancing up when he found an excuse to wander into the hall.

He was a man who prided himself on understanding women, but this one confounded everything he thought he knew.

* * *

When John walked into the hall late the next day, she rose, finally looking at him again.

'Here,' she said, holding the vest up to his chest, eyeing it as if wondering whether she had measured correctly. It was so heavy, it took both her hands. 'Try it on.'

He reached for it and slung it over his shoulders, shrugging it into proper position, amazed that, despite the weight, it was supple, moulding to his torso, more comfortable than armour would ever be.

She smiled and nodded at her handiwork, plucking and fussing with threads he could not see, pinching and tugging at the fabric to see whether she must do more work before it fitted him properly. 'I put new pieces down the side to hide them.'

The new material ran like a stripe from armpit to waist. Beside the rest, stained with sweat, snow and blood, it looked clean as a babe's bottom. '*I* am new to this.' He sighed. 'No sleight of hand will hide that.'

She reached for the ties, tucking the ends of the bows beneath the vest, her fingers flickering on his chest. He cleared his throat, forcing his arms to remain at his side.

'Whose was it?' he asked to distract himself. The previous owner must have been a long-waisted man, though narrower in the chest than John.

Silent, she finished the last tie, patted his chest and looked up, meeting his eyes for the first time. 'Red Geordie Brunson's.'

His father's vest seemed to sear his back. 'I can't wear this.'

'Why not?'

He fumbled at the ties, trying to free himself. 'It doesn't belong to me.'

She wrestled the strips of fabric away from his awkward fingers and tied them again, in knots this time. 'Red Geordie's got no more use for it. You do.'

'Rob would not approve.' *You're no longer a Brunson.*

'It's been hung in the armoury. That means it's there for the next man who needs it. That man is you.'

Everything tangled together, tight as the knots she tied. The raid, the feeling of belonging that had swept over him as he rode beside his brother, the man he'd killed. And then, there was Cate. No. First there was Cate. Cate was the reason he had ridden with them. Cate was the reason he had killed the man.

'I have not earned the right to wear this,' he said. He was no Brunson. Rob had made that clear. Donning his father's vest would not change it.

She shook her head. 'You do not have to earn it.' She finished the knot and stood back. 'You were born to it.'

He shook his head. 'Not me. Not this.' He turned away, without a word of thanks, leaving her alone in the hall.

But he still wore the vest.

Her nightmare came again that night, days after the raid was over and she was safe behind the tower walls.

Cate woke, eyes wide in the darkness, recognising the feel of her bed, the look of the ceiling and the sound of Bessie breathing beside her.

She had screamed only in her dream, then. Bessie still slept.

Cate did not rise to wander this time, but turned on her side and reached for Belde, reassured by the feel of his fur against her palm. She stroked his back, shook his ears and let him nudge her hand with his cold nose.

It had been two years. She counted herself cured.

But in those dreams, Braw Cate disappeared and only worthless, shivering fear remained.

'Are you going to tell him?'

Bessie's voice from the other side of the bed was calm and steady. Not asleep then.

'Tell him?' Caught unawares, Cate's cheeks burned and her heart pounded in her ears. 'Tell him what?' She did not need to ask tell *who*. 'He knows I have bad dreams.'

'I don't mean the dreams. Does he know what *causes* them?'

Cate lay in endless silence, eyes open, hand over her mouth, staring into darkness and realising that all this time, the secret she had gripped so tightly had been no secret at all.

'How did you know?' she asked finally.

Neither of them had moved. They lay, back to back, speaking softly in the darkness as if all would be ignored on the morrow, just as it had been until now.

She felt a shrug of Bessie's shoulders.

'Did I… In my sleep…?'

A movement against the pillow as Bessie shook her head. 'But I'm a woman.'

'Who else knows?' Panic now. 'The men, too?' She could not bear it if every man of them had looked at her, knowing, thinking, wondering…

'I've said nothing.' Bessie turned over on her back. 'And they would never expect it. Not from a Border man.'

Cate had a vision, suddenly, of Black Annie, silent, beside her husband. Bessie's mother had barely said a private word to Cate in the year she had been with them before the woman's death. But when Cate stood before Red Geordie, it was Black Annie who had lifted her gaze to her husband and nodded just before he said *yes*. Had Black Annie seen what Cate had thought hidden? Had she told her husband?

She sat up in bed, gripped with new fears. 'Did your father know when he gave me his word? Did Rob when he took it on?'

'Willie Storwick killed your father. They needed no more. That was enough.'

'Then it will have to be enough for Johnnie, too.' He had kissed her and he had killed for her, but this she would share with no man. For she would not admit to Bessie, nor to herself, that Johnnie's promise meant something different, something more, than Geordie's and Rob Brunson's ever had.

Chapter Twelve

A fortnight later, John wore the vest to Truce Day.

He and Cate had barely spoken since the day she finished it.

She had asked for no more kisses.

He had offered none.

Her eyes had expected too much that day, expected him to be a man he was not.

A Brunson. Someone who belonged here. Even someone who might stay.

But he rode as a Brunson today. Rob had called near all the men to come so they could fight if needed, but it was more than a war party. Cate was not the only woman with them, for Bessie had insisted they needed salt and a new cooking pot. Truce Day was a market day as well. Still, they rode every mile between the tower and Kershopefoote on alert, ready for an ambush.

'We should be meeting safely on Scots land,' Rob grumbled. The truce site lay on the English side of the river that served as the border.

'It was the only way they would consent to bring Scarred Willie.' John repeated Carwell's reassurances, but he had been in the Borders long enough to feel uneasy.

Or perhaps it was the October damp that chilled him. Gold-and-brown leaves littered the ground, but green leaves clung to most of the branches, drifting like clouds, blocking a clear view across the river.

The trees thinned where the river's ford was easiest and they pulled to a stop at Black Rob's grim nod. There, on the other side of the water, waited a group of mounted, armed men.

He pulled Norse closer to Cate, Rob to Bessie, and the rest of the men circled them. Belde growled, the hair on the back of his neck rising.

'I should not have let you come,' he muttered, as if Cate's coming had been his decision to make.

He did not take his eyes from the enemy to look at her, but her knuckles were white as she gripped the reins. Barely a breath escaped her.

The men on the opposite shore looked as ready for a fight as their own, but as he studied them, he realised the Storwicks must also have needed salt, for their horses surrounded a black-haired woman just as protectively as the Brunsons' circled Bessie and Cate.

John caught the eyes of the dark-haired woman for a moment and recognised uneasy apprehension. Then his eyes met those of the older man beside her, father, no doubt, and for just a moment, they were just two men, put upon by the foolish demands of their women.

But the gaze of the man on her other side held no such empathy. Perhaps ten years older than John, his face carried a scar from cheekbone down to his throat.

And something visceral shook John's gut.

'Who's that?' he whispered to Rob.

'The woman?'

John spared him a look. He'd never heard Rob comment on a woman before. 'The man with the scar.'

'Why, that's the man we're after, Johnnie boy. That's Scarred Willie Storwick.'

No wonder, then, that Cate sat silent.

'He'll not hurt you,' John whispered. He'd make sure of it.

She didn't answer.

When he turned to look, he could see that fear gripped her again. Eyes wide, hands stiff, she was so full of terror that she could not flee, even had she wanted.

And now, curse him for not seeing it before, he knew why.

It was Scarred Willie Storwick she feared. And now she had to face him in the flesh.

He wanted to cover her hand, to reassure her with a touch, but this was not the place. And right now, he wasn't even sure she would know his touch from that of the man she feared.

Rob stood in his stirrups. 'Back away and put down your weapons,' he said, voice raised. 'Then we'll come across.'

They could ford the river with weapons raised, but they would be at a disadvantage. On dry ground, the Storwicks could battle them back to flounder in the river.

'Do you not trust us, then?' The older Storwick spoke, but Scarred Willie had a smirk on his lips that clearly said they shouldn't.

'I would trust a man who gave me his word,' Rob answered. 'And I can see you have womenfolk with you. You wouldn't want any harm to come to them.'

John watched the chief on the other side of the river turn to look at the women beside him. Now he noticed an older woman next to the one he'd first seen, probably the wife and mother. Both of them lifted their chins, as if to dismiss the clan across the river.

'You're not threatening my women, I hope,' Storwick said.

Rob tensed, drawing the lance back as if he might hurl it across the river at the insult. A Border man might leave widows behind, but he'd never intentionally harm a woman. 'Not if you are not threatening mine,' Rob replied.

On Rob's other side, Bessie sat still and quiet as a carving of the Madonna, never releasing a ripple of fear.

But Cate bit her shaking lip, her hands tight on the reins. The fear beneath her bravado, the fear that had stalked her dreams was now real, before her, in the light of day.

'We're here for a Truce Day,' the Storwick answered. 'We threaten no one.'

'Well, then, why don't you put your weapons down in the grass over there?' Rob said, gesturing to the clearing safely to the right of the ford. 'That way, no sloppy Storwick with a spear will nick one of ours.'

The Storwicks' head man could judge the distance as well as he. 'I would certainly consider that if your men left your arms on that bank before you ride across. That way, you won't be careless, either.'

The suggestion wasn't worth Rob's breath to answer. So, on opposite shores, both families waited, silent.

'We've got to lay down our weapons anyway, as soon as we reach town,' John said.

'We're not leaving them on the Scots side of the border,' Rob snapped.

The sun moved silent overhead. The breeze fluttered. No one moved.

John looked downstream. 'Is there another crossing?'

Rob shook his head. 'They'd only follow us along the bank.'

'It's a smaller force than ours,' John answered, trying to assess their chances.

'That makes no difference when they are on land and our horses must flounder from the water to the bank. The warden should be here.'

Your warden, he might as well have said. As if the fault were John's.

'Where's your warden?' Rob called out to the Storwicks. There was a ritual. English and Scottish Wardens arrived the night before Truce Day. The next morning, the English Warden's men came to the Scots side to request a truce. The Scots would return the favour. The wardens would embrace to make the truce official. 'Has he no knowledge of how things are done?'

'I might ask the same about your man.'

The king had picked Carwell. John had met him face to face. But was he the right choice?

Then, hoofbeats.

John turned to see Carwell's green-and-gold banner flapping above a group of men riding fast from the west. Relieved, he released a sigh.

The new warden pulled up beside John, who introduced him to Rob and explained what had happened.

'We arranged this in haste,' Carwell said. 'The English man must have been delayed as I was.'

Rob rolled his eyes.

Carwell rode to the edge of the bank. 'Men of Storwick! I am Thomas Carwell, newly appointed Warden of the March, as my father was before me. Praise be to King James.'

A rousing silence met the mention of the king's name, on both sides of the water.

Carwell pulled out his sword and handed it to one of his men. 'Stay here,' he told the captain. 'And if they attack me, kill them all.'

Alone, Carwell urged his horse into the river.

'There goes an unarmed fool,' Rob said.

John smiled. 'He's still got his dagger.'

Halfway to the English side, Carwell's horse stopped and the man spoke again. 'Your warden and I have declared this a Truce Day according to Border Laws. Now lay down your arms and let me and my men across. We will collect your weapons and disarm the Brunsons when they follow.'

The Storwick leader hesitated. He shared a whisper with the man next to him—a son?—but not, John noticed, with Scarred Willie.

'Be ready,' Rob said. Each man put a hand on his weapon. 'Carwell hasn't enough men to take them all if they charge.'

The Storwicks' leader handed his sword to his lieutenant, then rode into the river until he faced Carwell. 'We agree,' he said, in a voice loud enough for both sides to hear.

John gave his brother a triumphant smile.

Carwell's men waded their horses across the river and collected the Storwick weapons. Then, Rob led his men across and, one by one, they disarmed and handed over their swords and spears.

Cate was the last. 'I'll not give it over,' she said, clinging to her dagger, as Carwell waited. Her eyes never left Scarred Willie. 'Not as long as he takes breath.'

'Let her keep it,' John said. 'I'll answer for her.'

'I can't begin with exceptions,' Carwell answered.

John knew that, but he fought it anyway. 'It's too small to use in battle.'

'It's large enough to take a life.' He turned to Bessie with a slight smile, as if a woman would be more yielding. 'Help me, won't you?'

Bessie frowned. 'I'll help you, but I'll hold you responsible,' she said, her brown eyes implacable.

Carwell nodded. 'You and every other Brunson on this bank.'

Then Bessie leaned towards Cate. 'Come on, hinny. Let him have it. Just a few hours more and this will all be over.'

Bessie kept her hand on Cate's arm and nodded to John, who pried open Cate's cold fingers, forcing her to release the hilt.

John handed it to Carwell, feeling as uncertain as Bessie sounded. 'If anything happens, the Brunson you'll need to answer to is *this* one.' He had convinced Cate to trust the warden. Could he?

They turned the horses towards the village.

Next to him, Rob, deprived of his weapon, looked naked and nervous and John saw, never so clearly as in that moment, that his brother knew nothing but riding and reiving.

What would such a man do if peace were thrust upon him?

Yet John felt no peace as he assessed the small village, protected by neither tower nor wall. Perfect for a Truce Day gathering, for there was nothing that could be captured.

But nothing that could be defended, either.

Three booths proudly decorated the crowded centre street, but the people were silent as they rode in, as if waiting for proof of peaceful intentions.

The mounted families filled the town square and they stood at another impasse, each waiting for the other side to dismount first.

'It's all wrong,' Rob muttered beside him. 'We always meet on Scots soil. The English Wardens come to us.'

Then the young Storwick woman, without waiting for leave, turned her horse away from the protection of her family, trotted to the booth of the seller of pans, dismounted and started inspecting his wares.

'Fool,' Cate muttered next to him.

Rob's gaze followed the woman. Strange.

Bessie cleared her throat. 'We'll be needing some salt, then.'

She did not demand. She did not defy her family as the Storwick woman had done. But her quiet statement was not a request. It was a stubborn, obstinate statement of intent.

Rob sighed. 'Off with you, then,' he said, motioning one of the men to go with her. 'Keep your eyes open and stay in sight.'

Bessie slid off her horse, looking to Cate to join her. Cate shook her head.

'We'll stay with her,' John said.

But the sight of women shopping relaxed them all. The rest of the men dismounted. A few idle words, even a laugh, drifted in the air. Cate dismounted, but kept a hand on Belde. The dog pressed against her, a bulwark.

John let himself breathe.

'Stay here,' he said to Rob. 'Watch Cate. I'm going to talk to Carwell.'

His brother gave a grunt. 'For all the good it will do you.'

Waiting for him to fail, he knew. Expecting it. Wanting it?

Well, he mustn't and Carwell mustn't, not only because he must not fail the king.

He must not fail Cate.

The world stopped as soon as Cate saw him on the other side of the river. Two years since that dark and terrible night, but still, she knew him.

John had seen her stare and seemed to understand it. Surprising, how much comfort that gave her. But then he'd betrayed her, siding with the rest of them, taking her weapons away.

She had barely slept the night before, not because of nightmares. No, this time, excitement had kept her awake. Finally, she would face him again. But this time, she would be armed and ready.

This time, she would not flinch.

Yet as she stared at him across the water, daring him to meet her eyes, his gaze had flowed over her with barely a ripple. He showed only the small bump of realisation that she was a woman and not the man he expected. Beyond that, she saw no recognition, no hint of guilt or shame, nothing to indicate he knew her at all.

Then they ripped the dagger from her hand and she was Braw Cate no longer.

Weapons held back the fear. Without them, she felt as helpless as she had that night. The night she *should* have kicked and screamed and bitten and scratched and done anything she could have to hold him off.

The night she could do nothing but lie stiffly in mortal fear like the worst fazart while he took her and took every ounce of power she possessed.

Now, she fought him in dreams.

Perhaps it was better he did not know her. If he looked at her again, *knowing*, would she be as helpless as she had been the first time?

If that were true, then everything she had done and been for the past two years had been for naught.

So she took comfort in Belde, warm and strong beside her. And she looked anywhere but at Scarred Willie.

Instead, she looked at John, exchanging words with Carwell. Her eyes rested on him, drawn as they would be by a green field or a starful sky. Drawn to a small momentary pleasure.

Like a kiss between a man and a woman.

She blinked at the thought and looked away. That was not a thought for today. Today, all she cared about was that justice would finally find Scarred Willie, even if not for his worst crime.

John followed Carwell into the ale-seller's house where the men were dragging tables and stools to the edge of the room for the Truce Day trial.

'Where's the English Warden?' John asked Carwell without preamble. 'He should have been here at sunrise. And so should you.'

A pinch of worry rumpled Carwell's smooth smile, but he gave no explanation of his absence. 'He should be here. Any minute.'

John looked out at the peaceful street. The women bargained with the merchants while a few Storwicks kicked a ball back and forth on the green with some of the Brunson men. A contest more harmless than fighting with blades.

For the moment.

'Can you give me your word he will come?' He

barely recognised his plea. Now he was begging for promises that would enable him to keep the one he'd made to Cate.

'I can't even promise that the sun will rise of a morning,' Carwell said, his voice disarmingly smooth. 'But the English Warden promised me. What more could I do?'

'I hope you do not have to answer that question, for I tell you, if we do not succeed, the king will have *us* at the end of the rope, instead of Scarred Willie Storwick.'

And somehow, that was less of a threat now than the chance that he would fail Cate.

Carwell looked grim. 'Border justice is only as strong as the allegiance men give it and they give it only if they think it will be administered fairly, so you'd better step away, John Brunson, because the longer we stand here running our tongues, the more the Storwicks will think we are plotting together and the less they will listen to anything I say.'

John turned away, but paused at the door. 'The English Warden. Is he trustworthy?'

'As much as I am.'

'How much is that, Thomas Carwell?' he asked, not expecting an answer. 'How much is that?'

He had trusted Carwell because the king did. But he'd been on the Borders long enough to wonder whether anyone beyond his family could be trusted.

Including Carwell and the king.

Cate did not join the others to look at the goods in the booths or cheer as the Brunsons kicked their ball down the green. John and Bessie took turns standing beside her. Each tried to tempt her away, but she would not savour a sweet oatcake or take a sip of ale. She just stood, Belde heavy against her leg, and watched Willie Storwick.

She had forced herself, finally, to watch him. Forced herself to watch his every move, thinking that, as long as her eyes were on him, he would dare nothing.

It was almost over. He was here. Hands bound, ready to stand trial. And she would watch him until he did.

But without the English Warden, no trial began.

The day grew long. Sun and clouds traded possession of the sky. Storwicks and Brunsons traded control of the ball. The chatter of the morning faded with the waiting.

Beside her, John, coiled with impatience, kept looking to the south.

'I'm going back to talk to Carwell,' he said when midday had passed, yet he paused, reluctant to leave her.

She raised her chin, Braw Cate again. 'Go. Tell him I am waiting and tell me what he says.'

With a glance back at her, he hurried his steps.

And in the moment she was alone, she heard the rustle of the leaves, saw the corbies take their flight, felt thunder in the ground beneath her feet, and realised, too late, what was coming.

Then the horses were upon them.

These men—three, if her head could still count— still wielded weapons and she cursed the trust that had allowed the Brunsons to give up their arms in perfect faith. Unarmed, on foot, there was nothing to do but run and hide unless she wanted to hold up a naked palm to stop a short sword.

But these men did not stop to fight. They rode down the street, directly for Scarred Willie, and cut the rope that bound his hands. Then they handed him a sword and the reins of a horse and kept riding for the other end of town before the rest of the men could regroup.

But before Willie put his boot in the stirrup and followed them, he came to Cate, pulled her to him and put his mouth on hers.

She reached for the dirk, now gone, then swung a fist at him instead. But it was Belde who tore into his arm, leaving the man bloody and howling before he mounted and followed the others out of the village.

And as he rode away, she stood in the dirt, doubled over, gritting her teeth to keep her breakfast bread in her stomach, and clutching a scrap of brown cloth that Belde had ripped from Scarred Willie's sleeve.

Chapter Thirteen

'You knew!' John's hand was on Carwell's throat, holding him against the wall of the alehouse. He was tempted to squeeze. Hard. 'You must have known!'

In the street behind him, villagers cowered and Brunsons and Storwicks ran to lay hands on their weapons.

He had first tried to reach Cate and, after, his sword. Too late for either. The men had ridden into the village and were gone before any one of them could retrieve a horse and a spear. Behind him, belatedly, three Brunson men mounted to follow.

He had little hope they would succeed.

And Cate? Bessie was with her. Cate would not welcome him now.

'They betrayed me, too,' Carwell said. His shifting greenish eyes usually hid more than they revealed, but now they burned with unconcealed fury. 'I swear on my father's grave.'

John forced his fingers away from the man's throat. 'I hope he meant more to you than mine did.'

'Storwick's defamed Carwell honour now,' the warden said. A Borderer's resolve had replaced his diplomat's mask. 'And I *will* discover whether the English warden helped.'

Out of the corner of his eye, John saw Rob and the Storwick head man face off, toe to toe. Rob had his sword pointed at the other man's chest, but instead of striking back, the man stood with open hands, sorrow weighing his shoulders.

'This was not of our doing,' he insisted, shaking his head. 'He is no longer a Storwick. He is a broken man.'

A broken man. Dead to his family. The worst curse a Borderer could inflict. A quarrel with Scarred Willie was no longer a Storwick matter. The family's head man had spoken.

John joined his brother. Slowly, Rob lowered his sword, then spat on the ground. 'There!' he yelled, raising his arms to encompass the day. 'Are you satisfied, Johnnie?'

Truce lay shattered. Men of both sides hobbled, bloody, to seek their horses, weapons and homes.

'Satisfied? Nay,' he answered through gritted teeth, itching to hold a sword again. The Border Laws and the King's Justice were not going to be enough. Even for him. 'Not satisfied by half.'

He had never felt so vulnerable, so foolish, so naked as when he stood, helpless, as they swooped in and took the man from justice. It was worse than when he had been the youngest boy, not big enough or strong enough or tough enough to beat the others.

And then Storwick put his hands on Cate.

Seeing the sickness on her face had been worse than all the rest. 'He cannot be far. We will ride after him. Now.'

'And if we do, we'll gallop into an ambush deadlier than the one we just survived.'

'Then we'll go home. Get help.' He tried to think. Failed. 'We'll bring a thousand men!'

'You're ready? To kill the bloody bastard?'

John wrestled with his emotions, realising he had been ready to violate every duty he had come to perform and cut off every opportunity the king might offer.

He took a deep breath, struggling to subdue his anger. He had already laid hands on the king's warden. If he murdered a Storwick outside the law, he'd be the one on trial at the next Truce Day.

'I am ready to track him down and take him to Edinburgh to stand trial.' There, at least, he could be sure that the judges had made no secret alliances.

Rob leaned back, arms crossed, looking at him as if he were Johnnie Blunkit again. 'If you think to do that, then you remember nothing and have learned less. You'll never take him alive, I can promise you that.'

'There has to be a way.' He wanted to argue, to tell his brother to put down his arms, and turn justice over to the king instead of holding tight into his own hands, but he had to convince himself, first. 'You must listen to me—'

'No! It's you who will be listening, Johnnie boy. I told you what would happen, but you knew it all. So I did it for you. I tried your precious justice. You see what happened. Now you can tell your king in Fife that allegiance to him and his laws is worth no more than a piece of parchment pierced by a sword. The sword always wins.'

Would Rob still send the king his men? Would they get there in time? None of that seemed to matter now. John had seen the truth the king was too far away to understand. There was no law, no justice on this frontier except that a family made for itself. And unless the king could change that, nothing else would change.

'Nevertheless, I will hunt him down and see him punished.'

Rob shook his head. 'Why? You made it clear this was not your fight.'

Why? Because he'd sworn a vow on the Hogback stones.

'Because I stood before you and vowed to Cate that I would bring the man to justice myself if the wardens did not do it.'

In hindsight, he'd given his word lightly, never thinking he would need to keep it. But now he was bound by more than words. He had seen the enemy, seen what he did to Cate.

Rob was silent, but a look of approval that John had never hoped to see crept into his eyes.

'Well, Johnnie me boy,' he said finally. 'You may grow into that vest yet.'

John shook his head. Cate would not agree. He had failed her and, until he could redeem that sin, he would be no Brunson. He wouldn't even call himself a man.

'Come.' Rob motioned him. 'We'll meet with the others. Decide what's to be done.'

He looked to Cate again. Bessie stood on one side of her, Belde on the other. 'I must speak to her first.'

Cate did not berate him as he approached.

She did not waste a breath on him at all.

She simply stood, stiff as a graven image with fury engraved on her face.

Bessie slipped away from her side and he was grateful for his sister's understanding. She, at least, did not look at him with judgement, though the dog's eyes held disappointment.

'Walk with me,' he said.

Cate didn't move.

He put his hand on her arm and pulled her with him, towards the river, out of earshot of the others.

Startled, she raised her head. 'I did not give you permission—'

He hated the fear in her eyes. 'I did not ask.'

'You did not ask when you came here.' She shrugged off his hold. 'You, who thought to stop the wind and change the path of the sun. Now do you see?' The anger in her eyes faded. 'It's as if God delivers him and punishes me.'

He hated her hopeless whisper. 'Man, not God.'

The words snapped her face into focus. 'Carwell?'

'I don't think so,' he said, though he was not sure.

'The English Warden, then. It doesn't matter. You can trust none of them.'

How well he understood that now. 'The Storwick head man has disowned him. Scarred Willie's a broken man now.'

'Yet he still lives. He rides free into the Debatable Land while I…' She squeezed her eyes against tears.

He forced himself to wait, not touching her, until she could speak again.

'While my father lies dead beside his fore folk.'

He had no argument for that. She had trusted him and he had failed her. 'I will hunt him down myself.'

They had reached the edge of the stream. Gold-and-green trees mingled side by side and fallen leaves littered the bank and floated on the water. Belde bent his head and slaked his thirst.

She looked at John, finally, doubt replacing the pain in her eyes. 'You would do that?'

For you, yes.

The thought came quickly, but he could not tell her that it was for her that he wanted to ride. Could barely tell himself. 'Did you not believe me when I gave my word?'

She searched John's face as if perhaps she had not.

Yet he had hardly believed himself.

He reached for her, wanting to touch her, as if somehow the feel of his hand on her arm would convey what mere words would not.

She looked down at his hand. 'Is your promise about Scarred Willie worth any more than your others?'

He dropped her arm and stepped away, wishing he had promised her nothing. 'I will bring him in.' He held up both hands, a surrender. And he'd explain it to the king later.

'Why now? What has changed? Is my father more dead today than he was afore?'

Nay. It was not the death of Cate's father that haunted him. 'The wardens, the Border laws, failed you.' *And me.* He wondered whether he could make the king understand that.

'Then I must be thanking you, Johnnie Brunson.' She met his gaze and took his hands in hers. 'For I know this is not an easy thing for you to do.'

He looked down at her hands, covering his. She had refused his touch. Now she sought it. Who was this Cate and what did she want of him? 'But Storwick's capture must be the end of it, the end of the killing.'

She shook her head. 'That's not mine to change.'

'But you could help. Help me convince Rob.'

She looked away, but her hands did not leave his.

After a day hard with anger and dark with fear, she looked as bashful as any young maid.

But her touch, innocent and light, lit the fire in his belly, a burning desire for something more than revenge. It was an ache to possess and protect what was his. What he *wanted* to be his.

Land. Family. Home. Woman.

'Think of it, Cate.' He swallowed, the words halting. 'Think of a life of peace—'

And then he could no longer think. Her lips coaxed him closer. He leaned forward…

And realised the last lips that had touched hers had been Storwick's.

Cate lifted her face and opened her lips to his. A kiss of thanks to seal the bargain they had struck. To let him know she understood the sacrifice this promise was for him.

Nothing more.

But it *was* more. It was a kiss to wipe away the taste of Willie Storwick. It was a search for hope that she might some day be done with revenge and fear and be like other women.

A dream she had never dared until Johnnie Brunson.

He hesitated, respecting her wishes and his promise. He took a breath, as if to speak.

She squeezed her eyes shut and leaned towards him. She did not want him to ask if he could kiss her or to hold his arms behind him. She wanted him to hold her, to protect her from the awful memory of the day.

Everything else must wait.

All day she had been Braw Cate, watching, waiting, muscles and nerves knotted so she would not run.

People can be happy, he had promised, *even when life is harsh.*

Show me it is true. Just for a moment.

And when that moment was over, she would be Braw Cate again, afraid of no man.

But he did not move. His arms stuck stubbornly to his side. She slipped hers around his waist, pressed herself to his chest, protected by the vest she had made, and lifted herself on to her toes, seeking his lips.

Finally, he gave a groan of surrender. His arms tightened around her. His lips met hers. And the world she knew dropped away.

The feeling of safety she had craved came first. His arms, impossibly strong and gentle all at once, drew a wall around her, closing out all the pain of the day.

But the moment of peace slid quickly into something more.

A rush of heat in her cheeks, a throbbing between her legs, a pounding in her chest like birds fleeing the hunt.

Desire. Her body like a runaway horse, galloping to join with his as if nothing else mattered. Not even her last breath.

And that was even more frightening that the tightness of his arms and the hunger of his kiss.

Her life depended on controlling her fear. If she lost her grip on her emotions, there would be nothing but a yawning, black pit before her.

She struggled against him. Ripped her lips from his. 'Enough.'

He looked at her as if she were mad. 'But you—'

'I know.' How could she explain? It was herself she rejected. Not him. 'Forgive me. You must think—'

He put his hands on her shoulders and held her steady, searching her eyes. She did not protest his touch.

Just moments ago, his blue eyes had been filled with fierce joy. She'd put confusion and anger there.

'Catie Gilnock, I must know what you want.'

She bit her lip and looked to Belde, calling him back, not wanting to face Johnnie's eyes, but he took her chin and turned her face to him again.

How brave are you, Cate? Brave enough to look in his eyes and tell him the truth? Brave enough to put yourself in hands other than your own?

She tried. She met his eyes, hoping for forgiveness, seeing only anger. And then, something else. Something she was afraid to name.

'It was I who broke a vow today,' she said, forcing steadiness into her voice. 'You had said men and women might grab some happiness. After…today…I needed to see if it were true.'

'Is it?'

Yes. But not for me.

He had her wanting impossible things. Peace. Love. A normal life. Better to hope for none of those things. Better to remember who she was.

'No,' she said. A lie that was easier than the truth.

He folded his arms across his chest. 'Then you needn't worry, Catie Gilnock.' His voice carried all the anger she had feared. 'I'll be inflicting no such unhappiness on you again.'

No such unhappiness. Only the loneliness she knew.

Too late to save her heart. She had let herself imagine she might be like other women some day, able to give her body to her man in joy and trust.

Today, Scarred Willie had proved her hopes a lie.

And for that, he would pay.

She nodded. 'And so, Johnnie Brunson, are you ready to track down Willie Storwick?'

Chapter Fourteen

John's flash of anger almost answered *no*.

He had not thought her one of those women who said come hither, only to say go hence. He had known those, the ones who would say *yes*, then *no*, then *maybe*, thinking that, eventually, a man would do anything she asked to have her.

Cate Gilnock was not one of those.

Or was she?

What did he know of this woman whose cause had become his? Her body said one thing, her words another. Yet yearning had filled her eyes, as if she saw a star, high overhead, and craved what she could never touch.

And there was something else in her eyes. Something too close to fear.

He sighed. Well, after today, she was entitled to her fear of Willie Storwick. And was he ready to hunt the bastard who had dared lay lips on hers?

The promise of his father and his brother had become his, the weight of it heavy, all because of this woman. He had taken on her cause and, with it, taken a step off the side of a mountain into a ravine deep and hidden as the one on Hogback Hill.

And he didn't know how far there was to fall, or what might await at the bottom.

Was he ready? 'Yes.'

She fell into step beside him. 'Then let's chase him down.'

Rob's reminders echoed in his ear. 'He's disappeared. We can't just ride into the middle of the Debatable Land and expect him to emerge and surrender.'

She shook her head. The grim, determined set had returned to her face. 'Belde will lead us to him.'

He looked at the dog. 'How? We have nothing to give him a scent.' He knew enough of the dog to understand that.

'Yes,' she said, calm as cold steel, 'we have.' She pulled some brown fabric from her pocket, holding it like a bloody captured flag.

'What is that?' Yet he knew, somehow. She was his Braw Cate again, a woman who feared nothing.

'He may have stolen a kiss, but I stole something better.'

John let Cate explain her plan to Rob. Sleuth dogs could track across water and rock with little more than a whiff, but this was a man on horseback. They must move quickly, so as not to lose the trail.

Bessie and most of the men would return to defend the tower. A smaller group, but enough to outnumber the outlaws, would chase after Storwick's band.

The street was near empty. The Storwicks had escaped into the hills and the poor folk of Kershopefoote had disappeared behind closed doors.

Carwell and his mounted men milled before the alehouse too far away for words, but when they rode past, the warden paused, looking down at John.

'I cannot countenance it,' he said, looking over the family, re-armed and ready to ride. He knew what it meant. The Brunsons would take their own justice now.

John grabbed the horse's bridle. 'You're an arrogant son of a bitch and I don't care what you think. Perhaps you countenance an English Warden in league with the Storwicks.'

Carwell's eyes flashed at the insult. He pulled his horse away from John's hand. 'I ride to find him now. He'll not go unpunished.'

'We'll meet again,' John called as Carwell rode away.

And it wasn't until the warden and his men were out of sight that John realised that though Carwell complained, he had not lifted a finger to stop them.

'Johnnie!'

He followed his brother's voice back to their gathering place: the spot where Storwick had grabbed Cate.

She knelt by Belde, tying him in harness, for once he was on the trail he would ignore even her calls. The dog already knew he was to hunt and was tugging at the leash, eager to start on the quarry's trail.

'Cool and damp,' Cate said, her head lifted as if she, like the dog, were catching a scent. She patted the dagger, safely back at her side. 'Good for tracking.'

'You're not coming,' John said. Out of the corner of his eye, he thought his brother smirked.

'It is my revenge we ride for,' she said. 'And the dog obeys no other.'

He looked to Rob, who shook his head. 'You've lost this battle before.'

'That was different.' John had seen her train with sword and dagger, watched her fight off nightmares, and even seen her ride a raid. But this would bring her face to face with Storwick again. Face to face with the fear that had turned her to stone already once today.

She did not look fearful now. 'I ride with you or I take the dog alone.'

'Bessie,' he called, a plea. 'Surely you know what she wants is impossible.'

'It's you who ask the impossible, Johnnie.' She hugged Cate and then subjected each of her brothers to the same before she took her horse again.

Rob gave last instructions to his second-in-command. Bessie hung behind as the others started for the crossing.

'God be with all of you,' she whispered, then followed the rest.

Cate pulled out the scrap of Storwick's sleeve and knelt beside the dog. Did her hand shake? He wasn't sure.

'Here, Belde,' her voice the loving, coaxing tone he had heard her use with the dog before, then murmured something he could not hear.

The dog sniffed so quickly, John could not believe he had a scent, but, tail wagging, he started sniffing the air. Then, the kind smile she'd had for the dog shifted into the hard face of revenge. 'Fetch Willie!'

Heavier than she, the beast lunged against her hold. She let out the rope and leapt into the saddle.

'I can take him,' John called, afraid the dog would pull free and they would lose him altogether.

With a tug on the rope, she slowed him a bit, then shook her head. 'It's mine to do.'

Rob and John fell in behind her.

Rob reached out a hand to John. 'Silent as moonrise.'

John clasped his brother's arm. 'Sure as the stars.'

And now, John rode as a Brunson.

* * *

They followed the dog back across the Liddel Water, then west. He loped, without hesitation, beside the stream as it ran into the thicketed valley that was called the Debatable Land.

Overhead, the clouds had turned grey-blue and, under foot, green grass was being slowly smothered by dying leaves. Wind chased them, rattling leaves and branches and magnifying the sound of hooves and harness, but Belde gave chase in silence.

She had trained him well.

John let the others watch the dog. His eyes were on Cate. She looked from side to side, uneasy.

From here, you could see anyone who might come. That's what she had said of Hogback Hill. Here, surrounded by trees and leaves, you could see no one until they were upon you. And they might come from any direction. This valley was crowded with bands of men, like animals in packs, coming out of their lairs to prey on civilised men.

At first, the dog had gone in a straight line. Now, he ran from side to side, cutting back and forth across the stream as if a squirrel were leading him on an aimless chase.

Rob rode closer and whispered, so Cate could not hear. 'The dog has lost the trail, then.'

'Have you ever seen him track before?' John asked.

Rob shook his head.

'I have.' The leaves, damp, did not crunch beneath the ponies' hooves, but he felt each sound as if they were an invading army. 'Storwick knows he's being followed.'

His brother's lips narrowed to a grim line. 'There's

no reason for him to stand and fight. He'll just keep running unless— Hold the dog, Cate!'

Ahead of them, the woods thinned. Once they rode out beyond the trees, they would have no cover. Cate kept Belde from running into the open and they gathered at the edge of the open valley.

'God's bells,' Rob said. 'Look at that.'

Rising from a knoll near the river was an ill-formed wooden tower, much smaller than their own.

And newer.

And bigger than six men could hope to take.

'Well, then,' Rob said, leaning forwards on his saddle to look at the rough fortress. 'It seems as if Scarred Willie has been planning this for a while.'

Chapter Fifteen

Belde whined and pulled against Cate's aching arm, ready to rush across the field and straight to his quarry.

'Sit,' she said, a waste of breath.

John reached to help her with the leash and she let him, grateful for the moment's rest.

They stared at the tower.

It rose only two storeys and had no outer wall or gate, but a layer of stones, and cast-off, ill-sized rubble climbed awkwardly up the outer wall, sheathing the lower storey.

'This is not Storwick land,' John said.

'It belongs to no man,' Rob answered. 'No country, and no king.'

Both Scotland and England claimed this narrow strip of wilderness. And since neither would give the other ownership, neither enforced order here. Not even the uncertain order of the Border Laws.

'But it's forbidden to build in the Debatable Lands,' John said.

Something near a smile touched her lips. John, who would still and always speak of what *should* be instead of what *was*. John, who almost made her believe that what *should* be, *could* be.

Rob made a dismissive sound that might, from another man, have been called a laugh. 'Welcome to the Borders, Johnnie boy.'

Belde whined, heaving himself against his harness. John, from the back of his horse, held the rope firm. Cate slipped off her horse to put both arms around the dog, adding her strength to John's.

She looked up, searching the men's faces for hope. 'Can we not…?' Her words faded. There were only a handful of them. An attack would be futile.

But Belde knew nothing of logic. He lived for the joy of the hunt. And the find.

And as she relaxed her hold, he broke free, running out of the trees and towards the tower, the rope slapping the ground behind him.

Cate had no time for fear. No time for thinking or hesitation.

She ran.

So near his quarry, Belde's speed was a match for a horse's and certainly faster than hers. And even if she caught him, she could not hold him.

None of that mattered.

Wind filled her ears, along with the sound of hoofbeats behind her, but she did not pause. The dog reached the tower's door, and frantic, jumped up, howling, knowing his man was inside. She grabbed the rope, jerking on it, trying in vain to pull him back. 'Good boy. Yes. Enough.'

She had boasted of his obedience, but he would not cease until he had delivered the man to her hand.

'Well, look who has come knocking at the door of my Hole House.'

She looked up. The hated face with its scarred cheek

looked out at her from an opening on the upper storey, above the door.

'You and your miserable beast.' He leaned out of the window, his arm bloody from Belde's attack. 'Have you come for more, then?' A grin, terrible as a demon's scream, creased his face.

At first, her lips refused to move. To look into his eyes was to see again what he had done to her. She became, like Lot's wife, unmoving as a pillar of salt.

He cannot hurt Braw Cate. She has kissed a man and wanted more.

'I've come to see my blade scar you anew.'

He blinked and looked away, his expression wary, as John pulled up beside her, dismounted and pulled Belde away from the door. 'I'm taking you to justice, Willie Storwick.'

A laugh echoed across the valley. 'You and the girl and the dog?'

Her fear abruptly doubled. Nothing must happen to Johnnie.

'Now or later, Storwick. We know where you are.' He had the sword in his hand and a mixture of fury and calculation in his eyes. 'No. Not Storwick. I can't call you that. Your family's disowned you.'

For the first time, she saw Willie's face shatter. 'They would not do that.'

With John at her side, her senses cleared. She listened for sounds from the tower, assessed the openings above them. How many men did he have there? Could they launch arrows?

'Oh, but they did, Willie. You've no family. No name. You're no one.' A slight burr, born of generations of Brunsons, shimmered around John's words.

She took the dog's leash, leaving John's sword arm clear. John, eyes fixed on Willie, let her.

'Call me what you like or call me nothing at all,' the man snarled. 'You're on my ground and I'm telling you to leave, not inviting you in for a brew.'

Never looking away from Willie, John put himself between Cate and the tower. 'Your ground? You've no right to this land.'

'Willie's Band gives me the right. We rule here.' He jerked his head towards the tower and the faceless men inside, but his eyes shifted, uneasy. 'Not the Storwicks, not the Brunsons, and certainly not wardens or kings.'

John eased the angle of his sword and looked down at it. 'Then again, you may not be worth dirtying my blade. You're nothing but a nameless fazart.'

Cate gulped at the insult and looked up. Storwick had raised a crossbow, pointed right at John.

She threw herself between them now, pressing herself against John's chest, her back to Willie. Belde, sensing danger, jumped on the door again, barking. The leash tangled around her legs, tying her to John.

She closed her eyes, the rapid thump of John's heart strong in her ear, and waited for the arrow to hit her back.

'Put it down, Storwick.' Rob's voice, behind them. 'Or I'll let mine fly first.'

Cate opened her eyes. Rob sat on his horse, his cross-latch poised to fire. The other men must still be hiding in the thicket. She and John had one horse and one dog between them. How could they outrun Willie's arrow and regain the trees?

'Come,' she whispered, before either Willie or Rob tired. 'We can do nothing today.'

John mounted, then pulled her on to Norse and, with

Rob and Belde, they galloped for the trees. An arrow, two, whizzed by and missed.

And Scarred Willie's laugh floated on the wind behind them.

It was full dark before they gained the tower's safety. Heedless of all else, John lifted her off her horse and carried her to her bed, leaving Rob to tell the tale and Bessie to feed the dog.

'Are you hurt? Are you safe?' They spoke together as he carried her inside and kicked the door closed.

And then there were no words between the kisses.

He laid her on the bed and sat beside her.

Promises disappeared. He searched her arms, neck, legs and back, as if she might have a wound he did not see. And she did the same, even wiggling each of his fingers, then crowning each one with a kiss when she found it whole.

Finally, relieved, he cradled her head in his hands, wanting to shake her for her foolishness. 'You ran unarmed to your enemy's door!'

I thought I had lost you.

'And you pulled a sword to storm a tower!'

They both laughed and he trailed his fingers over her cheek. Perhaps he had been foolish, but he would not admit it. When he saw her run, he thought of nothing but snatching her back.

And now, he thought of nothing but holding her close.

He took her lips, more precious now because he had near lost her twice today. No trace of that man's stain would remain when he was through.

Her hands still moved over him, rubbing his back as if she, too, were grateful he lived. He let his lips explore then, moving from hers, up her cheek to the delicate place above her ear where her fair hair grew, then traced the dainty curve of her ear with his tongue, proud when he felt her shudder in response.

How could he have ever thought her sharp edged? Her neck curved gracefully to her shoulders. Her skin tasted sweet. He wanted, oh, he wanted to see what lay beneath the thick vest, the rough shirt. He lifted his head and fumbled with the ties of her vest, smiling when she helped him, and unable to look away when she shrugged out of the fighting man's protection.

Beneath that, she wore rough, loose woven wool over her linen sark. For a moment, he imagined her in court dress: a white ruffle framing her throat and baring the delicate skin that tempted him to the breasts below...

No. That would not suit his Cate. No more than full polished harness would suit a Border man.

He slipped his hands beneath the wool and the linen to touch her skin. Warm against his palms, he felt life itself pulsing against him.

'Please...' Did he ask? Or did he simply pull her covering up and out of the way? But after that, after he bared her, he could not speak at all.

She had denied womanhood, but her breasts, round and full and pebbled against the cold, told a different tale. He reached, gently, so gently, thinking she might break if he was not soft with her. He cupped each breast, then stroked her, until his fingers met at the tips. Her eyes were closed, her head dropped back and a guttural sound rattled in her throat, no more coherent than his thoughts.

Now that he could see her, he thought he might never close his eyes again. All she had hidden beckoned, most of all the unseen places where breast became rib or shoulder turned into throat. He would study those places until he knew her so well, he would know when her waist became her hip and when her belly became the place between her legs...

He lifted her arm and bent to kiss the side of her breast, the imperceptible edge where it faded to become the skin of her side. She wiggled, closer, turning, tempting his lips with her breast, her body knowing, telling, without words.

And he answered.

Her hands, once content to roam his back, turned greedy. She pushed his shoulders, untying his vest with fingers clumsy as his own had been. He helped, shedding the heavy vest she had stitched so carefully, then stripping his shirt and sark without waiting for her help.

Now, she was the one to stare, gobbling him with her eyes. He had a strange feeling of shyness, something he had never felt with a woman before. Wondering what she thought and hoping he pleased her.

Then she touched him.

She stroked his skin from neck to shoulder to elbow to wrist and up again, doing the same on the other side and then across his chest, as if determined that every inch of him fall beneath her fingers, as if she were trying to engrave his shape upon her skin.

And he understood why she had closed her eyes.

But he could not blind himself for long. There was too much more of her to discover.

She still wore tall boots and he played squire to pull them off, along with his. Now, she was the shy one, covered in her last layer of tied-on hose.

He sat back on the bed, baffled. A woman in a skirt was always ready for tupping. He had never faced a woman in man's garb.

She rose from the bed, her hands fisted, and with her back to him, untied the strings where he could not see. Then, slowly, so slowly, she slipped the hose off, revealing bare hips, legs, more…

Did he breathe her name? Perhaps.

Still sitting on the bed, he reached around her, pulling her close, then slipped his fingers between her legs.

She let him take her weight as she edged her legs apart and pressed her hips forward, easing the way for him to explore.

Now. *Now*, his body screamed, stiff with reaching.

She, too, felt ready, slick, hot, her hips trying to meet his fingers' rhythm. He could wait no more. He wanted all of her.

He stood and scooped her up onto the bed and covered her, his lips on hers, her breasts against his chest, not remembering until he lay over her that he was still covered below the waist. He reached down, tried to free himself—

'No! No!'

The words had no meaning at first. Not until her fist punched his head, her nails scratched his cheek and her knee hit his groin.

He stopped, panting and dazed, then looked down to see he had pressed her against the bed. Dazed, he rolled out of her reach.

Eyes glazed, breathing heavily, he waited for his brain to return to his body.

His first thought was that the woman must be mad.

Or that he was.

But he had not mistaken her desire. She had been the one to let down the final garment, her final barrier. What had changed?

He looked back at her, still lying on her back, her

breath racing. She had turned her head and he could not see her eyes.

His desire had shrivelled, but the power of it still flowed in his veins. He stood, walked across the room, stirred the covered fire to flames and smacked the wall so hard his hand numbed.

'What, which, what…?' Damn. He was never so awkward with words. Or women. He raised his head to look at her. 'What is it, Cate? What would you have of me?'

In the firelight, the bold warrioress, the fearful spirit, the passionate woman he had glimpsed had all disappeared. A different Cate sat up in the bed. Not the one who disdained his touch. Not even the one who feared it. All that was left behind was this uncertain shell.

She looked instead around the room and towards the door, refusing to meet his eyes. 'Where is Belde?'

He released a sigh of regret so deep he thought it would never leave him.

'I understand,' he said, though he did not. 'You do not want me.'

He reached for his tunic and pulled it over his head.

'No!' She jumped out of bed and grabbed his arms as if she was afraid he would disappear. 'No. It's not that.'

Covered again, he searched her eyes, slowly, his memory returning. It had been like this before. Been like this every time they had kissed. First passion, then rejection.

Only when he had not held her had she wanted more. Only when he had stifled his own eagerness.

He struggled to make sense of it. 'What is it then, Cate? Tell me. Do you want me?'

As if suddenly aware of where she was and what she was doing, she let go and looked down at her feet. 'Yes.' Little louder than a whisper.

But she turned away and slipped on her shirt, so she was covered from shoulders to knees.

For a moment, he wished himself back on a battlefield. Surely it was easier to face an enemy's sword than this uncertain to and fro. He had walked away from women before. Why couldn't he leave this one?

But then she raised her eyes to his and he lost himself again. 'If it is yes, then say it aloud. To my face.'

'Yes. I want you.'

His anger was passing, but puzzlement remained. 'That sounds like resentment, not passion.' There was something here, something he should know if only he could make his mind work as hard as his tarse for a moment.

'I want you.' It was Braw Cate speaking now. The woman whose eyes would clash with his as bravely as her sword. 'And I do not *want* to want you.'

Anger, still close to the surface, escaped. 'What am I to do with that?' It hit him, then, as if he had run into a wall. 'It's marriage you're wanting then, is it?' A strange word on his tongue. It came to all men, eventually, but he had avoided all thoughts of tomorrows because tomorrows meant decisions he was not ready to make.

'No! All I want is Willie Storwick's death.'

'Storwick! I'm sick to death of hearing his name. Must he follow us into the bedchamber?' He paced again, afraid that if he stopped, he would lay hands on her in frustration. 'Why can't you leave him be for a night, or even an hour?'

Cate watched John turn away and lift his arms to heaven.

Why can't you leave him be?

For those few, precious minutes, she had. She had

faced the man today, looked him in the eye, talked back and made him blink.

Then, she had been able to lose herself in John, in the two of them together. Craving his lips, eyes, fingers on her, in her. Nothing but the two of them and this room. Finally, she was free…to love.

And then, the weight of a body crushing her, stiffness between his legs, wool scratching her belly, fingers fumbling below her waist—and it was no longer John she was loving.

It was her nightmare alive.

How could she tell him that?

John still prowled the room. 'Why does he obsess you so? Brunsons have died by Storwick hand before and we did not give the whole of our lives to hatred.'

Are you going to tell him?

How could she tell him what she had told no one? How could she explain that when she tried to love Johnnie Brunson, her body still fought Willie Storwick?

Before the fire again, he stopped and looked at her, hands on his hips, a demand that she answer.

And a slow dawning of suspicion in his expression. 'I asked you once whether your father's death was all. You told me there was nothing else. Did you lie?'

She swallowed, unable to speak. Suspicion was not certainty. If she told him, everything would change.

She let her eyes wander the face that had delighted her days. She wanted to savour him one more time, to look at his rumpled hair and grey-blue eyes, to admire the arms that had held her gently and attacked those who would threaten her.

'It *is* more than my father's death.' With each word, she was unsure she could say the next. She kept her eyes on his, as if she wanted to see the exact moment he stopped loving her.

His anger melted at her stillness. He dropped his hands from his hips. Then he was beside her, pulling her to him in a gesture part-protection, part-seduction. 'Tell me.' His whisper, insistent in her ear. 'How much more?'

She swallowed and opened her mouth. 'He…'

Nothing else came.

She shook her head.

He straightened his arms, holding her so he could see her face, and she saw in his eyes that she need say nothing more.

That he *knew*.

Cupping her face in his hands, he forced her to meet his eyes again. 'Say it. You can trust me.'

'Trust you?' Those were the words. The words that freed her.

She brought her arms up between his and knocked his aside, striding away again to the opposite wall. But trapped. Still trapped as she had been all this time. Always trying to walk away and hitting a wall every time.

She *had* come to trust him, as she had trusted no other man. More, she had begun to trust herself when she was with him.

She had let herself be lulled by the days beside him, a man who had not known, or guessed, her past. Tricked herself into believing that they could go on like this. Riding beside each other. Planning for a grand revenge and dreaming of what would come after.

Dreams that included Johnnie Brunson because she had hoped, had believed, had prayed that she would be able to join with this man, unlike any other.

That she would be alone no more.

Foolish dreams. From that day, she had known that she could never again be like other women. Well, she had fooled herself too long. She must cut out her heart. Cut off her hope. Confess and let him ride away and shun her.

She could not face him now, could not face his *knowing*. She turned away, walking to the window.

'Every night, I pray to God,' she began, looking west towards the valley where Willie Storwick rode free, 'to rain down flame and fire and flood and pestilence on his head and then to give him a death of unspeakable horror.'

She took a deep breath and looked back at John's love-touched face, as if for the last time.

'And I must kill him,' she said, 'because he raped me.'

Chapter Sixteen

Rage washed through him. Red-hot hatred followed by a cold, black determination.

The reasonable man, the king's man, the man who had argued for laws and justice, that man ceased to exist. In his place stood a Brunson, ready to kill because of what his enemy had done.

Not to his family. To *her*.

And for that, Scarred Willie Storwick would die.

He should have known, should have recognised the truth earlier. But at first, his promise to bring the man to justice was dispassioned, designed to sway Cate and spare his brother a difficult decision. Whether the wardens let Storwick live or die mattered not. It had been a bargain. A means to an end.

Now, nothing would stop him from killing the man.

Not even his king.

'I will tell the men. We will ride now. Tonight. We will find him, no matter where he hides. He will not live to see the dawn.'

Instead of the gratitude he expected, her eyes filled with horror. 'No. You mustn't tell them. You must tell no one.'

Halfway to the door, he paused. 'Why? They'll avenge you. You needn't have borne this alone.'

She grabbed his arm, the strength of her hands reminding him she had wielded a sword. 'No. Please. What I said was only for your ears. Don't tell them.' Here was yet another Cate. No longer the hard, harsh woman he knew, nor the one sightless with fear. This woman was pleading, desperate. 'If I had not thought you would keep the secret, I would never have told you.'

He reached to stroke her hair, for just a moment relishing her womanly worry. 'Don't worry. I'll be careful.'

She practically threw him from her. 'It's not your hide that worries me.' Though she bit her lower lip, so he was not sure she spoke true.

'What, then?' Every muscle, every nerve was bent to Willie's death. His brain had room and time to comprehend little else.

'Do you not understand me? If the men know he… know I was…' She broke her gaze, unable to speak the word again, and looked towards the fire. 'They may not even believe it.'

Where was his Cate? The woman ready to take on an army? 'Why would they not?'

Her eyes met his again. Here, finally, was Cate without armour. The real, vulnerable Cate.

She cleared her throat and tried. 'What he did. It is not the way of the Borders.'

In that, she was right. A Border man might leave a woman widowed, but she would not be touched. That was why it had taken him so long to see the obvious truth. 'But some men—'

'And what would happen to him,' she interrupted, 'if he were to be named for forcing me?'

'He would be hanged.' Too kind a death.

'On my word alone? I had no witnesses. No wounds to show. By the time I came down from the hills, my bruises were gone.'

How could anyone doubt his Cate? 'But—'

'And after I accused him, then what? Perhaps, after I had been poked and questioned and made to feel as if I had enticed him away from the cattle with a comely stare, perhaps he might be branded and exiled. Or perhaps, to make things right before God and man, we would be wedded for our sin. And afterwards, because a marriage across the Border is forbidden, we could both be strung up for violating the law and swing side by side from the hanging tree. Is that what you want?'

He opened his mouth, but it took some time before words escaped. 'None of those things will happen. I won't allow it.' A simple statement. As simple as the ideas he had brought home with him. Justice. Order. Obedience. But here, justice was complex. Family loyalty was simple.

'Once they know, they will not treat me…as they should.'

'Once they know, they'll avenge you, as they are sworn to do.' Angry again, at himself this time, for not seeing, for not understanding before. 'And from now on, we'll protect you, which is what we should have done all along.'

We. As if he were a Brunson, too.

She shook her head. She had calmed, as if accepting that, finally, someone else knew the truth. 'What do you think of the women you and the king have tupped?'

He shrugged, not understanding. 'They're fickle, changeable.' Not worthy of the time he had wasted on them.

'Is that what the father says of his daughter? Does her brother use those words?'

A glimmer of light pierced the red haze in his brain. 'You think they will think—'

'I *know* what they will think.'

She had kept them away, all of them, for so long he could see why it had taken so long to let him in.

'And that's why...' He felt as slow as the biggest dolt. 'Why you didn't want to touch or kiss or...' His every touch must have been torture. 'I should have known.'

She shook her head. 'I did not want you to know.'

Those final words shattered her calm. She turned away and curled in on herself, shoulders shaking, hands to her mouth, trying to hold in all the pain she had borne alone. My God, how had she lived with this?

He picked her up, sat on the bed and rocked her. And with the tears, finally, she released a cry, near the sort of scream one might hear from a mortally wounded animal. But even that she stifled, to be sure the others would not hear.

So she bit her lip, buried her face in his shoulder and sobbed. And he held her in his lap and let her cry until there were no tears left.

'But you told me,' he whispered, much, much later, after he'd wondered at all the reasons why.

She raised her head, her small smile a mismatch for eyes still red from her tears. 'You are different.'

'Ah, Cate.' He pulled her close and wrapped her in his arms, as if that would be enough to keep them both safe. 'You say I'm different at the very moment I've become a Border man.' Full of blood lust that wanted nothing more than revenge.

The woman in his arms needed healing, but that would have to come later. After.

Holding her, holding back the kisses he wanted to give her, he felt her relax and finally heard the breathing that said she slept, trusting, in his arms. And he watched the waxing moon rise over unchanging hills.

Only the land remained the same. Everything else had changed.

He felt no different towards her. More loving, more tender, more protective if anything. She was at once all he had ever thought of her and more, for now he understood what had made her his brave and angry Cate.

Yet as he held her in his arms, waiting for dawn, it was the man wearing John Brunson's skin that he no longer knew.

At court, he had been surrounded by constant plots and shifting loyalties. He had taken things lightly—missions, women, promises—not wanting to care for something that might be lost, expecting that tomorrow, everything would change.

But this man who held Cate Gilnock in his arms had no intention of tracking down Scarred Willie Storwick and turning him over to the Border wardens. No interest in peace on the Borders or a position as Pursemaster or a wealthy wife.

He had one intent now. He was going to kill Willie Storwick. And if he were caught and hanged for it, he would die a happy man.

This man was a stranger, but he lived squarely inside John's body now, never to be escaped, no matter how fast the horse.

This man was a Brunson.

Impossible to rest safely in a man's arms.
Impossible that he knew. And accepted.
Would that change after he had had time to ponder?

Cate opened her eyes and felt her lashes flutter against his skin and breathed the man smell of him. The hair on his chest was soft on her lips and she let lose a sigh, grateful to Bessie for finding another bed for the night and leaving them alone.

She raised her head, slowly, wanting to look at him, to see who Johnnie Brunson was now.

The sweet face that had ridden home just weeks ago was tempered. He had been determined, yes, and even bitter when he arrived, but careless and light, he had looked over the world as if he thought the worst could never truly happen.

Now, lips that had curved in a smile were set in a harsh, straight line, as if they might never kiss again.

She stretched a finger, tracing their lines, but he caught her hand and pulled it away. 'Ah, Johnnie. Have I stolen your smile for ever?'

He blessed her with it, then. 'I want to see you smile, too. Must I wait until Scarred Willie's dead?'

She shook her head. The name of her dreaded enemy drifted past her ears, no heavier than a feather. What was real was this man. The face she loved to look at. The touch she craved. The belief that, finally, she could trust someone other than herself. And trust herself when she was with him.

'Not nearly so long, Johnnie.'

And then she smiled. And raised her lips to his.

She had kissed him before, yes. But this was different. This time, she had no secrets.

She melted into him, her body no longer hers, responding, feeling, wanting. Now that she had shed her secret, she ached to join with him in a way that could wash away the taint of that other joining, a baptism to cleanse her of that sin.

Now that she had let it go, she recognised the weight of the secret she had carried. When she shared it, it had tumbled off her shoulders, splashed into the water.

Her lips, his, both eager. She pressed as close as she could, as if flesh itself were a barrier that could be overcome. Now, finally, she could become one with him, no longer alone...

Then, fear fluttered again.

The secret had not floated away on the current. Instead, it bobbed on top of the water, staining the stream with poison.

It was not gone. It would never be gone until Willie was.

He paused, breaking the kiss. 'It does not bring you joy, still.'

She shook her head, hating Willie, hating herself because before she could stop it, willing lips and eager arms had stiffened against him again. 'I want it to. For you.'

He smiled again. A smile tinged with sad knowledge she knew would never leave him, either. 'Ah, Catie, I cannot find joy unless you do. And you cannot find joy while you think of him.'

And even when Willie was gone, what if that were not enough? What if nothing changed even then?

She swallowed. 'There's never been anyone else to think of.'

Pain crumpled John's face as he saw, finally, fully, the enemy he faced. At first, he had thought it would be as easy as letting his anger loose and taking revenge. He would track the man and kill him and Cate would be free.

Now he saw that death would not be the end. Scarred

Willie, or his memory, still lived inside of her, where he could rise like a powrie spirit.

There, inside her, Willie's ghost might live for ever.

He would kill Storwick, yes. And for stealing the joy she should take in joining, he was going to make that death very, very painful.

Chapter Seventeen

Thomas Carwell appeared at their gate the next day.

John's first urge was to lock him out, but Rob, surprisingly, overruled him. Still, they let him come no further than the small hall off the courtyard, meant for conducting business with strangers.

John glowered when Bessie brought them ale. Carwell deserved no such welcome, and, judging by his expression, the man knew it.

Rob sat at the head man's table, leaving Carwell to perch awkwardly on a stool.

John refused to sit at all. Bad enough he was forced to share a brew with the man. 'I'm surprised you dare to show your face.'

'I thank you for opening the gate. It is more than the English Warden's men did.'

Rob shook his head. 'A waste of horse feed, that trip.'

'His steward said he was gone,' Carwell said. 'To Truce Day. Where he never appeared. And then he expressed "utter dismay" to hear of Storwick's escape, an emotion I sincerely doubt.' He took a gulp of his ale. 'I don't know where the man is.'

'Well, we know where Storwick is,' John said, pac-

ing. A plume of smoke from the central brazier slug-
gishly sought the ceiling vent. 'He's built himself a
tower in the Debatable Land. Calls it his Hole House.'

'Hell House it is,' Rob muttered.

Carwell raised his brows. The man was listening,
at least. 'Anything on those lands after sundown belongs to all.'

John looked at Rob, then back at Carwell. 'He says
the English Warden gave him leave to build.'

'It was not his to give.'

'You said he was as trustworthy as you.'

'I must have lied.'

John faced him, studying the unreadable expression,
trying to determine whether Carwell could be trusted
at all. The king had named him, yes, but had the king
ever looked the man in the eye? 'I don't trust either
one of you—'

'John,' Rob interrupted, 'he's the warden. Hear him
out.'

'Have you gone mad?' he yelled, but not the words
he wanted to scream. *Do you know what Storwick did
to Cate?* 'After he betrayed us?'

'I did not,' Carwell said. 'I swear it.'

John turned away in disgust.

Behind him, Rob spoke up, sharp, but calm. 'Prove
it.'

Carwell rose, putting his tankard on the table. Just
by standing, he had taken control of the conversation.
'We make the rules work to our advantage.'

John stared. How to judge the man rightly? Older
than Rob, but not by much. Courtly manners that hid
both emotion and thought. He showed nothing a man
could get a grip on. 'Willie and his band don't care for

rules. They tie them in a pretty bow and throw them on the dung heap.'

Carwell smiled in that way that hid a secret, an expression as dangerous as Rob's scowl. 'Then we'll set the heap ablaze, won't we? The land is common by day, but his tower is there after dark. By law, anything left there after dark can be seized.'

John looked at Rob. They looked at Carwell. And Rob nodded.

'We'll need at least a hundred men to take it,' John said, finally willing to sit. 'Three would be better.'

'The Brunsons will bring half,' Rob said.

John looked at Carwell. 'You must raise the rest.'

It was a challenge. Carwell had already sent many of his men to the king. There would be few left to guard his own keep.

After a moment, he nodded. Then, arms crossed, he studied John. 'And the Brunson men the king waits for?'

Days had slid into weeks. He had postponed the decision, thinking to satisfy Cate and then the king. Now, the men would be late.

If they rode at all.

John looked at Rob and shook his head. 'We ride for Storwick first.'

Carwell raised his brows. 'What's changed?'

'Changed?' He knew the man's meaning, but Cate's shame was not his to share.

'What happened to the man who served king before kin?'

He tried to remember. Tried to summon up the arrogant, careless man who had ridden into the valley wearing a badge of thistle, expecting that alone would entitle him to respect.

'Gone. Vanished. Disappeared into the Border mist.'

Cate. Cate had changed him.

A smile flickered between Carwell and Rob. 'Welcome home, Johnnie Brunson,' Rob said.

Then Carwell frowned, silent. John did not press him. They could well be on opposite sides after this battle, when Carwell must again enforce the king's will.

The warden pulled a map from his bag and unfolded the parchment on the table showing the shaded no man's land near the river. 'Now show me where Storwick's built his Hell Hole.'

It took weeks to prepare their invasion. October slid into November. Leaves slid off the trees. When there was not work that kept them apart, Cate and John were side by side.

Each day, Cate trusted him more. She had shared her secret and he revealed it to no one. But now that he knew the truth, her pain was not halved, but doubled, for she saw it ever reflected back at her when she met his eyes.

They did not speak of it. And they did not share a bed again.

But on the night before the men were to leave, she lingered in the tower's hall as darkness fell, sheltered in the meagre privacy of the alcove near the west-facing window.

He sat beside her, his body shielding hers from prying eyes, his hand resting on hers. The hard stone seat released the warmth of the day slowly.

'Tomorrow it will all be over,' he said.

She nodded, fervently hoping it would be and that she would be free.

He started again. 'I do not want to go without...'

There was the pain again. She did not have to ask

what he meant. 'Aye.' She squeezed his hand. She must try once more. Even if she could not join with him, she had to touch him, to hold him, her touch a talisman to keep him safe. 'But where?'

Men who would ride tomorrow over-spilled the tower. Between Carwell's men and the Brunsons, they could crush whatever band Storwick had collected around him.

Belde had been banished outside after he growled at too many strangers and even the room she shared with Bessie was full of wives and daughters who had come to prepare food for what had become near an army.

'Rob sleeps with his men tonight. If he sleeps at all.'

She looked at him, eyes wide. 'The master's chamber is empty?' Curtained bed. Roaring fire. Chest and chair. What luxury the tower could boast was in that room.

And the last time they had been in it together, his father had lain dead in the bed.

Aye, they would both face ghosts in that room. 'Are you sure?'

'Yes.' No hesitation in his voice, or in his eyes.

No one watched them climb the darkened stairs. No one saw them open the door to find a wasteful, crackling fire warming an empty room.

'Bessie,' she whispered, taking in the fire, the freshly made bed and small plate of oat cakes and tankards of ale. 'Bessie has been here.'

He hugged her from behind, then turned her to face him. 'There will be no one in this room tonight but me and thee. No one.'

That was what she wanted. To banish the ghosts. To bury the nightmares.

She reached for his cheek, loving the feel of it against her palm. 'No one but John and Cate.'

'Let us be slow. Just let me make you happy.'

There are ways for men and women to be happy. Perhaps it was true, for those blessed with good fortune and luck. She wanted to believe it. 'What must I do?'

'You must do *nothing*.' He picked her up and laid her on the bed.

She stiffened against the softness of the feather mattress, then forced her fisted fingers apart.

He put a hand on either cheek and she clung to his eyes, as if they could save her. *As long as I know it's Johnnie, I'll feel safe.*

'I will tell you everything I'm going to do, so you won't be afraid. And if anything feels wrong, just hold up your hand and I'll stop. And if there's anything you want, just tell me.'

'I understand,' she said, not sure she did.

But the fire and the bed sheltered by blue fabric made it easier. Outside, there was hard ground and soft heather and nothing to keep a raider away. Inside, protected by the walls, her memories were of John.

He lifted her left hand and kissed each finger, then turned it over to press his lips to her palm.

She studied each movement.

'I would recommend closing your eyes.' He smiled, still, soft, reassuring.

She shook her head. Last time, she had closed her eyes. 'I like to look at you.'

He threaded his fingers through her hair. 'I like to look at you, too.' His hand reached the end of tresses too short to touch her shoulders and he tugged, as if he might help them grow.

She had cut her hair up to her ears and, until recently, had forced Bessie to keep it short. Never again would a man grab her braid so she could not escape.

'I can let it grow,' she said, wondering how it would feel. 'If you like.'

He shook his head. 'I will not force you to do anything because of what I like.' He did not speak of her hair.

'Do what you want. I will like it.' A lie she wanted to believe.

'You may like me without liking it all, but I will be gentle. I promise.'

She nodded, but still, her body braced itself. He trailed his fingers down her cheek, slowly, then to her neck and throat. They bumped against her shirt. 'Help me.'

Kind of him to give her control. Did he know how much she needed it?

Without her shirt, the cool night air slipped over her. His warm fingers followed, stirring her skin like swirling water. He took his time, letting her adjust, running his fingers over her shoulders, then down the valley between her breasts, then up her sides to her shoulders again and down her arms until they reached her fingers and tangled there. Everywhere he touched was warm. And when he withdrew his touch, she chilled.

Too slow. She did not want to wait. His touch must erase the past. 'You needn't dally.'

'Ah, Catie, my love, the dallying is where the joy is.'

My love. Said as easily as he had, no doubt, said it to other women.

'But I…' What? She both wanted it to be over and never to end.

'We went too fast the last time. Just lie back.'

So she stretched out on the bed, trying to feel nothing but his touch, be nowhere but in this room, and with no one but Johnnie Brunson.

His lazy fingers played over her skin until it shimmered, as if ready to dissolve. But beneath, her body still warred with her, muscles tight, ready to fight. Ready to run.

He started to slide her woollen hose off her hips. She froze again and gripped his wrists. 'No.' Thinking he would ignore her.

Instead, he let go.

Now she did close her eyes, squeezing them tight against the tears. Down there. Down there was where that man had been. Last time, it was the feel of wool breeches on her bare skin, the feel of a man fumbling for himself just before—

She opened her eyes to see his smile gone. 'It's too soon,' he whispered. 'I'll wait. Until you're ready.'

Her body relaxed at his words, as if given a reprieve from death. But death might come to either of them tomorrow.

And even if death came to Willie Storwick, would that be enough? What if his death did not free her?

She could see herself, years from now, still locked in the prison her mind had made. Years after Johnnie Blunkit had gone back to his king and his court and she was left alone with everything below her waist still in Willie's grip.

'No!' She laced her fingers in his, refusing to let him go, afraid this chance would be gone. 'I *am* ready.' She met his eyes.

John took her hand, playing with her fingers and studying her eyes. 'Show me,' he said finally. 'Show me what you want, what you are ready for.'

'So you'll do only as I say?' She felt herself ease at the thought.

'Until you no longer know what to ask for.'

She could share a smile with him, then, grateful to think there were parts to come beyond her experience.

'And still, if there is anything, anything I do that you do not want, you need only say "nay".'

A word had stopped him before. She could trust it would do so again.

He had touched her arms, her throat, her ribs and waist, but her breasts ached for the same.

She looked down. 'Here.'

He smiled. 'Where?'

She pointed to the valley between her breasts.

He stroked the place she pointed to, not the place she wanted, but his fingers spread to either side and she moaned, turning to thrust her nipples under his fingers.

'Here?' She could hear the smile in his voice.

She opened her eyes, trying to catch her breath. 'I did not think you were a man who would need instruction on a woman's body.'

He laughed, then, and she joined him. Laughter. Who would think laughter and loving could be joined?

'Ah, but you are no ordinary woman, my love.'

My. Such a large word.

His fingers slid across first one breast, then the other. Then his lips followed. Warm, wet, exciting. This must be what they meant when they said 'love making'. It was so different from…

From things she did not want to remember.

The skin below her waist burned, impatient. She must know. She must know if she could ever be a woman again. She pushed him away and pulled her hose down, wanting to feel his skin on hers. Something escaped his throat. Not a word. Something between a gasp and a groan.

She faced him, seeing joy and pain mixed on his face.

'What…' Then he coughed, as if the word could not find its way up his throat. 'What do you want?'

Waiting. Waiting for her to say. 'I want your clothes gone.'

He stood, shedding the tunic. His chest, broad, strong, dusted with hair, made her smile. There, she had nested, snuggled and safe.

And so much more.

He reached to strip the rest, but suddenly she was not ready.

'Stop.'

He did, instantly.

She swallowed, licked her lips. It had been easier the first time, before she knew what might happen, both for good and ill. 'I want to feel your skin on mine.'

He sat on the bed and held her gently, as if she were a chalice. 'Like this?'

She nodded. This, this closeness, surely this could wipe the memories away. Yet her stiff body refused to yield to the promise. It fought him still, along with the comfort and pleasure he offered.

His lips met her forehead.

'Cate, listen to me. I will not take you tonight. Do you hear? Do you understand?'

She nodded, shakily, unsure whether she was relieved or sad.

'In order to do that, I need to keep my tarse in my braies, but I'll be sure you don't feel either of those things. Do you understand?'

She knew neither what he promised, nor how he had known why her body had rebelled, but trusting him, she nodded.

His words rumbled, close to her ear. 'What I am going to do is show you something of how it can be. How it can be wonderful. Will you let me do that?'

'Yes.' A word, only. But the right one.

His lips, warm, trailed down her neck and his fingers drifted lower. She let herself lie back, eyes open, as his lips and fingers played over her skin, at once lulling and exciting.

His kisses floated to the curve of her belly, reached the spot between her legs she had protected for so long. Some mix of fingers and tongue, she could not sort it out, focused on a nub of feeling she'd barely realised existed. A place no one had ever touched.

The rest of the world fell away, leaving only his lips meeting that secret place.

Everything within her rushed towards that spot, as fast as the Liddel Water towards the sea, and she thought she would die rather than stop it.

Then, as if a rock stood at the confluence of two rivers, the feeling, like the rushing water, hit it and broke into uncountable drops, sparkling in the sun, only to fall back to join the larger river.

The one river that was two joined together.

He held her for as long as she shook. Then she felt him move up and touch his lips to her forehead. That was not enough. That could hardly contain what had just happened.

She searched for his lips, met them with hers and let her kiss say what words could not.

The kiss ended only when his lips curved into a smile. 'And that, my love, is how it can be between a man and a woman.'

Not *a* man, she thought. Not *any* man. That's how it could be with *this* man.

Chapter Eighteen

Cate held him tightly for those few hours after the crescent moon rose, wishing neither of them had to leave each other or the bed. Once they left this room, nothing would be certain.

Not even their return.

Light touched the sky and she forced herself to stir. Belde must be fed. The horses prepared to ride when night fell.

She sighed and threw back the covers, searching for her clothes. 'I will pack food for us,' she said, wanting to speak of ordinary things. As if this were a day no more important than any other.

He sat up, crossing his legs, leaning his arms on his knees. 'Not this time. I won't let you go this time.'

A different kind of fear fluttered within her. 'But I must! I must face him. I must see him dead or I'll never—'

Never be able to love you as I want to.

He shook his head, wearing an expression that would have been at home on Black Rob's. 'No. I'll listen to no argument.'

'But now you know. You know why I must face him

myself.' Her fear had a name. Eyes, nose, ears. And she must prove that she would not do what she had the first time. What she had done in Kershopefoote. Freeze.

'You have faced him already.'

'It's different now.'

'Why?'

Because of you.

But she could not say that. Could not tell him she had hope she had not had before last night, hope she couldn't even breathe to the man who had given it to her. 'Why will you not let me see it to the end?'

'Because if you come, I'll worry that you're going to ride across a field like a target for their practice! Talk of it no more.'

'I can't stay here wondering, not knowing whether you—'

'I'll tie you down in the caif with the barrels if I must, but you will not ride with us.'

He would not be swayed. He had become a Brunson in truth and stubborn as any of them.

She straightened her shoulders against sharp disappointment. 'Then bring me his body. I must see him.' For she would not believe the man dead unless she witnessed it herself.

'Will that be enough for you, then? To see him dead?'

He paused and she lifted her chin. She would not let Johnnie cajole her from this. With Willie dead, she could put the past behind her.

But that left the future yawning, empty and uncertain.

'Yes. It will be enough. It will be the end.'

'Aye, then. I'll bring him.' Hands on her shoulders, he kissed her forehead. 'If there's a piece of him left when I'm done.'

* * *

They left at gloaming, riding towards the River Esk, where they would join Carwell and his men. His father's vest hung heavy on his shoulders. Norse moved steady and silent beneath him.

The plan was set. There was no more need for words.

It was comforting, riding shoulder to shoulder with Rob. An unfamiliar feeling, to be a brother again.

He and Cate had shared a final kiss before leaving the sanctuary of the room. As the men mounted, he glimpsed her across the courtyard, standing next to Bessie. Belde paced beside her, looking up at her as if expecting orders to join the hunt. His sister wrapped her arms around Cate, as if her grip was the only thing keeping Cate from mounting her pony.

She would stay safe and he would kill Storwick. He refused to think beyond that. To the men. To the king.

Yet, each step he had taken, each kiss they shared, each gallop over the hills, had drawn him closer to the land he was born to until, now, it was difficult to imagine leaving.

Carwell and his men joined them at the meeting place. 'Shall I call you Black John, then?' Carwell's question told John he was wearing his mood.

'I'll smile when this is done.'

'Then you'll smile this time tomorrow,' Rob said, his tone a match for John's, 'when we've wiped Scarred Willie's Hell House off the earth.'

The next leg of the journey took them into the valley land, crowded with trees with night air so thick with mist it felt as if they rode through the river.

When they finally reached the edge of clearing, Willie's tower stood in sight, just as it had been before. Still hidden by the trees, they paused to light their torches, tonight's weapon, more deadly than a sword.

There was a reason towers were built of stone.

Rob, Carwell and John exchanged glances, but not words. Actions would be their measure tonight. Of Rob as the head man, of John as a Brunson, and of Carwell as an ally.

Rob nodded and they galloped towards the tower.

A thousand hooves thundered against the earth. Spears and pikes pointed straight ahead, ready to gut any man who ran from the burning building.

Close now, close enough that they should have heard some clash of steel and stone as the defenders roused from sleep.

Nothing stirred within.

No time to wonder at it. They were there.

Rob hurled the first brand, which landed on the parapet. Bad throw. A guard could throw it back. But they followed with the rest, a dozen or more, raining into the wooden structure like stars falling from the heavens.

The horses shied, uneasy at the smell.

Nothing stirred inside the tower but flames.

Fire licked the damp walls until the exposed wood above the stone sheath smouldered, sending roiling clouds of smoke into the dark, damp sky.

Still, nothing.

Then, flame by flame, the tower erupted into an inferno. Behind the stone sheath, the wooden shell disappeared.

And as the empty tower burned, John turned to Carwell. First Truce Day. Now a new betrayal.

He pulled the man from his horse, then jumped off his own and started pummelling Carwell as if he were Willie Storwick. Ashes drifted over them. Acrid air seared his lungs. Caught by surprise, Carwell was bested at first, but he landed a punch to John's jaw before they were pulled apart.

Soot streaked Rob's skin; anger strained his frown. 'You'll not resolve your quarrel here. They may still be close. Waiting.'

'Or worse.' John staggered to Norse and mounted, unsteady, head finally holding his emotions in check. 'They may be at our tower.'

The tower was intact. Cate was safe. But the cattle they had stolen from the Storwicks a few weeks ago had vanished.

He thought Rob was going to put his fist through the stone.

Carwell had returned with them, not asking permission.

John turned on him. 'Why is it that every time we trust you with a plan the Storwicks discover it?'

Carwell's usual secret smile had turned to stone. 'I don't know. But I intend to find out.'

'Hold him,' he said to Rob, not stopping to ponder his assumption that Rob would need no further words to know his meaning.

'Don't be a fool,' Carwell said. 'He's on his way to my castle.' One he'd left lightly defended. 'Come along if you don't trust me.'

'We will.' But first, he must face Cate.

And his failure.

Still covered with ashes, he wrapped her in his arms and they clung to each other, together and alive. Relief that she was safe warred with anger that he had failed her.

She did not ask, but lifted her face, now smudged with soot, and waited.

He let her go, undeserving of the privilege. 'He was gone.' Spare. Stark. True. The only words he knew how to say.

'He came and was gone before we knew. If I had come, if you had taken Belde, we could have—'

'Do not think of could.'

They had retreated to the wall walk and she paced, restless as the dog, looking towards the hills as if expecting a new threat.

He could not blame her. Too late he had learned the Borders' lessons.

'He knew,' she whispered, looking to the west. 'He must have known.' Her eyes met his, then, strong as a comrade in arms. 'What happens now?'

'We find the traitor. And then, we find Storwick.'

'Do you think it is Carwell?'

Did he? He no longer knew who to trust. 'I don't know.' And if it were true, what did that mean? Was Carwell disloyal to the king or was it just the Brunsons he deceived? Or was the king himself playing a different game? What kind of personal congratulations had been in that envelope he had put in Carwell's hand? 'But I intend to find out.'

Strange, to echo Carwell's own words.

And to do that, he must go to Carwell's castle to see whether Storwick had attacked it or sought shelter there.

Carwell was ready to ride, but Rob and John insisted the men be allowed to sleep first. If Storwick had attacked, they were too late to stop him. Then, while Rob stayed with a contingent at the tower, John rode with the rest to Carwell's castle.

Enough to fight the rest of Carwell's men if need be.

Rob clasped his arm in farewell. 'So go see how loyal your king's warden is.' His tone was as sceptical as his words.

John felt the same.

There was time and space to do no more than kiss Cate before he left.

Again, he had forbidden her to come and this time, she did not argue. 'You won't find him there,' she said, her voice calm. 'It's not the time.'

He hugged her, and neither asked nor argued, hoping she was right. She could not possibly know where Storwick was, but sometimes, hunter and prey became linked in some way impossible to understand. Hunter never able to capture prey and prey never able to escape hunter.

Carwell pushed them without ceasing and they were within sound of the sea by nightfall. They approached the hold cautiously, wondering whether Storwick's men might have overpowered Carwell's.

But as they came closer, it was evident the raiders had come and gone. The moat had protected the castle, but an outbuilding on the flat land that sloped to the bay was a charred hulk.

'There.' Carwell waved his arm to the ruined hut. 'There's your answer.'

His voice held a bitterness that belied every smooth syllable John had heard him utter.

'That's no answer. You might have agreed that he would torch something unimportant.'

Carwell turned his back, riding across the drawbridge and into the courtyard. 'Yes, I might,' he called over his shoulder, too smoothly for John's taste. 'But I did not.'

Inside the gate, the man dismounted, arranged for the steward to see to the small army that rode with him and instructed his lieutenants to meet him in the hall and tell him all that had happened.

As they walked across the courtyard and into the hall, Carwell's stride now had the urgency of his own.

'It's more likely,' he began, as if the conversation had not been interrupted, 'that he discovered our plans another way. Maxwell men have married Storwick women. No doubt Brunson women have married Storwick men. It would only take one.'

Was that an explanation or an excuse? 'But his family disowned him.'

Even in the uncertain light of the fire, he could see disbelief in the man's expression. 'His blood is unchanged. There are Storwicks who would shelter him if he rode to Stirling and bent a knee to King James.'

Aye, he'd been the naive one, the one who believed in laws and kings and pronouncements, none of which were as strong as blood. 'If that's true, where is he now?'

Carwell's look was weary. 'He could be anywhere. He's got my fish and your cattle. He can feast for months.'

'I've not got months to wait.'

'Neither does the king,' Carwell answered.

And neither did Cate.

'The king will have to wait a few weeks more,' John said.

In fact, the king might have to wait for ever.

Chapter Nineteen

Home again, he went directly to Cate, having to admit the quarry had escaped again. The two of them left the tower and walked to the stream alone. Along the banks, beneath leafless trees and a pale sky, the grass clung to its summer green.

She bent down to pick up a stick and flung it across the water. Belde splashed in to chase it. 'I'm glad you didn't find him.'

'Why?' She had said they would not. Was she glad to be proven right?

'I must be there when you do.' She spoke with harsh finality. 'I must kill him myself.'

'I told you I would find him,' he said. 'And I will.' All this talk of being there, of killing him herself, would fade when Storwick was gone. There was no moving on, for either of them, until then.

'I know.' But she did not meet his eyes when she said it.

John put an arm around her and she let him, leaning against his chest, watching the dog. Belde's tail wagged one way, his legs moved another, and then he pounced on the stick, grabbed it in his jaws and shook it, playful as a child.

His antics coaxed a smile from Cate.

Belde bounded back into the stream and up the bank, then shook all the water off his coat and on to them.

Laughing, Cate knelt down, wrestled the stick away from him and flung it back towards the tower.

Her smile faded when she stood. 'Is it Carwell?'

He had told her the story on the way down. 'I'm not sure.' The man was full of his own secrets, but that did not make him a traitor. 'But until I am, there'll be no trusting him again.'

They started back to the tower. Belde ran towards them and John, without thinking, held out his hand. The dog brought him the stick, nudging John's palm with a cold nose.

'He's not done that for anyone else,' she said. 'He must trust you.'

Do you? He wondered, but did not ask.

He played tug of war with Belde, then threw the stick halfway up the knoll. The dog bounded away, tireless, ran past its landing place, then loped in circles trying to find it.

Cate laughed again.

The sound warmed him. 'Happy?'

Happy. A foreign word.

Was she?

She smiled back at him. Ordinary women must have many moments like this. Sunshine. A man beside them. Dogs, children, laughter.

A man and woman can be happy, he had promised, *even when the world is harsh.*

She had thought he was talking about a man and a woman, intimate and alone in bed. That was happiness she thought never to have. But the closeness she had shared with John in bed, imperfect as it was, had made this moment possible.

It reminded her of the way she had clawed her way back from numb despair. Being grateful for a stray sunbeam. Appreciating a scarlet sky at sunset.

And somehow, happiness now touched a man as well, something she had been afraid to ever hope for. Would it ever be more than this? Would she ever be able to love him fully?

And still, fear nipped at the heels of the thought. Somewhere in the hills, Willie Storwick rode free. He, too, had laughed.

But I am here. And I am not the woman I was before Johnnie came. Think of what is now, not what is past or to come.

Was she happy?

Her smile broadened. 'Yes.'

John met Rob in the small, windowless chamber off the public hall where they had met Carwell. Where their plans would be private.

'This time,' John began, 'we search for Storwick without Carwell.'

Rob nodded. 'Can't be trusted.'

His brother did not berate him. Rob had trusted the warden last time, too. No more.

'Carwell claims Willie knew we were coming because Brunsons have married Storwicks.'

'Any Brunson traitor enough to marry a Storwick would be traitor enough to do it.'

'But once married, they would not go home again. How would they know?'

'They are family still. Women sometimes visit.'

Rob's good humour had fled. 'But if I find the traitor, I'll kill him. Or her.'

Rob was a blunt instrument, John thought, whose first and only impulse was to fight. Sometimes, there was no enemy. Sometimes, disaster was accidental, not deliberate.

'Scarred Willie had to expect we'd come after him,' he began. 'What if a Storwick usually visited her cousin married to a Brunson on a Sunday? And what if she had word not to visit that day? That would be enough for him to know, even if no one else understood.'

'Or it could be Carwell and the English warden.'

John nodded. 'First we find Scarred Willie. Then we find who betrayed us. You talked to the Storwick head man. Would he help?'

'No.'

No need to say more. Disowning a family member and handing him over to the enemy were two very different things. 'What if Carwell is right? If word spread of our plans among the family, even accidentally, we could discover Willie's whereabouts the same way.'

Rob studied his face. 'Is everyone at court so devious?' His voice held a hint of admiration.

A good sign. At least he might listen. 'So, do we have any Brunsons married to Storwicks?'

'It's banned.'

'So is reiving.' His brother was not usually so concerned with the law.

'I don't mean by the king. *I* won't have Storwick blood under my roof.'

John sighed. *Stubborn as a Brunson*, they said along the Borders. He knew where the phrase came from. 'A Brunson woman married to a Storwick man, then. Living on their land.'

'A few.' A grudging admission, as if somehow he'd failed. 'But we can't just ride up and ask. There'd be an arrow in your chest before you reached the door.'

'No, not you or me. Perhaps one of the Brunson women married to a Storwick man?'

'Not if we don't know whether there is a traitor.'

Who *could* be trusted now?

They sat, silent.

'No,' Rob said, 'it must be Bessie.'

'Bessie!' He tried to picture his quiet sister as a spy. 'But she can't—'

'She's the head man's sister. Mother used to visit every family member at least once a year. Even...' he sighed '...those.'

It would be the perfect excuse. 'She's calm and quiet, but I don't know whether she could tell a lie.'

Then he thought of all the truths she had withheld and paused. Bessie might make a better spy than he thought.

'Do you want Cate to go?'

He glared at his brother. Cate could not even breathe Storwick air without gagging. 'She'd fool no one.'

'Ach! Enough of this. Let's just ride across the hills and attack them.'

'And if he's not there, then what?' They would have escalated the feud while Willie still rode free.

Rob sighed and put a hand on John's shoulder. 'We'll try it your way, then.'

The hand on his shoulder was a blessing. Acceptance. His plan. It was a slender one, but without some direction, they could ride the hills for years, chasing a ghost. 'I'll tell Cate, then we'll ask Bessie.'

And he found himself, guilty, hoping Bessie would say yes, for without her, they had no plan at all.

* * *

John found Cate in the empty hall, mending the rips on his jack-of-plaites vest as if it were her right to do so. As if she would do so for years to come.

He explained the plan. 'We're going to ask Bessie,' he said, finally.

'Why Bessie? I'll go. I'm not afraid.'

'I know you're not.' He knew she did not want to be. 'But no one will question why she has come, but you...'

'They know I would as soon kill a Storwick as look at him.' She sighed. 'Why would a woman do that? Marry her family's mortal enemy?'

Because she loved him. Yet he made no glib reply. Love was not enough to keep a man from his duty. Or shouldn't be. Not at court. And not on the Border.

Yet he had let Cate keep him from his.

He blocked the thought. It was not to be dwelled on now.

'Will you help me explain it to her?' he said. 'Bessie's not like you. She's...' And he realised he was not sure what Bessie was. Quietly labouring in the background like that sister in the Bible who worked while her sibling listened at Jesus's feet. She did what was asked and even what wasn't.

Cate nodded finally, and rose, meeting his eyes. 'She'll be in the kitchen.'

They walked down the stairs and into the west courtyard. 'Cate,' he said, 'you said he would not be at Carwell's. Do you...' what was the word? '...sense, where he is?'

She looked to the hills, her eyes dark and far away, as if trying to see. 'Out there. Waiting.'

He was not sure whether to be disappointed or grateful she knew no more than that.

The smell of lamb stew drew them into the kitchen. Since Willie Storwick had stolen the cattle, the meal would have more broth and less meat.

Bessie glanced up at them, but her rolling pin did not stop. 'Out with it. What have you come for?'

His sister would not be fooled by a Storwick, of that, he was certain. 'We need to find Willie Storwick. Rob and I, and Cate, have talked and we have an idea.'

'You want me to visit the Storwick Brunsons and see what I can discover.'

He felt his jaw sag. He thought, not for the first time, that his sister might be fey.

Bessie and Cate exchanged smiles. 'Don't look so surprised, Brother. Even a woman's head can follow that logic.'

'You'll do it?'

Her hands never stopped working as she put down the pin and pinched the dough at the edge of the crust to build it up, thick and sturdy enough to hold the lamb and carrots.

'It's better than sending three hundred men into the Cheviot Hills searching for one man hidden in the heather.' Bessie reached for another ball of dough and attacked it with the rolling pin. 'I've gone every year since we lost Mother. Now that Da is gone…it's time.'

'Thank you,' Cate whispered. 'For braving those *savages* for me.'

Bessie paused with a sigh to push a strand of red hair off her forehead with the back of her hand. 'I was alone with a Storwick once. Just the two of us.'

Cate leaned forwards, hand on her dagger. 'When? Where?'

John studied Bessie's smile. It held the shadow of

the one his mother had given to her foolish young sons. 'Long ago. I was no more than twelve, thirteen.'

'Did he hurt you?' Cate held her breath.

Bessie shook her head. 'It wasn't a "he". It was a lass. I was sent to the burn for water, but I left the bowie on the bank and wandered. Followed the stream past the burial ground, picked flowers.' She brought her gaze back to the kitchen. 'It was a lovely spring day and I didn't want to work.'

John swallowed astonishment. He had never known his sister to shirk a duty.

'A little farther down, I looked across the stream and there was a girl, maybe a little older than I. She saw me, too, and we both just stopped, afraid.'

'Did you know she was a Storwick?' Cate asked.

'I wasn't sure, but I knew all the Brunsons and she wasn't one of us.'

'What happened?'

'We were on opposite sides of the stream, too far away to do each other harm. "Who are you?" she said and I said, "You first." She told me she was a Storwick and I told her I was a Brunson.' She smiled again. 'That was so surprising we were struck dumb for a while. Later, we talked.'

'Talked?' John said. 'What was there to talk about?'

Bessie's smile turned tart. 'As I recall, we shared stories about her arrogant cousin and my overbearing brothers.'

John felt his jaw sag, as if she had just confided she'd flown to the top of Hogback Hill. He had never thought of the Storwick women much at all and had certainly not imagined them as sisters with kin who might tease them.

Next to him, Cate gnawed her lip, as if she, too, were

struggling with a reminder that even Storwicks were born children of God. 'Did you ever see her again?'

His sister didn't speak at first.

'I'm not sure,' she said, finally, picking up the rolling pin and turning back to her work. 'I'll visit the Storwick Brunsons. On Sunday.'

And as they left the kitchen, John pondered what his sister had said. Women were ever full of secrets.

A few days later, Cate helped Bessie collect oat cakes and load them into bags, hanging on either side of the pony. Unable to settle, Cate picked up too many, too fast, handing them to Bessie before she needed them, and so was forced to put them down again.

'I could go with you,' she said again, finally. 'They wouldn't be afraid of me if I were with you.'

'Yes, they would.'

'I could disguise myself. I could put on woman's clothes. I could—'

'No.' One word. As definitive as her brother's.

'I'm not afraid.'

'No one said you were. But you should be.'

'But I shouldn't be,' she protested without thinking.

'I would be, if I were you.'

'But you're never afraid.'

'Am I not?'

She stared at Bessie, not sure how to answer. This woman had never spoken a word of protest against any duty that had been given to her, but only lifted it to her shoulders, one more rock on a back already over-burdened. A woman younger than she by two years, but who seemed infinitely older. 'But you never say a word.'

'Nor do you.'

But she was silent out of shame, not valour. 'I want no one to know how...afraid I am.'

Wordless, Bessie lifted her brows, saying, as clearly as words, *And neither do I.*

Before Cate's eyes, patient, quiet, calm, knowing Bessie became a different person. One who accepted the burdens handed to her without complaint not because she had none but because, for reasons of her own, she dared make none.

Cate wrapped her arms around Bessie, hoping an embrace might say all she could not. 'Be safe,' she whispered.

Against her shoulder, she felt Bessie nod.

John frowned as Bessie mounted the pony. 'You must take more than one man with you. What if you're attacked?'

'Mother always travelled this way,' she said. 'If I come with an army, they'll not let me close.'

With a suspicious look at the man beside her, he pulled Rob out of earshot. 'Can we trust him?' Which man had gone before?

'I think so, yes,' Rob answered. 'But there's something you must learn on the Borders, Johnnie. You can think and work and plan and scheme with all your might, but in the end...' He shrugged. 'In the end, your life is in the hands of fate. Just like that of the First Brunson.'

Left for dead and found alive. Both by chance.

He looked at Cate, as she gave Bessie a last hug. Yes, fate seemed to be meddling with his best-laid plans.

And he had a feeling that fate was not finished.

No work was done for the rest of the day.

Rob sat near the great hearth in the hall, staring into

the flames, saying even less than usual. John paced. Periodically, he climbed to the parapet, walked the perimeter, then stood by Cate, looking towards the hills, straining for a glimpse of a woman on a pony and her sole guard.

Cate had taken the warm seat next to the chimney as soon as Bessie left and had not moved since.

All day, she huddled there, watching the hills stretch to the south, rising and falling like waves. Above them, grey rolling clouds reflected the rounded hilltops and hidden valleys.

The days were growing shorter, the sun set sooner. When he mounted the stairs at day's end, the sky had turned blood red, spilling colour on to the clouds.

Cate, unmoving, looked out into the darkness. Belde, who had not left her side, raised his head. The dog's drooping, mournful eyes held both a plea and an accusation.

'We can't expect to see her until tomorrow,' he said as much to himself as to Cate.

'I should have gone,' she muttered, not moving her eyes.

'Do you not think I've said the same?'

She turned to him, then, some private agony darkening her eyes. 'But it's my fault, all of this. I'm the reason someone must go at all.'

My fault. As if *she* had caused everything to happen instead of a man so unredeemable that he had been outcast by his own.

'It's not your fault,' he said, putting an arm around her shoulders and pulling her near. 'And you cannot solve it alone.'

'I'm not alone,' she answered, a small smile curving her lips. But wrapped in a faded blue blanket, her fair hair mixing with the wind, she looked as solitary as the ancestor who'd been left behind. 'I'm a Brunson.'

A Brunson. With a sister in Bessie who would ride through the Valley of Death for her and a brother in Rob who would take up the sword to right the wrongs done to her. No distant king cared whether this woman lived or died. King James had not broken bread with her or seen the anguish in her eyes.

Or shared her bed.

No king cared for the things that meant most in the world to John. And there was the choice he had not wanted to make: between Cate and his king.

He crouched down, fending off a friendly nudge from Belde, to savour the sight of her face. The planes of her nose, the edges of her cheekbones were still as sharply drawn as he had first thought, but her lips... Ah, how had he ever thought them less than perfect? The top one softly bowed, the lower, lushly curved...

'Aye,' he said. 'And you're the bravest of us all.'

Chapter Twenty

Bessie didn't return until after moonrise the next day. Cate bit her tongue to keep from asking questions until Bessie had been settled by the fire and held a bowl of hot soup. The day had been raw and the ride long.

They had gathered in Rob's bedchamber with the door closed and Belde outside to keep prying ears away. Bessie took the stool by the fire, John the one by the bed and Rob sat on the chest.

That left the bed for her. She perched uneasily on the high mattress, avoiding John's eyes. Just to sit on it reminded her body of what they had shared here.

Bessie took a sip of the soup, sighed deeply and dropped her head back, letting her long, red hair hang behind her, as if she were letting the strain of the trip fall away.

Then she put down the bowl and leaned forwards. 'He has been disowned. It is true. The head man has told the rest not to treat him as a Storwick.'

Cate shuddered. Thrust from the family. A living death.

'Don't believe it,' Rob said. 'He and the head man

both must be in league with the English Warden to take possession of the no man's land.'

'If so, they've not told the rest. They've no more love for the man than we have. Word must have come to him by accident. No one warned him deliberately.'

'How can you be certain?' Johnnie asked.

Bessie looked at Cate as she answered. 'He's...' she swallowed '...he's made enemies among his own.'

Horror chilled her. Unthinkable that his own kinswomen might have suffered as she had. Did some nameless Storwick woman wake with nightmares, too?

John, on the stool below her, reached over to put his hand on her leg in reassurance. 'But did they know where he is?'

Bessie shook her head. 'No. And they seemed uneasy with that.'

'There's only one place he can be,' Rob said. 'Back in the Debatable Lands, rebuilding his tower.'

'I don't think so,' Bessie said. 'Rumour is that his men blame him for the loss of the tower. I think he's closer.'

'Why?'

She looked at Cate, then John, joining them with her glance. 'Because they say he's hunting for you.'

John felt Cate tremble, felt her swallow, felt her trying to speak...

Nothing came.

His job now was to protect her, to complete the vow. If he'd made an enemy of Scarred Willie, all the better. It would keep the man away from Cate.

'It could be a trap.' He trusted his sister, but not the Storwicks.

She shook her head. 'The women told me all this when we were alone.'

As if a woman would not lie to her.

'If he's made enemies of his own, we could hunt him together, Brunson and Storwick.' He looked to Rob. If the families rode together, it would be punishment of a criminal, not reiving and raiding and revenge.

At least, that's what he would tell the king.

But it was a scowling Black Rob who returned his gaze. 'I'll not ride beside any Storwick for any reason. They'd send us into an ambush. Just you and me this time.'

'No,' John answered. 'I'm the one he wants. This time, I go alone.'

Rob tensed. 'You don't trust me?'

'I do, Rob. With my life.' And he had not realised it until now. Yet he still did not know whether their truce was more than temporary. 'But this will end with Willie dead and the king in a rage. Better to restrict his wrath to Johnnie Brunson.'

'You expect the king to know one Brunson from another? That's more than a Storwick can do.'

'He can tell this one.' The one who had been his friend. Once.

'Just look at your eyes, eh?'

They shared a chuckle.

'Don't worry,' Rob said, serious again, 'I care nothing for the king's wrath.'

I'm not afraid. That's what Rob was saying.

'I know. And I know you don't believe me, but some day, it will matter. One of us ought to stay on his good side for the sake of the family.' For the family. Words he never thought to say. 'Besides...' he looked at Cate, the vow now his '…I've reasons of my own to want him dead.'

Rob studied him. 'The vow was the family's, no matter who fulfils it.'

It rushed over him, the sense of belonging. Yes, it was his own vow to Cate, but he could feel his brother's support in those words. Rob would let him fulfil the family's vow. And Rob would stand at his back to lift the sword should John falter.

And behind Rob, generations of Brunsons.

He cleared his throat and swallowed against the lump there. 'Next time, I'll let you face the king's rage.'

Was that another laugh from Rob? Despite everything, things seemed a little easier between them.

'But this time,' he concluded, 'I'll ride alone.'

'No, you won't,' Cate said. 'You'll ride with me.'

No was all they told her. *No* and *no* and *no* as they planned in whispers and speculated where Willie might be hiding. In the hills along the border. Farther into England. No, back in the Debatable Land.

And she kept silent, finally, because she knew where he was hiding. Knew it as if she had the sight.

He had gone back to the beginning. Back to Hogback Hill.

And she would go back alone to find him.

But before she did, there was something else she must do. Something that required even more bravery.

The master's chamber had been left open and empty for them. No one had to explain.

John would ride out alone tomorrow.

But while Rob and Bessie intended to give them the gift of a last night, Cate needed something more.

Needed to prove to herself that she was Braw Cate—brave enough to face both of her enemies.

John walked in without hesitation, crouching before the hearth to stir the banked fire. Behind her, Belde stretched out on the floor outside the door, as if to guard against intruders. Resting his head on his paws, he closed his eyes as Cate shut the door and turned around.

Bed.

A place that still held terrors. A place in which her courage failed.

But in the fading light of the sunset, she saw in John's eyes more than desire. She saw belief. Belief that here, too, she could be brave.

She hesitated, torn between fear and want. She wanted to love him. Wanted to have him. Wanted to believe that loving him could eradicate her past. Wanted to be brave in the bed and on the battlefield.

And she feared, still, that she was neither. And until she could slay Willie's demon in the bedchamber, she would never be able to defeat the man himself.

John turned to see her frozen at the threshold. 'We will do, or not do, whatever you desire.'

Kind, gentle, tender, respectful. All the things she had discovered him to be, so unlike the man who seized that first, unwanted kiss from her a few weeks ago as they crossed swords. But that man, that passionate lover, was John as well.

She wanted to relish that urgent, eager side of loving, too. Tried before. Failed. But tonight, yes. Tonight, she could. She *would.*

Drawn across the floor, she stood before him. 'Come,' she said, swallowing. 'Let me…'

But there were no words for what she wanted. Only

her fingers slipping under his tunic, searching for his skin, wanting to see him in his fullness.

'Tell me.' His voice already husky. 'Tell me what you want.'

'I want to see you.' Last time, the feel of wool on her legs had taken her back. This time, he would be naked. 'All of you.' She pointed at the bed. 'There.'

First, he flashed a quick, wicked smile that spoke of private delights. Just as fast, hesitation touched his eyes and hovered on his lips. 'Are you sure?'

Anger flashed over her desire. Now her fear had infected him as well. No more. Scarred Willie would claim no more victims.

She lifted her chin and squeezed his hand. 'Yes. I'm sure.'

His smile returned and he reached for the edge of his tunic.

'Wait! When I tell you.' Before, he had acted, while giving her the power to say *no*. This time, *she* would direct *him*.

He dropped his arms, the expression on his face suddenly uncertain.

She slipped her hands under his tunic again, savouring the feel of his skin, hot against her palms, then moved from his back to his chest, where the soft, curly hair tickled.

And her fingers stumbled upon his nipples.

So unlike a woman's. And what did a man need with them?

She rubbed them, slowly.

He moaned.

She smiled. Sensitive, then, as hers were.

'Now,' she whispered. 'Take it off.'

She helped him, but kept one hand on his skin. With

the tunic gone, she could admire his chest, his shoulders, the curves that shaped his arms. She had seen bare chests before. Working men shed their shirts often enough, but when she glanced at the others, all she could think of was how strong their arms were. Strong enough to heft a sword or hurl a spear.

Worse. Strong enough to hold her down.

John's arms were strong enough to protect her, even from himself.

She stroked him, lightly, with the tips of her fingers, as if she might learn to draw him in the air.

He groaned, eyes closed, then shivered as she trailed her hand down the inside of his arm, to that sensitive skin inside the elbow.

He opened one eye. 'Can I touch you now?'

She shook her head, though she hungered for his touch already. 'In due time. When I have done all I want.'

A ripple of unease wrinkled his brow. How much worse she must have looked, cramped with terror. Easy to see, now, how uncertain he must have felt as he tried to bring her pleasure.

She smiled. 'You can say "no" any time.'

'I understand.' His smile belied the solemn tone, telling her more than words that he did.

She wrapped herself around him, cheek to chest, hip to hip. And below his waist, that part of him still hidden was stiff already.

She steadied her breath. His naked chest had been the easy part. Now, she needed to face what was below.

She pushed herself away and clasped her fingers together, steadying them for the task. Then she reached for the ties holding his chausses, aware her fingers were shaking. He was strong and hard and she hesitated, afraid to pull the string and to let the monster loose.

He held up his arms, palms towards her, as if making himself her prisoner. 'Do with me what you will.' His light tone warred with the want on his face. 'But be braw, Cate.'

She swallowed, unable to speak. *What if I scream and kick and claw at him again? What if the fear has not gone away?*

What if it never goes away?

She pulled the tie.

The chausses fell down, but they snagged on his tarse and she was forced to free it, astonished to find it warm against her fingers.

She raised her eyes to his face. He opened his mouth, waved his hands to give her permission, since he seemed unable to speak.

She wrapped her palms around him, as if she could subdue it, but instead, it swelled larger against her hands. He had kissed her, there. Perhaps he would like the same.

Had she that much courage?

She knelt, amazed at how the position put her lips at precisely the right place, to taste...

She released her grip, then stroked gently, curious. Now it tempted, rather than frightened, her.

'Cate, love.' The words were strangled. His boyish smile was gone. 'I want you to do anything...' He cleared his throat. 'Anything you want, but there will be a time I won't, I can't, I'll just...'

She suddenly realised his meaning and scrambled to stand. No, she was not braw enough for that. Yet.

Clothed beside his nakedness, she clenched her fists as if gripping the control she needed. Then, she pointed to the bed. 'Lie down.'

'May I take my boots off?' The smile was in his voice again.

She looked down at the fabric, tangled around his boots.

'Sit,' she said. 'I'll do it.'

And it felt more like power than servitude, to kneel before him to wrestle with leather and cloth until he was naked.

He stretched on the bed and she stood again, towering over him. Her gaze travelled the lean length of him, from his strong legs to his hips, and up his chest, until she was ready to meet his eyes.

He will be impatient, she thought. Irritated at the waiting.

Instead, his blue, beloved eyes held nothing but adoration.

She caught her breath, basking in his gaze. He had put her needs before his own, yet he looked at her as if she gifted him with a treasured chalice.

How many men would do the same?

As she watched him, she saw a man with true power. The power to control himself.

'Tell me.' His voice was in his control again. 'Tell me what you want.'

She no longer knew.

She had expected joining to be a battle, one body invading and conquering the other. So she planned to direct him through the motions so she would not feel threatened or forced into submission.

Instead, the battle was within her own body.

John would wait on her command. She could punish him for Storwick's sins, for being born a man, sky to her earth.

That was not what she wanted now. The Cate who

had clung to control and thirsted for revenge and kept every man at arm's length now seemed the ghost of something long dead. Beneath that Cate was one who wanted something very different.

To join with him.

Within her, something had broken apart like the ice shifting on top of a stream in spring, revealing the rippling water beneath, flowing unchecked towards the sea.

As she wanted to rush to him. To merge, as two streams meeting, mixing together, creating something of both of them.

Could people do that?

Tell me what you want.

'I want…'

If she lay down on the bed, one of them must be on top, conquering. Yet to join with him the way she wanted would mean putting aside the armour, taking off the bravado, casting away the false fearlessness. It would mean surrender.

'Tell me.'

How could all that become words? 'I want to be… with you. But it must be different.'

'It will be different because I am different.'

'So am I,' she whispered, barely able to believe it. But he had been willing to trust her. To put himself at her mercy without question.

Could she be that strong? Did she trust him that much?

'It will not be as you fear,' he said. 'I promise.'

She smiled. 'I've lost track of your promises, Johnnie.'

'I haven't.'

A smile fluttered at her lips. 'So you swear on the grave of your ancestor?'

'On something more sure than that. Because this promise is the most important of all. I swear by my feelings for you.'

She bit her lip, but could not hold back the tear that streaked her face.

He held out his hand. 'Come to me.'

That meant she must be naked, too, so she lifted her tunic. He let her do it alone, only helping when she was trapped behind the fabric as she tried to pull it over her head. When she struggled, panicked and blind, he made it easy, whisking it away, gently, as if he knew that something had changed.

She looked down and hesitated. Even as she was stirred with desire, removing her men's garb meant more than simply shedding clothes. Unlike a woman's skirts, which left her always open to a man who might lift them, pants with two legs protected what was between them.

He rose from the bed and pulled her to him, so tight that she could feel him, stiff against her. Wanting, yearning.

'A man is vulnerable, too,' he said, holding her snug against his hips while above the waist, he leaned back so she could see his eyes. 'When I desire you, you and all the world can see. But what you want is hidden, even from me. So unless you tell me, unless you show me, I'll not know you are ready or what you want.' There it was, now. Johnnie's smile. 'But you'll certainly know you've left a man dangling.'

She laughed, the sound, the feeling unfamiliar. Johnnie had taught her that, that laughter could be a part of the loving and as it rippled through her, it loosened the last of the tight places.

'Then we must be sure,' she said with a smile, 'not to leave you hanging, Johnnie Brunson.'

She tugged off her chausses and kicked them aside and he lifted her onto the bed. Sinking into the softness, she stiffened again as he stood, looming over her.

Yet something loving mixed with the desire in his eyes and he shook his head, as if he had read her fears.

'Not this time,' he began. 'A woman can be taken, yes, forced to mate.' The burning look of vengeance passed over his eyes and he shook his head, sending the bad memories from the room. 'But not forced to love.'

Love. Something she'd been afraid to dream of.

She nodded, giving him permission. He nudged her over and stretched out beside her, holding his head with one hand, leaving the other free. 'Now you.'

She lay on her side, able to see the whole of him, each open to the other, neither above, neither below.

No longer willing to simply look, she opened her arms to pull him in and he did the same.

She closed her eyes, letting her lips find his, letting the feelings sweep through her, no longer frightening. He did not devour her. They devoured each other, her need as strong as his.

Her demons slain.

John kissed her, cradling her in his arms, trying to be as mindful of her feelings as of his needs.

Everything about this woman was different, and so was the way he loved her. She was at once the fiercest and the most vulnerable woman he had ever met, let alone bedded. That alone had warred with his desire for her over the past weeks.

He broke from her lips only so he could kiss her nose, her cheeks, her temple, her forehead, to put his lips everywhere on her. Then he pulled away, feeling breath he could not control heaving through his chest.

'I know,' he swallowed. His mind was bare of words. 'I know you do not want to be…possessed.' He watched her eyes when he said it, not wanting to see them fearful again.

Instead, wide-eyed, she raised a hand from his back to stroke his cheek. 'Aye, but…'

But he wanted to possess her. To take her. To make her his and never let her leave his side again. Wanted it more than he had wanted anything in his life.

She smiled. 'But it will not be like that with you. I know that now. To do this will mean I am…free.'

Free. No ghosts, no strings, no ties, no promises. Everything he had wanted for her.

He wanted that no more. Instead, he wanted to mark her so that she would never be free of *him.* Yet he could not do that now. Tonight, his future must be banned as completely as her past.

'So,' he began, the words struggling to leave his throat, 'Tonight, there'll be only John and Cate. Nothing behind us, nothing before.'

'No yesterday,' she whispered. 'No tomorrow.'

Brain silenced, his body took control. He took her lips again, lost in fingers and lips and tongues, not sure who touched who. He felt himself swell, hot and hard and ready for her, suddenly aware he had not been careful to ready her as well.

He reached down to find her slick and wet on his fingers.

'Yes.' Her word a breath on his lips.

'Are you sure?' How did he manage to speak? But he must be sure. This time must be different. That, he had promised.

She pursed her lips and nodded.

And then, he knew what he must do.

Holding her tight, he rolled onto his back, leaving her on his chest, her back to the air. She lifted her head to meet his eyes, her gaze uncertain.

'There you are, love. You are in charge. You may take me.'

He prayed she would, quickly.

She pushed herself upright, eyes still on his, realisation dawning on her face. She looked down at him. 'Can it be done?'

He laughed, partly in pain as he throbbed beneath her. 'Oh, yes, it surely can.'

'And will it feel as good as when you...?'

'I'll do all I can to make it so.'

And so she spread her legs wider and he guided himself into her, loving the mix of confusion and joy on her face.

'I feel...full.'

He swelled inside her; she tightened on him in response. He reached for her centre of feeling, bringing her with him, and she writhed on top of him, in her own rhythm. He kept his eyes open to watch her face, flushed, mindless, thinking of only the pleasure he had promised.

She fell on his chest then, taking, demanding his lips, and he held her tight and started his own rhythm and she joined him, feelings, bodies, struggling to merge into something no longer separate. Then, a rush, his, releasing into her. Her spasm in reply.

And a torrent of feeling deeper than any he had ever felt in joining before.

One that said he was home.

The raging river slowed to a trickle. He held her close

to his chest and listened to her breathe, slow and even and drifting towards sleep.

Aye, he thought, satisfied. *The ghost she carried is gone.*

But as he watched the glow of the embers, the future intruded again. For now he realised that, somehow, nothing his parents or his brother or his sister had said or done, nothing in this tower or in the land itself had bound him as tightly to this place as this act.

And this woman.

Chapter Twenty-One

Later that night, Cate lay awake next to Johnnie, watching the full moon cast sharp shadows on the floor.

Waiting.

She must truly be Braw Cate now.

She had leaned on family for too long—on John and Rob and Bessie and the rest—coercing them to join in retribution. The debt Scarred Willie must die for was owed to her alone.

She would say aloud that it was for Johnnie's sake. He was right in wanting to go alone to protect the family, though wrong to think he was the one to do it. She knew nothing of the king, not enough to know whether he was to be feared or not. But disowned or not, Storwicks would not let Brunsons hunt down one of their own and ride away unscathed. They would take retribution. Black Rob would retaliate.

And the killing would go on without end.

But if *she* alone slew Scarred Willie, they would call her mad. She could surrender herself to judgement and let justice do its worst. She was brave enough to face it.

Yes, she could tell them all that, but the truth was far different. The truth was that she must slay the man herself or she would never be whole. Only then would it be enough.

Then it would be *over*.

She had thought joining with Johnnie would heal her and allow her to find someone else. Now, she could not imagine trusting herself and her secrets to any other man. But he deserved someone whole. Someone healed. Even tonight, when she had wanted to give him all, he had been careful, he had made accommodations. She had been unable to lose herself in him.

A doubt floated and she squashed it. This was how it must be. If she were to have any hope of a life with Johnnie, she must defeat all her demons and there was only one way to do it.

Kill Scarred Willie.

Of course, there was another possibility.

Scarred Willie might kill her.

And that thought bothered her now in a way it never had before.

She slipped out of bed, donning her outer layers against the cold. Johnnie stirred and opened his eyes.

'Garderobe,' Cate whispered.

He nodded, his eyes drifting closed again.

Belde was harder to convince. He pushed himself to his feet, ready to follow her.

She hesitated, biting her lip. There was no reason to take him, no scent to follow. But Belde's greatest gift to her had been courage.

Well, time to find her own. To keep him, all of them, out of harm's way.

She put her arms around him. 'Stay. I'll be right back.'

He sniffed her face, as if to reassure her. As she

closed the door, closing him in with Johnnie, she wondered whether the dog had smelled her tears.

The hound's howls woke him.

John sat straight, hearing Belde's bark echoing against the walls of the room empty of her.

And in the distance, hoofbeats.

Immediately, in the moment of waking, he knew Cate had gone, as well as where and why. And he cursed himself for not realising she would.

Belde paced to the door and back, whining, trying to hurry John along.

'I'm coming, boy.' He threw off the covers and reached for the vest she'd made for him.

She must have walked the horse out, he realised, trying to organise his thoughts. What idiot guarded the gate and let her go?

Some of the other men might have been awakened by now, but there was no time to waste organising them. He had planned to go alone. Instead, he would go with the other creature who loved her.

Hand on the dog's head, he tied the halter on him. Then, he knelt on her side of the bed, thinking even his poor, human nose could recognise the scent of someone he loved.

He held the sheet to Belde's nose, quickly, as he had seen her do. 'Fetch Cate.'

Belde turned, ears flying, and pulled him out the door and down the stairs.

Chapter Twenty-Two

As the pony plodded up the snow-dusted hill, Cate wished she had brought Belde. Instead, she was alone with the moonlight.

And the hated scent of heather.

She shook her head, knowing that could not be. Frost had come. The scent could be no more than a waking dream.

But she was in that dream again. Back in the hills where all this had started, riding to face him again, her nightmare come alive.

Passing the place where her father's small hut had stood that night, she shivered, and not with the cold. Covered with snow, there was not even a dent in the ground to show where it had stood. But her memory of it was as vivid, and as solid, as the ground beneath her.

She had expected, somehow, that he would be standing in this spot, waiting for her. She had been so sure that he would be here. Instead, there was only the wind, and memories.

She kept climbing. Maybe he was hiding. Somewhere close.

The circle of stones rose before her, strange shadows

in the moonlight. Once, she had feared the place. Now, the memory was sweet. When she and Johnnie had sat together, looking across the valley to the hills beyond and she had felt for the first time...

A dark shape moved among the stones. Haunted, her father had said. Was that the ghost of the ancestors she saw?

Or worse?

She dismounted as quietly as she could, and left the pony to stand. Without thinking, she reached down, expecting her hand to meet Belde's coat, warm and soft. If he were here, he would be growling, low in his throat, the hair of his neck on end, ready to protect her.

But she was alone.

She pulled her sword and stepped forwards, snow seeping through her boots.

But in the moment she had shifted her eyes, the shape among the stones disappeared.

And she muttered a prayer to the fore folk.

They must have been busy elsewhere, for the next thing she knew, a lance was pointed at her.

'Another move, lad, and this goes straight through your belly.'

No wraith haunted these stones, but Scarred Willie.

She stilled, not speaking, not wanting to give him a clue that she was not the man he thought.

He circled her, keeping the pike close, as if turning a wagon wheel. 'What's your name, boy? How did you find me?'

She followed him with her eyes, but he disappeared behind her. 'Who are *you*?' she answered in the lowest tone she could muster. At least he had not disarmed her. 'And what are you doing on Brunson land?'

He stopped, squarely behind her, an invisible menace. 'You!'

She tried to swallow. Couldn't.

'All alone, are you?'

Bravado deserted her. Stomach churning, cheeks hot, then cold, she could only stand, helpless as the first time, and wait for him to grab her again.

'Been missing me since Truce Day, have you? Well, your beast gave me a new scar. One you must pay for.'

Her stomach curdled. 'No.' The word shook.

You must do this. Or when you next lie in Johnnie's arms, you will see this man instead.

'No!' She yelled this time, to be sure the ancestors knew she was no coward.

She jumped away, then whirled to face him, blade up, her sword strong and solid in her hand. 'I came back to make sure you never hurt another woman.'

And that you hurt me no more.

He stepped to one side, forcing her to do the same, recognising her as a threat. 'You're going to fight me, are you?' He laughed. 'Even better. More exciting than before.'

She gripped the hilt of the sword. Her fingers numbed.

Before. When she had not fought at all.

He teased her sword with his pike, the staff so long he could easily knock her blade away, while keeping her well at a distance.

Furious, she grabbed the hilt with both hands and swung the sword, leaving herself open on the other side. His pike blocked her easily, throwing her off balance. She stumbled backwards into one of the stones.

He waited, smugly, while she steadied herself.

Fear, anger, something beyond thought throbbed in

her head and pulsed through her veins as she raised her sword again.

Scarred Willie felt none of those things. Scarred Willie was laughing.

Moving before he could prepare, she knocked the pike from his hands and pointed her blade to his chest.

Now. Thrust it through his black heart.

But now he was close to her. Close as he had been that night just before...

He dodged under the sword. Reached for her.

She ran, or tried to. Her arms and legs, useless stones, too heavy to lift, holding her back, dragging her down.

She tripped over the hogback stone and fell into the snow.

Then he was on top of her.

This time she kicked and screamed and punched and scratched and fought with all the fury she'd been saving for two years. But no matter what she did, he was bigger and stronger and heavier than she would ever be. Her knee could not connect with his groin. He held her arms safely away from his face. And all her puny efforts weren't enough to throw him off.

Now, her nightmare lived in truth.

John, on Norse, raced beside Belde, who ran directly up Hogback Hill.

I have not been on this hill since...

What a fool he'd been not to realise it then. She feared more than spirits on this hill.

He urged the horse faster, knowing the dog would keep up. As he gained the rise, he saw them, amidst the stones, two black figures, fighting. She swung her sword. He blocked her blow.

She tripped. Screamed. Storwick was on top of her...

John leapt from the horse and pulled his sword. There would be no waiting this time. No pretence of taking the man for trial. There would be only justice: quick, sure and final.

In the time it had taken John to dismount, Belde was at Storwick's throat. Barking, teeth bared, the dog ripped a new scar on his face.

Storwick yelled and rolled off Cate. Staggering to his feet, he stumbled into a run. Belde was on him in an instant. Rising on hind legs, tall as a man, the dog knocked Storwick to the ground and pinned him to the earth.

John rushed over, sword drawn, ready to plunge it through the bastard, piercing his black heart and letting his blood soak the soil. Rage drove him now, the same fury that had kept Cate going these two years. This man had hurt her, hurt her so deeply that John was not sure she would ever recover.

And for that, he raised his sword…

The man beneath the dog's paws curled in on himself, eyes shut, shaking.

John paused, his arm raised, sword ready to descend. *No. Not like this. This was no better than murder.*

The furious, boiling rage in his blood cooled enough for him to look down at the craven coward. The man deserved no better death than this for what he had done.

But it was not the Brunson way.

John lowered the sword and kicked Storwick in the ribs. 'Get up.'

The man opened his eyes. Belde growled, but did not move.

John looked down at Storwick, thinking one more time of running him through. 'Get up, fazart.' He dragged him up by the shoulders of his vest and pulled

Belde away. 'Take out your sword and face me. I'll give you a fighting chance, but only one of us will come down from this mountain alive.'

He snarled at Storwick's snivelling, cowardly face, 'And it won't be you.'

Cate cringed, hiding behind the carved stone as John stood over the man, sword raised. Eyes closed, she waited for the scream of pain that would tell her Willie was dead.

It didn't come.

She opened her eyes to see Storwick standing, sword in hand.

No!

But the scream stuck in her throat.

Move. Do something.

But she was rooted to the ground and the small voice in her head seemed to come from as far away as the scene before her eyes.

Belde, removed from his prey, paced around the two men as they circled each other with drawn swords. She called the dog, afraid he would get too close and John might trip.

Slow, reluctant, he obeyed and she locked her arms around his neck, as the men drew sword and dirk and faced each other. The dog's chest rose and fell and she wanted to make her legs work, wanted to rise, grab her dagger and thrust it into Storwick's neck, to save John from his own foolish honour.

But as she watched the dark shapes move against the pre-dawn sky, she hesitated. Moments ago she had tried to fight Storwick and been overpowered. If she interfered now, would she help John or put them both in danger?

She had faced John's sword, knew how good he was. Willie preferred to use a pike from horseback, or a latch to send an arrow, killing while he remained out of reach. She had never seen him face a man with a sword.

He swung it like an axe. Rough, blunt, strong as if hacking through trees, not caring where he hit. But if the sword connected, it would be a mortal blow.

John, on the other hand, fought quickly and lightly, shifting his stance, switching his thrust too quickly for Storwick to defend against him. Fuelling the dance was his rage, controlled, but ready to channel the blade for a death thrust.

Beside her, Belde growled and tugged against her hold.

Storwick swung his sword, forcing John to back up. She saw the stone behind him, stood to shout a warning, too late. John tripped and fell to his back on the other side.

And Storwick stood over him, sword raised.

Chapter Twenty-Three

Sword gone from his hand, wind knocked from his chest, John looked up to see the point of Storwick's blade hovering an inch above his chest.

'I'm the one who'll be coming down from the mountain,' the man said, with a smirk. '*With* the girl.'

Honour, John thought, had had its chance.

He lifted a boot, aiming squarely between Stowick's legs, and kicked.

Storwick staggered. John rolled out of reach and sprang to his feet.

Yet he was armed only with a dagger now. Storwick had stumbled, reached down to cradle himself, but managed to hold on to his long sword. John stepped sideways, hoping to reach his sword before Storwick could swing again.

And then John saw a blur lunge from behind a stone.

Belde had ripped himself from her arms and run.

Willie dropped his sword and stumbled up the mountain, leaving the circle of stones. The dog gained on him quickly and the man looked back over his shoulder, eyes wide with terror.

And because he was looking back, he did not see the edge of the ravine.

The echo of his scream was cut short by a distant thud.

John shook his head, trying to clear his eyes and his brain. Belde paced at the edge of the precipice, as if ready to leap into the chasm to be sure Scarred Willie Storwick was a threat no more.

John staggered to the edge and looked down.

Done. It was done.

His word kept. Cate avenged.

He turned, expecting to find her at his side, smiling, arms wide, raising her lips to be kissed.

Instead, he saw only the sculpted stones. Heard only the whistling of the wind.

She heard the scream, and its end, and knew it was over.

She waited for relief. For joy. For peace.

It did not come.

Storwick's death did not free her limbs or allow her lips to move. In the uncertain light, she could only stare at the diamond shapes carved into the stones, eyes fixed on them as though they might have meaning.

When John pulled her gently to her feet, she did not resist.

'It's over. He's dead.'

She did not raise her eyes to his.

He grasped her in a fierce hug, but she did not return it. It was as if her spirit had left her body, leaving only the husk of a woman. Scarred Willie Storwick lay dead. She had been avenged, yet it was as Johnnie had warned her.

It was not enough.

But not for the reason he thought.

'I fought him this time.'

His arms did not leave her, and he rocked her tight against him. 'I know you did. It's all right now.'

But it wasn't. And she couldn't make him understand why.

She shook her head, buried against his chest.

'It didn't matter. Everything I've done didn't matter.' And because it didn't, she was not worthy of this man. 'If you had not come, he would have taken me again.'

John held her, shaken not by the battle now that it was over, but by the despair of the woman in his arms.

'But I did come.' The quest was over. His promise fulfilled. Her revenge taken. She should be grateful, relieved, joyful.

But the woman in his arms was none of these, her expression bleak, empty, as if life held no more purpose. He had expected…what? Happiness. Joy. Celebration. Not this inner deadness, as if killing Scarred Willie had also killed something within her.

'And then the dog had to save you,' she muttered, looking at Belde. The derision in her eyes directed inwards. 'A dog chased Scarred Willie over a cliff while Cate the Bold cowered behind a gravestone.'

Her words made no sense, so he put his arm around her shoulders and led her to the horses. 'Come. Let's go home.'

Wordless, she let him guide her.

Trailed by Belde, they returned to the tower as the sun cleared the eastern hills. Helpless to make her smile, he kissed her forehead and turned her over to Bessie, who would put her to bed.

Cate was tired. She needed sleep. He must give her time. It was only natural for her to be numb with shock. When she woke, she would be his Cate again.

And even as he thought it, he knew he lied.

'Is she still abed?' John whispered to Bessie as the sun left the sky.

Cate had slept the day while he had been hailed a hero. Tankards were raised. Ballads sung. A new verse tested.

Braw Johnnie Blunkit, blue-eyed Brunson
Faced his foe on Hogback Hill...

And when he told the men that the dog deserved full credit, they laughed, and spun a verse of 'Belde's Ballad', as well.

It was enough to make him feel as if he had come home.

As if he wanted to stay.

Then he would look up to see Rob, standing by the hearth, silent. The only man who had not wished him well.

And all through the day, there had been no word from Cate.

He had left the celebration when he saw Bessie at the hall's door. His sister kept her voice low. 'She's not moved since she lay down. Nor that great beast beside her.'

'Should we wake her?'

She sighed. 'I don't know. She was like this once

before, when she first came, right after he…' She bit her lip.

Right after he raped her. That's what she had almost said.

The realisation surprised him. 'She told you?' He thought he had been the only one.

Silent, Bessie studied him, as if judging what he knew and whether he was worthy to know the rest. 'She told no one,' she said finally, as if accepting that they shared Cate's secret.

No one but him. 'Then how did you know?'

A shrug was her only answer.

They were women. They shared a room. A bed. And while women seemed ever talking, he had discovered that it was the things they knew without speaking that were the most mysterious.

'What happened last time to bring her…back?'

'I never knew, but I remember the day she rose. She came to the kitchen door, wearing men's clothes for the first time, and stood, not even looking at me, but staring at something I couldn't see and said, "Next time, I will kill him myself. Next time, there will be no fear."'

'But he is dead. There's nothing more to fear. Then why…?'

'You're asking me again, Johnnie. Things you should be asking her.'

He would have taken me again. And even conquering her fear had not been able to change that. Was that why? Yet it was easier for him to face Storwick's sword than to see Cate so helpless. And to face the possibility that even with Storwick dead, Cate might not be free.

He sighed. 'I'll let her wake on her own, then, before I ask her.'

He looked back at the group around the table. They

waved him to join them again. He nodded, but the hours weighed on him now. He needed sleep.

Bessie's fingers gripped on his sleeve. 'There's something else you should be asking, Johnnie. Something you should be asking yourself.'

'What's that?'

'How much you care for her. And whether it's enough.'

Cate squeezed her eyes tight, not wanting to wake to her life. But her eyelids fluttered open of their own, seeking the waning sun.

She was alone in the room. Bessie had got up hours ago, working on her daily tasks, leaving Cate to face the truth.

Storwick was dead. And still, she could not rejoice.

She had searched within herself, looking for the joy she had long expected at his demise. She had imagined that when this day came, the sky would open, a rainbow would appear, perhaps an angel would even descend from the heavens. She had expected to be crowned with glory, or at least with peace.

She had expected to feel as if, at long last, she was a woman who deserved the love of Johnnie Brunson.

Instead, she felt only as if she had failed. Storwick was dead. And she was still the same woman.

Belde sensed that she had waked and lumbered to his feet. He had not left her side all day, a hardship for a dog who lived to run. Now he looked at her without judgement, as if he were glad to have saved her life and John's. As if he were ready to do it again.

She turned her head away, eyes burning. Dumb beast. Yet he had shown more courage than she.

She had lived the last two years only so she could

set things right. This time, she would fight back. This time, she would strike. This time, she would make him pay for what he had done to her father.

To her.

But when the time came, nothing had changed. She'd fought this time, yes, despite her fear, but not only could she not save herself, she had put John at risk. He had been saved by an animal's courage, not her own.

Her trousers, her blades, her swagger, all for show, a disguise over an empty shell.

As she tried to imagine her life now, it yawned empty before her. For the past two years, every breath had been dedicated to revenge. Every small joy a rung on a ladder that had lifted her out of despair and kept her alive long enough to slay her demons.

And at the top of her ladder, the demons still lived.

She reached out to pet Belde. He sniffed her face, as if her scent could explain her sadness.

She shut her eyes again, but the tears escaped. She could not face Johnnie knowing she had failed him. Perhaps she had braved the imaginary demons in bed, but that had made no difference in the end. He had almost died for a worthless shell of a woman.

If she stayed abed long enough, he would be gone when she emerged. He would take the men and ride back to king and court and she would never have to face those blue eyes again.

She buried her face in the pillow to shut out the light.

How much you care for her. And whether it's enough.

Bessie's words hit hard as a broadsword.

John staggered, resting his palm on a stone wall that no longer felt solid. Behind him, the words of the new song came through a haze.

Braw Johnnie Blunkit, blue-eyed Brunson
Faced his foe on Hogback Hill...

Aye. He'd been brave. Hunting Willie Storwick to
the death, risking the king's wrath as well as his life.
Telling himself, telling all of them, that he did it only
so he could leave home and return to court.

It was not brave to face those things. Men did. Every
day.

But he had not faced his true fear.

In coming home, everything about his life had
changed. Who he was. What he wanted. He was a
Brunson. He wanted a life with Cate. Here. Home. He
wanted nothing that he had thought he wanted when he
first caught sight of the tower again.

Was he brave enough to face that?

Seeking quiet, he left the hall to settle in the stair-
well, on the very step where he and Cate had talked
alone in the dark.

He had delayed thoughts of the future. First, find
Storwick. Then carry out the king's orders. But surrounded by the warmth of the tower, the voices of his
fellows echoing off the stone walls, he realised he had
made his decision, unawares, weeks ago.

Somewhere, the king went to war without Brunson
men.

When he vowed to hunt Cate's enemy, he had cast
his lot with the hills of his birth. He must have known,
even then, that he would not see Stirling again, but he
had been too blind to see it. Or too cowardly to admit it.

He had told himself Cate was a means to an end.
No longer true, if ever it had been. Cate *was* the end.
Whatever her wound now, they could heal it together.

Don't ask me questions you should be asking her, Bessie had said. Questions like 'will you share my life?'

But he could not ask her that question. Not as things stood.

You're no longer a Brunson. I won't have you here.

Rob had said the words days and miles ago. Since then, they had ridden side by side and fought shoulder to shoulder. But Rob's words still stood. He had not taken them back.

And John had not asked him to.

He looked out of the opening in the wall. The ground was hard and frozen and dusted with fresh snow. The wind, raw and cold, blew fitfully through the valley. Damp air penetrated all the way to his skin.

And there was nowhere on earth he would rather be.

On the ground of his birth he was strong and sure as he had never been by the king's side.

Was he the Borderer Rob was? No. If he stayed, they would still quarrel. But Rob must know by now that Johnnie Blunkit was no longer the little blue-eyed boy who dragged his blanket down these stairs.

Johnnie finally did.

He sighed. He had planned to return home in triumph, flaunting the king's badge. A man to be respected.

Now, in order to stay, he must do the thing he'd sworn never to do.

Humble himself and ask Rob if he could come home. Unless...

He rose, smiling. There might be another way.

Chapter Twenty-Four

Assured by Bessie that Cate still slept, John found Rob on the parapet, searching for the next threat.

Willie Storwick might be gone, but the rest of his clan were not.

John leaned on the wall beside him. Silent, they watched the sky turn the blue of church glass.

'So you kept your word,' Rob said finally.

No thanks. No praise. And none deserved, he thought. A man says what he will do and does it. Bit by bit, over a lifetime, that earns respect.

'I had help,' he answered.

'So it's the dog I should be raising a mug to?'

Hard to ignore the insult in his brother's words. *Steady. You're no longer a lad and unless you bite your tongue now and then, you and Rob will be quarrelling when Christ rises.*

But today, he had reason to pick a fight. 'Do you doubt me?'

'Should I?'

John rested his hand on the pommel of his sword, holding back a smile. 'Go a round with me if you've doubts. As we used to.'

'I'll beat you now as I beat you then.'

He drew his sword from his scabbard and passed it from one hand to the other. 'Well, we'll see about that, won't we?'

The corner of Rob's mouth twitched. 'What stakes, in the unlikely event that you win?'

'To stay here. As a Brunson. In my home.' Nine words to describe a lifetime.

No smile on Rob's unmoving face now. No hint of whether his brother was pleased, surprised or opposed. 'And if I win?'

John shrugged, as if it didn't matter. 'Why, then, I guess I'll turn myself over to his Majesty the King to be put on trial for treason.'

'Lead the way.'

They descended to the corner of the courtyard they had used as boys, the corner where the last daylight lingered.

Rob pulled his sword. 'First touch.' His nod as firm as the way he hefted his sword. 'Begin.'

They circled each other with slow, deliberate steps, assessing the other. They had not lifted swords against each other in ten years. A lifetime.

Since then, they had fought beside each other in battles of life and death, yet this seemed more important than any of those.

He waved his sword slowly in Rob's direction to see what he would do. Rob was broader and heavier, John quicker.

That would have to be enough.

Each tested the other, gauging the length of his blade and the reach of his arm, determining just how far he would have to stretch his sword.

Rob had the advantage, his blade longer by inches.

Facing him in the waning light, John felt the shadows play tricks on him. Felt as if he were little Johnnie once more, about to be pummelled by his older brother.

He battled the shades of memory. If he expected Cate to move beyond her memories, so must he. He must be Braw Johnnie to her Cate.

Rob thrust first, just missing him. Mindful of the scar Rob had marked him with years ago, John had donned his father's vest. *His* now. Battleworn and comfortable. Rob had inherited Geordie the Red's title, but John felt his father's protection in the padding, Cate's love in the stitches.

He dodged and swung back, careful not to put his strength behind the blow, nearly making contact.

Rob scowled, surprised.

'I learned a few things from the king's sword master,' he called out, smiling.

Now settled to it, the two were evenly matched. The light faded. The fight did not.

John began to feel the burden of the last day. His eyes burned, his muscles shook, the wound from the first raid was throbbing again, and his head and stomach were carrying on a private war. He had risen in the middle of the night, chased Cate to the mountain, fought Willie Storwick and returned to share celebratory toasts.

A wiser man might have waited to challenge his brother until he'd enjoyed a night's sleep.

He summoned his strength to swing again, a move he had used against Rob when they were boys. It had not worked then, and he didn't expect it would now, but he hoped to force Rob back two steps and give himself a moment to think.

But instead of blocking the swing as he always did, Rob flinched or bobbed or did something so quickly that thinking back on it later, John wasn't sure exactly what happened, but the next thing he knew, he'd nicked Rob's shoulder and drawn blood.

And what was even stranger, Rob was smiling.

John's jaw dropped as Rob held up his hands in surrender. 'Well,' his brother said, 'I guess we'll not be rid of you now.'

Engulfed in Rob's strong arms, John gritted his teeth against threatening tears.

Home. He was home.

Released as quickly as he'd been grabbed, John searched his brother's eyes for answers. Had Rob deliberately allowed the win? Was that secret delight or regret in his eyes?

'Thank you,' he said finally.

'For what? Being a bad swordsman? You won't thank me for that when the Storwicks come riding again.'

'Well, when they do, there'll be men enough to take them.'

Rob tipped his head, puzzled.

'The king will be fighting his battles without any Brunsons.'

This time, Rob smiled.

John pounded his back. 'Come. Let's have Bessie patch you up before the corbies start circling.'

They walked back into the tower, but just before they entered, Rob lifted a hand to John's shoulder. 'And, Johnnie, it's not my permission you need.' He jerked his towards the upper floors. 'It's hers.' He patted John's shoulder, then pushed him inside. 'Go.'

She rose, finally, as darkness fell, and donned the one gown she still owned. For two years, she had known who she was and what her purpose was. Now, Cate was bold no more.

The dark skirt barely reached her ankles now and without sturdy pants the cold swirled between her legs. Instead of walking the earth with two good legs, she had to kick the skirt aside with each step.

Belde sat, head tilted in confusion. She crouched before him, cupped his muzzle with one hand and petted his head with the other.

'Belde was the name I called you. And that's what *I* wanted to be—bold and brave and never helpless with fear again.'

Tears now, hot on her cheeks. She buried her face in his coat, muttering against his fur. 'And then, the time came and it wasn't enough. I kicked and hit and scratched and—'

'Cate, you're awake.' John's voice, behind her.

She swiped her tears with the back of her hand as Belde ran to him, sniffing toe to chest in greeting.

Cate stood, dizzy and wobbling on her feet, reaching for something to steady herself. She had been abed for so long she was unaccustomed to being upright.

In a moment, John was by her side, steady and sure, as if she was the kind of woman who could not even stand without protection. Well, perhaps he was right. Her cowardice had nearly killed him.

'Let me go,' she said, the words rusty as an unoiled hinge.

He did and she stood alone again. Thus it must be. She had not earned the right to stand by his side.

He looked her up and down, a puzzled crease wrinkling his brow, but did not question the skirt.

Belde jumped for John's right hand. 'Down,' he said, holding it out of reach. 'Sit.'

Astonished, she saw the dog obey, though he swung his head, looking at Cate and then John, confused.

John handed her a lumpy bannock. 'I thought you would be hungry.'

Suddenly, she was, as if her stomach had taken up arms against her heart, determined to keep her alive.

The first bite tasted of honey and love. Oat cakes were not usually so sweet. Bessie must have made this batch especially for her. She closed her eyes, savouring the flavour on the tip of her tongue.

When she opened them again, John was still studying her. 'Are you well?'

When had Johnnie ever been awkward with words?

She chewed slowly, stealing time. There was no answer to that question. Or none that she wanted to give to this man. Swallowing, she had no excuse for silence. 'Well enough.'

'Then you'll come ride with me.'

It was not a request, but before she could refuse, Belde gave a *woof* and trotted to the door, tail wagging.

Poor faithful beast. She should not punish him for her sins. Besides, she did not want to stay in a room with John and a bed and memories.

No doubt he was going to say farewell and ride off with the men to meet the king.

John draped a cloak over her shoulders, straightening it square as if she were incapable of the simple task. Yet she needed his arm as they descended the stairs. Her legs, unused for the day, had no more strength than dry grass.

Belde, quivering with excitement, bounded down the stairs ahead of them. When she followed him into the yard, a blast of cold wind cut through her, making her long for the protection of a man's garb on her legs.

Yet the crisp air made her feel truly awake for the first time. Beside her, John stayed close, his blue eyes serious, yet as always, a smile lurked just out of sight.

The gate loomed before her like a threat. 'Are there Storwicks near?'

'The men have just returned from a sweep of the hills. None to be seen. You'll be safe.'

You'll be safe. No. She would never be safe. Because she had not been able to save herself. Or him.

They mounted the ponies, the gate opened for them, and Belde ran in delirious circles around and ahead of them.

And it wasn't until it was too late that she realised John was taking her to Hogback Hill.

Silent, John watched her ride beside him, unsure how to speak to this strange woman who resembled Cate's ghost more than the woman herself.

He could tell the moment she realised where they were going. Saw her turn and open her mouth to protest, but he urged his horse ahead and let the wind whip her words away.

She had lost herself on that mountain, so that's where they must go to find her.

He kept his horse just out of earshot so she could not protest, hoping she would not turn back without him. Instead, shorn of Cate's spirit, this woman simply followed him.

When they reached the place of stones, he dismounted and waited as she sat, unmoving, on top of her horse.

'Cate, come down. I must talk to you.'

She slid off, as if no longer making her own decisions, then stood, staring vacantly at the ground.

He wondered at the man he had been when he arrived home months ago, thinking he knew something of women. On top of this cold and windswept mountain, faced with a Cate he barely recognised, he knew nothing at all.

Well, if they claimed him as a Brunson, the fore folk would have to help him now.

He took her shoulders. 'It's done, Cate. It's over.'

She looked towards the ravine, then a nod, imperceptible.

'You had your revenge.'

'Aye.' Yet she shook her head as if to say no.

'And I kept my word.'

Her eyes met his finally. 'That you did.'

Well, nothing to do but say it. 'And now, I'd like you to be my wife.'

He held his breath, though he did not know why. True, he had not spoken of marriage before, but he had avenged her for more than his family's honour. He knew that now and she must surely have known it long ago; else why would she have trusted him with her body?

Then why was he so uncertain of her answer?

'Wife?' She said the word as if she did not know it.

'Yes, dolt, wife!' The words came out more harshly than he had intended. He was the doltish one. Why could he not smooth things with this woman?

She blinked. 'Why would you want a woman who has been defiled?'

Now he was the one who blinked. He had taken her body, yes, but given her his as well. And so much more. 'That's no word for what we did.'

'Not you.' She looked towards the ravine. 'Him.'

He followed her glance and her thoughts, finally, back to the night she had confessed, fearful that the others would know. Afraid of what they would think. 'I don't care about that.'

'You cared enough to kill.'

'I cared about *you* and the promise I made you. I *don't* care about what happened before except that it makes you sad.'

'Sad?' She looked up at the snow-filled clouds. 'What a strange word.'

He stifled the urge to shake her from her stupor. Her words wandered without purpose. What had this shell of a woman wearing a dress done with the brittle warrior he loved?

But with his hands still tight on her shoulders, he paused. Which was the real Cate? Had the warrior been no more than her armour? What if this were the real woman?

Could he love this one, too?

'Tell me then,' he began, gentling his tone and his touch. 'Tell me the right word.'

She met his eyes then, the first time she seemed to really see him. 'A fazart. It makes me a fazart.'

Two syllables, ugly. They seemed to turn the very air putrid.

'I will let no one call you that. Not even you. How can you think that?'

'Because I am!' She flung her arms wide, knocking loose his hold.

At least she was fighting again. At least her spirit lived. 'Storwick is dead,' he said. 'God took his justice.'

'I don't care about God's! *I* wanted justice!' She pounded her chest with her fists. 'Me! Mine!'

He started to speak, but she didn't wait.

'It was supposed to be different. *I* was supposed to be

different. But it didn't matter. I still couldn't stop him. I couldn't even save myself. And I couldn't save you.'

He recognised his Cate now, the one who had thirsted for revenge. But it wasn't revenge she wanted after all.

She wanted to change the past.

And because she could not, all the hate she had carried for Willie had turned inwards.

'Did you think that killing Willie would make you a maiden again?'

She stared at him, white with shock at his words. 'I thought...' she began, then swallowed. 'I thought it would make me worthy of you.'

'But you are! Did I not just ask you to be my wife?'

She shook her head. 'Go back to your king, Johnnie. Go back to your ladies at the court. Go find someone who can share your bed without seeing demons and fighting dreams. Someone who can...'

She pursed her lips against the tears.

He took her hands and shook his head. 'It's here I'll be staying.'

'Why?'

Such a simple question. And the answer, now, was simple, too. 'Because it is where I belong.'

She shook her head, cloaking herself in calm once more. 'Don't be staying on my account, Johnnie Brunson. I haven't earned the right to you.'

She tugged the cloak around her and turned back to the pony. He helped her mount and she started down the hill without waiting. Belde trailed her with a mournful, accusatory look over his shoulder.

He yelled before she was out of earshot, 'When you are ready, I'll be here.'

Here for as long as it took for Cate to become Cate again. But as he rode down the mountain, hunched against the cold, he heard no comforting whispers in the wind. Unless she believed in herself, she could not believe in them.

And even love couldn't change the past.

Chapter Twenty-Five

I'd like you to be my wife.

Alone and hiding in her bedchamber again the next day, Cate turned the strange words over in her mind. All that she had been afraid to hope for was laid before her, yet she had not the courage to grasp it.

She had fought Scarred Willie in life only to discover he had defeated her in death. If she bedded Johnnie again and again and again, the memories might still rise, holding her in fear's grip.

She would not risk that. Not for herself, but more, not for Johnnie. He should have a wife in truth. One who could laugh and love and surrender and create those moments of happiness with him.

The ones she had cherished.

A soft knock and Bessie entered the room, carrying clean laundry. She glanced at Cate with a brief nod, then lay the stack of white on the bed, moving quietly to put the clean sarks in the chest. 'Will you help me with the sheets, then?'

Listless, Cate rose and started stripping the bed-clothes from her side of the bed.

On the other side, Bessie whipped the blanket back

with brisk efficiency, then pulled the sheet loose. 'If it's skirts you'll be wearing from now on, you'll need to sew a new one.'

Startled, Cate looked up. Bessie, leaning over the bed, was not waiting for her answer. But that simple statement seemed to force a choice.

She could not hide in this room for ever.

'I don't know,' she began, 'what to do now.'

Bessie paused. 'I could not have... I was not called on to have the courage you've shown since...' She did not say since *what*. She did not need to.

'Fear has haunted me every day and every night.'

And haunts me still.

'You have awakened to face every day and lain down at night to face your dreams. You have put one foot before the other and carried on in spite of your fear. I would call that courage.'

Had she not said the same to John?

She shook her head. 'It's not the kind of courage I need now.'

'What are you afraid of now?'

Failing him.

She smoothed the sheet over the bed. The bed where she and John had done what men and women do. He wanted a wife, yet she would not bind him to a woman who would freeze in fear or scream in terror beneath him.

Thoughts too intimate to be shared. 'I am afraid to be his wife.'

Bessie, patient Bessie, tugged the sheet smooth, tucked it under her side of the bed, then straightened with a sigh. 'We're given the kind we need. The kind you need has nothing to do with swords or dirks or riding into Storwick lands. You need the courage to say "yes".'

Yes.

Lying with John in the darkness. *Yes.*

Joining with him. *Yes.*

Letting his body overpower hers. *Yes.*

Letting him see her, fears and all. Could she say *yes* to that?

If she could not, then even with Scarred Willie dead, her future would be no different from her past.

'Would you...' Cate cleared her throat and tried again. 'Tell John that I am ready.'

After Bessie left, Cate stood beside the newly made bed, keeping her fingers fisted so they would not tremble, reminding herself there was nothing to fear.

Nothing to fear.

It was Johnnie, she told herself, when the door opened and he stood there. Johnnie, who said he loved her.

And he looked at her, silent, giving her all the time she needed.

She swallowed. 'You said, when I was ready, you would be here.'

'Aye.'

Cruel man. He did not ask whether she was ready. Did not leave her with only the *yes* to breathe. Instead, he waited for her to say it. 'I am ready.'

'Are you now?' His voice echoed with the edge of the hurt she had done him. 'What exactly are you ready for? Are you ready for a lifetime? Are you ready for joining without that jack-of-plaites that shields your heart? Are you ready for surrendering your body to your husband in the dark? If you are not ready for those things, I'm not ready for you.'

The very litany made her tremble. What if she froze or screamed or fought him when it was time for their joining?

What if she stood here for ever afraid, never discovering the truth?

'I am ready,' she began again, 'to face my fear. If you will face it with me.'

And then the light returned to his face and he pulled her into his arms, which felt strong and safe. 'That's all a man can ask.'

'I'm afraid I will always be afraid.'

He smiled at the tangled words. 'As long as you are not afraid of me.' He pulled back a little then, as if to give her space, not wanting to rush her too soon. 'I can be gentle.'

No. That would be worse. That would make her his burden, not his partner. 'Willie Storwick has no place in our bedchamber. I want no special treatment.'

'But what if—'

'No! We can make no life if my fear becomes yours. You are Braw Johnnie and I am Bold Cate!' She lifted her chin and opened her arms. 'As brave in love as in battle.'

The grin flickered across his face then. 'Then cross swords with me, my Cate. We both shall win.'

He took her lips without delicacy. Strong and urgent, his tongue explored her mouth, a sign of what was to come. She kissed him back, searching his mouth as he had teased hers, until each was inside the other, neither invading, both surrendering.

Desire surged within her, ready to devour him, as she had felt devoured, new and raw and raging out of control, refusing to accept separation.

She tugged at his tunic, pushed at his braises, unwilling to wait. This would not be the cautious joining of their past. She wanted him all at once. Beneath her greedy hands, his skin was hot, his muscles hard, the hair of his forearm soft and the skin of his belly, that never saw wind or sun, softer.

She helped him wrestle with the unfamiliar dress, her skin impatient for his. And when the clothes were shed, piled on the floor, her nakedness felt only his lips and his skin and air.

Now, he kissed her neck. Now, she kissed his shoulder. Now, he teased her breasts. Now, she stroked his thighs. Now, he moaned. Now, she gasped.

And then he took her lips again and they were on the bed.

No time for thought. No hesitation. Not until he lay with his body on top of hers, pinning her beneath him.

She stiffened.

He rolled off her, gasping for breath, for control.

She wanted to beat her stubborn, stupid body. 'No! Do not stop.' Tears of frustration threatened and his beloved face blurred before her eyes.

But she could still see the doubt in his.

'I cannot...not if...'

Then she saw it in his face, that she possessed him as completely as he possessed her. Even when she had sat astride him, he was not conquered. Nor would she be now. Joined in love, there was no greater, no lesser. Only the one they became together.

'You are Johnnie Brunson,' she said. 'The man I love. The man I want. The man I will allow to take me. And the man I will take in turn.'

'Now you are truly Braw Cate, for what you do this day takes more courage than facing forty long pikes.'

'Make me new memories, Johnnie.'

And he took her lips and took her body and swept them both into a dark, safe world that was theirs alone.

She woke with the sun, feeling the welcome weight of his leg and a new sense of strength. Perhaps her wound would heal as some of the body did, stronger in the broken places.

He opened his eyes, his wonderful, soft blue eyes, and smiled. 'We must declare a marriage, I think.'

His wife. Her very toes were smiling.

Relief. Then reality. 'You want to stay?'

He leaned on one elbow, grinning. 'King James will not be in a forgiving mood. I'll be a lucky man if our esteemed warden doesn't decide I deserve hanging.'

She clung to his careless smile. None of them knew whether Carwell was friend or foe. 'But if the king forgave you, then what?'

He shook his head, suddenly seeing her fears. 'I would still stay home.'

Home.

But if Rob did not agree, they would be exiled to the same lawless lands Scarred Willie had roamed. 'Where will we live?'

His fingers reached out to tug her hair, as if to make it grow. 'Well, Rob and I had a little talk.'

From his grin, she knew there was little talking involved. She put both hands on his shoulders and shook him. 'And what did Rob say?'

'Rob said to ask you if dividing the master's bed-chamber would suffice.'

And she laughed and rolled him onto his back and took his lips and they did not talk again for a long, long time.

Epilogue

He always hoped you would come home.

John stood on the parapet a week later, trying to catch an echo of his father's voice in the wind.

'Was Bessie right, old man? Is this what you wanted?'

There would be no going back. As word spread of Scarred Willie's death, John would be a hunted man, one who had walked away from all the titles, wealth and power a king could offer.

And yet, as he surveyed the snowy hills, he felt himself more than a king. Soon to be husband of a woman like no other. One he would protect with more than his life.

That might be necessary. Carwell would come for the man who had killed Scarred Willie. And if they told him it was a dog instead, who would believe it?

He smiled. Let the ballad singers concoct a better story. Let them sing of Bold Cate, brave as the First Brunson.

'Johnnie? Would you have supper?' Bessie stood at the top of the stair, not stepping up to the windswept parapet.

'Come look,' he said. 'The wind's died down.'

Sunset had turned the sky gold over snowy hills and she leaned on the ledge beside him, watching as the sun disappeared.

'Did he really want me to come home?' No need to say *who*. He had waited a long, long time to ask, afraid of the answer.

'Aye.'

A single word. And it brought the peace he'd searched for nearly half his life.

'But he sent no word. Asked nothing of my life.' The hurt rushed back, blunted only slightly by long years.

Bessie shook her head. 'What if he had? What if we had sent you word of Rob's tumble from his horse or my first woman's birthday? You would only have longed for what you were missing instead of turning to meet your life.'

Did they not think he longed for his family anyway?

'I think,' Bessie said, 'that he hoped you would come back, just as you did.'

'Demanding he send men to the king?'

'No.' Her crooked smile was kin to Rob's. 'He would have greeted that news even less cordially than Rob did.'

'Are you sure he didn't just want to be rid of the son who didn't fit?'

She turned away from the darkened hills to face him. 'He knew you had to go to a place where you were not Johnnie Blunkit.'

A place where he could become himself, before he became a Brunson.

Geordie the Red was a wiser bastard than he had thought.

'He loved this life,' she said. 'And Rob was born to it. But he wanted you to be free to choose something else. If you wanted.'

He drew a breath of Borders air. 'I could want nothing more than this.'

He turned to smile at his sister and in that unguarded moment, saw something flash across her face. Longing? Envy? He wondered again what life awaited his sister.

'Bessie—?'

'Johnnie?' Cate's voice preceded her up the stairs. 'Are you up here?'

She joined them on the parapet and the sight of her alone made him smile.

'Now come to eat. I've made lamb pie and if you don't get there quickly, Belde may eat it for us.'

Bessie raised her brows and started down the stairs to rescue dinner.

'I've a taste for something else tonight,' Cate said with a smile, glancing down.

His body responded instantly to her invitation. 'Do you, now?' But he tempered his smile. It was all still new to her. He did not want to rush. 'But you can say no whenever you want.'

She lifted her eyes to meet his. 'Yes. Yes. And a thousand times yes.'

He took her lips, thinking supper might wait. Aye, where Cate was, he was home.

And if the king's men came to take him? Well, he and Cate and generations of Brunsons would be ready for them.

Now let me sing of Cate the Bold
Who rode the hills with her brave dog Belde

In later years, after all those who knew her were gone, they still sang of the Warrior Woman of Liddesdale and how she crept out alone when the moon was dark to track and kill her enemy. And then the song told how the king thundered into the Borders to punish the man responsible for Willie Storwick's death.

And found a woman.

But that is a song for another day.

Afterword

This story takes place in the Borders of my imagination. Certain events are true. The King of Scotland, James V, did assume his 'personal rule' at age sixteen and, from then forwards, struggled to control the Borders, among other parts of his kingdom.

Borderers held themselves above kings of either country. They were driven by family loyalties in much the same way as Highlanders and as likely to feud with a family on their own side of the border as they were to ally with one on the opposite. Kings, Scottish and English, were far away and viewed with all the disdain I've shown here.

For at least two hundred years, the Borders operated much like a separate country, a buffer between England and Scotland. As I've outlined, they had their own laws which the wardens, English and Scottish, had the near-impossible job of enforcing. 'Reiving', the stealing of sheep and cattle and goods, was constant and, in many cases, more vicious than I described.

Modern litanies of the Reivers' sins typically list rape among them. In actual historic accounts, however, rape is so rare as to be non-existent. An assault such as the one in Cate's past was so unusual that I was unable to find a specific report of one in the history. Is this because they did not exist, or because women like Cate did not make them public? The answer, as so much of women's history, is hidden.

I studied the landscape, the towers, the laws and the raiding carefully, though I did take liberties. There were three 'Marches', or quasi-political divisions on each side of the Border. The Brunsons lived in what would be the Scottish Middle March and their warden would have lived there, too. But the warden in the book, Carwell, lives in what would actually be the West March and would have had jurisdiction over that geography.

My Brunsons were inspired very loosely by the Armstrongs, Carwell by the Maxwell family. There *was* an invasion of the Debatable Lands in 1528, but it was the English Warden who led it.

'Sleuth dogs', forerunners of our bloodhounds, are well documented during this time. The wardens often used them to track raiders back to their hiding places.

There was no Brunson family. No legend—that I know of!—of a lost Viking. There are, however, 'hogback stones' scattered on both sides of the Borders, like the ones I described on my imaginary 'Hogback Hill'. They date from five to six hundred years earlier than this story and are nearly as mysterious to us as they were to John and Cate.

Who's to say they could not sing to us of the past?

* * * * *

Look for Bessie's story in
CAPTIVE OF THE BORDER LORD,
coming soon.

OKLAHOMA WEDDING BELLS
Carol Finch
Independent Josephine Malloy is determined to stake her own claim during the latest Oklahoma land run. But to fend off the countless suitors seeking a wife and a homestead she needs a fake fiancé for cover. Enter horse trader Solomon Tremain...
(Western)

SOME LIKE IT WICKED
Daring Duchesses
Carole Mortimer
Risqué behavior is beyond Pandora Maybury, widowed Duchess of Wyndwood. If only the Ton knew just how innocent she really was... including Rupert, Duke of Stratton, who, after rescuing her from a compromising situation, seems intent on wickedly compromising her himself!
(Regency)

BORN TO SCANDAL
Diane Gaston
Scandalous Lord Brentmore is in need of a reputable governess. Anna Hill is too passionate, too *alluring*, but she fills Brentmore Hall with light and laughter again—and its master with feelings he'd forgotten.... But a lord marrying a governess would be the biggest scandal of all!
(Regency)

WARRIORS IN WINTER
The MacEgan Brothers
Michelle Willingham
Spend Christmas with your favorite warriors—the MacEgans! Three tales of warriors, Vikings and passion!
(Medieval)

REQUEST YOUR FREE BOOKS!

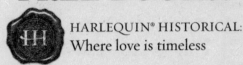

HARLEQUIN® HISTORICAL:
Where love is timeless

2 FREE NOVELS PLUS 2 FREE GIFTS!

YES! Please send me 2 FREE Harlequin® Historical novels and my 2 FREE gifts (gifts are worth about $10). After receiving them, if I don't wish to receive any more books, I can return the shipping statement marked "cancel." If I don't cancel, I will receive 6 brand-new novels every month and be billed just $5.19 per book in the U.S. or $5.74 per book in Canada. That's a savings of at least 17% off the cover price! It's quite a bargain! Shipping and handling is just 50¢ per book in the U.S. and 75¢ per book in Canada.* I understand that accepting the 2 free books and gifts places me under no obligation to buy anything. I can always return a shipment and cancel at any time. Even if I never buy another book, the two free books and gifts are mine to keep forever.

246/349 HDN FEQQ

Name _____ (PLEASE PRINT) _____

Address _____ Apt. # _____

City _____ State/Prov. _____ Zip/Postal Code _____

Signature (if under 18, a parent or guardian must sign)

Mail to the Reader Service:
IN U.S.A.: P.O. Box 1867, Buffalo, NY 14240-1867
IN CANADA: P.O. Box 609, Fort Erie, Ontario L2A 5X3

Not valid for current subscribers to Harlequin Historical books.

Want to try two free books from another line?
Call 1-800-873-8635 or visit www.ReaderService.com.

* Terms and prices subject to change without notice. Prices do not include applicable taxes. Sales tax applicable in N.Y. Canadian residents will be charged applicable taxes. Offer not valid in Quebec. This offer is limited to one order per household. All orders subject to credit approval. Credit or debit balances in a customer's account(s) may be offset by any other outstanding balance owed by or to the customer. Please allow 4 to 6 weeks for delivery. Offer available while quantities last.

Your Privacy—The Reader Service is committed to protecting your privacy. Our Privacy Policy is available online at www.ReaderService.com or upon request from the Reader Service.

We make a portion of our mailing list available to reputable third parties that offer products we believe may interest you. If you prefer that we not exchange your name with third parties, or if you wish to clarify or modify your communication preferences, please visit us at www.ReaderService.com/consumerschoice or write to us at Reader Service Preference Service, P.O. Box 9062, Buffalo, NY 14269. Include your complete name and address.

HHI1B

HARLEQUIN® HISTORICAL:
Where love is timeless

Fill your Christmas with three tales of warriors, Vikings and passion with author

MICHELLE WILLINGHAM

IN THE BLEAK MIDWINTER

It's a year since Brianna MacEgan's husband was killed, and she remains coldly obsessed with avenging his death. But Arturo de Manzano is intent on distracting her with his muscled fighter's body.

THE HOLLY AND THE VIKING

Lost in a snowstorm, Rhiannon MacEgan is rescued by a fierce Viking. Her lonely soul instantly finds its mate in Kaall, but can they ever be together?

A SEASON TO FORGIVE

Adriana de Manzano is betrothed to Liam MacEgan, a man she absolutely adores. But she's hiding a terrible secret.

Look for

Warriors in Winter

available November 13 wherever books are sold.

"OH..." PANDORA HAD NEVER FELT SO HUMILIATED.
"I apologize if I have caused you insult, Your Grace—er—
Rupert," she amended as those furious silver eyes narrowed
in dire warning. "It was not my intention to do so. I merely
wished to—"

"Refuse the *dubious honor* of becoming my mistress
before I felt compelled to voice it."

She had said that, Pandora acknowledged with an inward
wince. A remark he'd obviously taken exception to. "Well.
That is... Of course, I'm sure that many women would be
deeply flattered to so much as be considered—"

"Oh, give it up, Pandora." He bit out the words harshly.
"And accept that there's no going back from your insult to
me."

Her wince was outward this time. "I was angry when I
made that remark—"

"Because you had assumed *I* meant to insult *you* by
making such an offer!" A nerve pulsed in his tightly
clenched jaw.

"Well...yes."

Rupert felt some of his initial anger begin to fade as he
considered the amusement of their present situation instead.
Pandora Maybury, with her unusual beauty, golden curls
and mesmerizing violet eyes, had minutes ago insulted him,

and his honor, more roundly, more completely, than any other living person. Perhaps because any gentleman who had ever dared to speak to him like that would have very quickly found himself at the other end of Rupert's dueling pistols.

His amusement faded somewhat as he recalled that to have indeed been the fate of Pandora's husband *and* her lover....

He moved away from her until he stood with his back to the room, looking out the window into the street below. His carriage and four still stood on the cobbles below, waiting to take him back to Stratton House, an option he would perhaps be wise to take.

If not for the presence of the woman who awaited him there...

His shoulders stiffened with renewed resolve as he turned back to face the now cautiously watchful Pandora. "Contrary to general belief, the offer I intend making to you is not of becoming my mistress—but my wife!"

Read more of Carole Mortimer's
SOME LIKE IT WICKED, available from
Harlequin® Historical November 13, 2012.

And catch the next installment
SOME LIKE TO SHOCK
in January 2013.

When legacy commands, these Greek royals must obey!

Discover a page-turning new Harlequin Presents®
duet from *USA TODAY* bestselling author

Maisey Yates

A ROYAL WORLD APART

Desperate to escape an arranged marriage, Princess
Evangelina has tried every trick in her little black book
to dodge her security guards. But where everyone else
has failed, will her new bodyguard bend her to his
will…and steal her heart?

Available November 13, 2012.

AT HIS MAJESTY'S REQUEST

Prince Stavros Drakos rules his country like his
business—with a will of iron! And when duty demands
an heir, this resolute bachelor will turn his sole
focus to the task….

But will he finally have met his match in a world-
renowned matchmaker?

**Coming December 18, 2012,
wherever books are sold.**

HARLEQUIN® *Desire*

ALWAYS POWERFUL, PASSIONATE AND PROVOCATIVE.

A brand-new Westmoreland novel from *New York Times* bestselling author

BRENDA JACKSON

Riley Westmoreland never mixes business with pleasure—until he meets his company's gorgeous new party planner. But when he gets Alpha Blake into bed, he realizes one night will never be enough. That's when her past threatens to end their affair. So Riley does what any Westmoreland male would do…he lets the fun begin.

ONE WINTER'S NIGHT

"Jackson's characters are…hot enough to burn the pages."
—*RT Book Reviews* on *Westmoreland's Way*

Available from Harlequin® Desire December 2012!

HD73210BJ